of MAGIC

WISH QUARTET BOOK FOUR

AGE

of

MAGIC

WISH QUARTET BOOK FOUR

ELISE KOVA & LYNN LARSH

Silver Wing Press

Published by Silver Wing Press
Copyright © 2018 by Elise Kova

Cover Artwork by Elise Kova
Editing by Rebecca Faith Editorial

eISBN: 9781642372083
Print ISBN: 9781720208297

*for the friendships that
span time and space*

CONTENTS

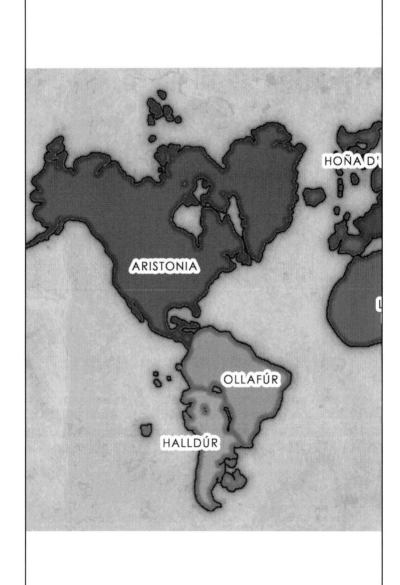

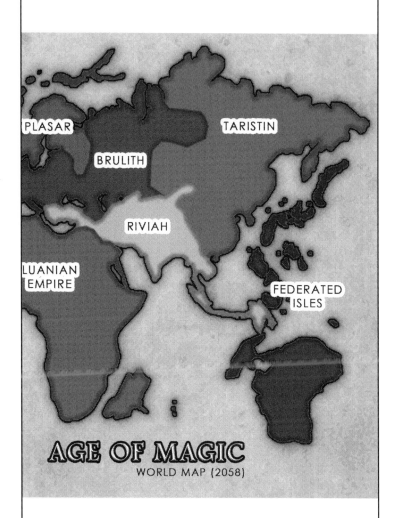

1. FAR FROM OVER

"Just what're you talking about? 'This is far from over'?" Wayne repeated Jo's sentiment with a level of confusion, agitation, and exasperation that she'd never heard from the man before.

"Exactly what I said: the Society may have been destroyed, but we still have work to do." Jo took a deep breath, letting it out with a sigh. She was still wrapping her head around everything; it seemed almost impossible for her to fathom. How could she hope to explain it to them? Where would she start when it felt like something she should've told them long ago?

"Just how was the Society destroyed, Jo?" asked the magical projection of Takako. Her voice was gentle enough that Jo wondered if the astute woman could sense her inner turmoil. "From our perspective it was all a bit . . . confusing."

Wayne scoffed at the last word, though his demeanor

remained serious. "Yeah, Takako and I didn't run into the room until *after* the Door was broken."

"Eslar and I saw it," Samson added. "But even I don't understand."

"We've been trying to put it together for nearly a year, doll."

"A year," Jo mused. "You said that before . . . What do you mean, a year?"

For Jo, it hadn't been a year. From her perspective, the past twenty-four hours comprised a series of events that competed with each other for maximum impossibility. The Society had crumbled—thanks to her unleashing her destructive magic on its foundation—and then she'd woken up yesterday in this time, in the front yard of a serial killer's house—one who, thanks to a piece of resistant code in his AI mainframe, had helped her get her bearings.

Her bearings—there was another oddity. The whole world around her was a strange transformation of the time she knew. There were skyscrapers, and elves roaming the streets. The earth itself was a familiar map, but with notable changes to the land, along with kingdoms and empires she didn't recognize atop it.

Oh, and then she'd ridden on a Dragon. Couldn't forget that, could she? Yeah, the past twenty-four hours had been a day for the record books. But just a day—at least, from her perspective.

"We all woke back up, already solidified in—as far as we can tell—the lives we would've had in this world had we not been pulled from it." Once again, Takako was the one to answer, but Jo could see that even she was struggling with a response. Comprehending their odd twist of fate was like trying to read a book backwards, up-side-down, and written in pig Latin. "Eslar was the first, then Samson."

"I think we woke up in the order we joined the Society," Samson chimed in, only briefly looking up from his bauble. He had yet to fully recover from Jo's initial mention of Eslar. Another oddity that needed eventually to be addressed.

"I'll tell you what, it *was* a bit jarring. Waking up to a life I've supposedly been living for twenty years and having no memory of it . . ." Wayne motioned to the office. "Though I can't rightly complain about how I turned out in this world."

Twenty years. That was how old Wayne was when he'd made his wish, Jo remembered. So, the Society had been destroyed, they were all subsequently dropped back into a new world, in the order they'd joined the Society, and they were already settled into the lives they would've been living. As if the Society had never even existed. As if *none* of their previous timelines had ever even existed.

Jo couldn't help but wonder if she had a mother in what had been Texas but was now some corner of Aristonia. Something in her said she wouldn't; they were returning to timelines as they "should've been" and for her, that was as a demigod, not as Josephina Espinosa. Now, all she would carry of her 2057 would be her name, and the memories she'd never let go of.

"So . . . this is what 2057—I mean 2058, looks like now for all of us." Jo turned away from the table and the projected images of her teammates, looking out through the windows that dominated one of the walls

3

of Wayne's office.

It was New York City. *Yorkton*, Jo mentally corrected. Charlie hadn't known what New York City was, but Yorkton made perfect sense. And, just like the name, it was similar, but not the same as the "original" Jo recalled. But what was ever original in a universe that could be entirely remade?

She saw winged creatures landing on rooftops. The sky was filled with a mix of animal and technological flying systems. The buildings were skyscrapers, but not quite as she knew them. Impossible feats of architecture hollowed out cores of buildings where lush gardens cascaded down, striking a contrast against the industrial glass-tones below.

"A new Age of Magic." Wayne stated the obvious and rested a hand heavily on her shoulder. It summoned Jo's attention away from the sights and back to her team.

The Age of Magic had once given way to the Age of Man—Jo's original time. But it seemed that when the Society was destroyed, so too was the world reset to the year of the Society's creation: the beginning of the Age of Magic. Somewhere in this time was Snow . . . Jo's chest tightened at the thought, and Wayne's next question had Jo wondering if he could sense it.

"Now, what did you mean when you said, 'It's not over'?" Because from what we've managed to discern, life is pretty great not being beholden to wishes, or Snow, or, you know, watches."

Jo couldn't help but notice that, even still, he wore the gaudy golden timepiece on his wrist. She also couldn't help the small smile that threatened to pull at the corner of her lips at the sight.

"We're all here, yes. But the Society was—"

"The Society ended, but the fight hasn't," Jo interrupted Takako.

"What fight?" Samson asked. Jo hated the tremor in Samson's voice, an obvious reluctance to hear her response. But he needed to. They all did.

"A fight for the power to destroy the world."

"Pan." Samson surprised her by being the one to say it. Seemed to surprise everyone, in fact, as he elaborated for Wayne and Takako's benefit. "Pan was the one going after Jo . . . I'm guessing she'll keep trying, but I don't know any more than you do."

The moment Pan's name was brought up, Jo felt the sickening feeling she'd come to associate with pure loathing. But it also brought up a different feeling—the phantom sensation of being watched. A feeling that had haunted her in the Society, that had kept Pan's name off her lips, and seemed to linger even now.

"How secure is this?" Jo asked Wayne.

"What?"

"This communication." Jo motioned to the desk so oddly reminiscent of the briefing room table. "I'm still learning about this world, but video conferencing could be hacked and listened in on in my original timeline."

"I'm pretty sure it's secure."

Jo put her hands on her hips, thinking a long moment. She could see how the communication could be broken into and listened in on with a blink. But Jo didn't know if it was because of her magic, or because it was actually a risky connection. She took a deep breath and decided to err on the side of caution. It wasn't exactly a far leap in logic to see Wayne as someone who wouldn't understand a good security system from a bad one. He likely had people to take care of that for him, but looking at the office, she trusted them even less.

"*Pretty sure* isn't going to cut it," Jo muttered. That same sensation of being watched still lingered with her. She shook her head, her mind made up. "We need to meet, in person. I have so much I need to tell all of you, but for now, you're all going to have to trust me on this. The one you suspect *is* a danger, not just to you, but to everyone you love, and the very fabric of the world itself."

"You don't have to convince me." Takako was the first to respond. "I'll get to Aristonia as quickly as possible."

"Where are you now?" Jo couldn't help but ask.

"We know it as Japan, but it's now the Kingdom of Hajisha . . . Part of the Federated Isles."

If Jo hadn't known Takako so well, known her to be a level and serious person—especially when the situation called for it—she would have suspected the woman of making up the names. But this was not her world and it was not a practical joke. This was the Age of Magic, the earth overlaid with thousands of years where sorcery had never left the landscape of human history.

"I guess it's a good thing I always sucked at history," Jo mumbled. "Gonna have to re-learn it all anyway."

Wayne made a soft noise of amusement. "I can coordinate travel for you both," he offered to Samson and Takako.

"Thank you," Takako said.

"One or two, Samson?"

All eyes turned to their craftsman.

"I'll try to get Eslar." He didn't even notice they were all looking at him, his head never rising to meet their gaze.

"Thank you, Samson," Jo said gently. She could see something was breaking him down, though without more information, it was impossible to tell what it might be. Just that it had something to do with Eslar. "He's one of the team, after all."

Samson just nodded.

"All right, I'll get on the arrangements, and we'll all wait on pins and needles until Jo feels confident telling us what, exactly, is going on." Wayne leaned over his desk. "See you all soon." With a wave of his hand, the call ended.

Jo turned, leaning against the edge of the desk. Looking back out the window, she squinted into the setting sun, wondering just where Pan was now. She didn't know what it would take to bring the woman down, but Jo was confident that their first step was the right one—getting the team back together.

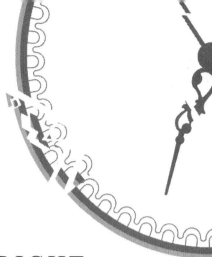

2. JUST ALL RIGHT

THE BREEZE THAT wafted past the balcony brushed the hair out of Jo's face with gentle yet chilling fingers. Even as she tightened the heavy blanket around her shoulders, Jo couldn't help but lean into the feel of it, closing her eyes to the sensation, soaking it in

It wasn't until she was finally sitting down, glass of way-too-expensive scotch in hand, that it hit her. She hadn't had a chance to really process what being in this new world, free of the Society's constraints, might mean. But now, as she felt the breeze against her face, heard the sounds of the city below her in its un-muted cacophony, she allowed herself a moment to simply *feel*.

The chair beneath her was comfortable and sturdy, the cushions a soft and cradling contrast. The air was rich with the tangy scent of a busy city, muted by both the crisp chill of the mid-January weather and the distance provided by the penthouse balcony—because of *course* Wayne would live in a fancy penthouse above his own company. Some things not even a brand-new world could change, it would seem.

And, while she'd never admit it to him, some things she didn't *want* to see changed. There were few precious constants she could depend on in the jumping timelines and shifting worlds; the members of the Society, Wayne specifically, counted among them. He'd been by her side from the very first moment, after all.

At the sound of the sliding glass door opening behind her, Jo let her eyes flutter open as well, taking in the flickering lights of the buildings surrounding them. Soft jazz spilled outside for a moment before it was dulled once again by the door sliding shut. If Jo listened intently enough though, she could still hear it amid the backdrop of the city's ambient noise.

"Someone looks cozy," Wayne chuckled by way of greeting, sitting himself down in the chair to Jo's right. He'd forgone a blanket of his own for a scarf and an expensive-looking coat that managed to cling to his frame in all the right ways. Jo just shrugged, pulling the thick, probably-also-hideously-expensive blanket tighter around herself out of spite. When she glanced over at Wayne, it was to find a look of unexpected fondness on his face. One that he hastily schooled into something more teasing once he noticed, motioning with his chin towards her glass. "Liking the giggle juice?"

Though the lingo felt more teasing than Wayne's usual bravado, Jo still felt warmth bloom at the center of her chest. She hadn't realized how much she'd missed the easy rapport they'd once had, hadn't realized how long things had been getting rougher and messier between them as a result of her not-so-secret mission to end the Society. Jo raised the glass to her lips, lamenting her role in inflicting those old wounds.

As she sipped, mulling over where, how, and when to attempt to suture her past mistakes, Jo allowed herself to focus for a moment on the way her fingers felt against the cool glass of the tumbler, the way the rich and smoky flavor of the scotch coated her tongue, tingling all the way down her throat and warming her chest and stomach. It was the most delicious liquor she'd ever experienced in any of her lives, she was certain, but after another quiet sip and a brief moment to lick the remnants of the amber liquid from her lips, she just shrugged again. And smirked.

"It's all right, I guess."

"*All right?*" Wayne gaped at her, which only made her smirk grow into a full-fledged grin. With an over-dramatic flourish of his own glass, Wayne said, "I'll have you know this single malt was aged for twenty years in Aristonian oak and another *fifteen* in Brulithian wine casks, and that's not even taking into account the . . . Wait. You're just razzin' me, aren't you, dollface?"

Jo finally gave in to the bubble of laughter she'd only just held at bay during his tirade.

"You got me," she said, holding her glass out for a toast. "It's amazing, Wayne, even if I don't understand half of what you just said. Thank you for sharing it with me."

With an exasperated sigh that was only half-feigned,

Wayne shook his head, eventually smiling softly in return and clinking the edge of his glass against hers. "Pleasure's all mine, doll. When you're given a second shot at life, you learn not to get hung up on formality. What's the point of having nice things if you aren't going to enjoy them?"

"Sure, Mr. Twenty Years in Aristonian barrels." Jo rolled her eyes, but even she could hear the amusement in her voice.

"What can I say? If you're going to *have* nice things, you've also got to know *why* they're nice, don't you think?"

Jo took another small swig of the nice thing in question and hummed her approval. She braced herself. "Wayne, I'm sorry."

"For what?" The man likely knew exactly what she was trying to say, but . . .

"For how I handled everything in those final weeks, maybe even months, of the Society." Jo passed her glass from hand to hand, eyes locked within as if trying to find the right words shining true in the sheen of the city lights off the amber liquor. "For keeping my powers a secret and endangering everyone.

"I had reasons," she added hastily. Then sighed. "But they're all just excuses . . . I think. I should've trusted the team more. I should've just put everything out in the open." Jo dared to look Wayne in the eye then. His face was passive, expressionless; there was nothing for her to read in his visage. "I should've trusted you more." A beat passed, enough for Jo to grow nervous, and then—

"Doll." Wayne leaned further back in his chair,

looking at the city skyline, a deep furrow in his brow. "I know you had your reasons and I trusted them without explanation. But I think I can speak for all of us when I say I'm looking forward to finding out what those reasons are."

"More than fair."

"Plus, it seems like you learned your lesson." He looked back at her, a small smile on his lips. Jo hoped he was referring to her instinct to get the Society back together, her plan to tell them everything.

"I think I have. So . . . are we good?"

"Yeah, we're good." Wayne hoisted his glass and Jo did the same. They both leaned over their chairs and, for a brief moment, she was reminded of another balcony they'd once shared after a night of satisfying bliss.

Their glasses made another soft *clinking* sound, and they both drank.

After that, a comfortable silence fell, both of them staring out past the glass railing of the balcony and into the shimmering city night. Even with the threat of the unknown hanging over all of them, it felt oddly peaceful—like if Jo closed her eyes, she could convince herself that the world wasn't in danger. If she pretended hard enough, she could imagine that this was a world without Pan, without any dangers at all outside of the ones that come with any normal, human (humanish?) life.

She could imagine that Snow was there, wrapping her up in his loving embrace, enjoying this moment of temporary peace, too.

At the thought of him, of how much he'd sacrificed

to give her this chance, Jo felt the cocoon of that faux-peace begin to unravel, a weight settling firmly back over her shoulders. She had no idea what position Snow was even in right now, if he was hurt or being tortured by Pan, or worse. And here she was drinking fancy scotch and pretending everything was going to work out just fine. Guilt churned low in her gut as she pulled her eyes from the city and into the reflective pool of liquor in her glass.

Had she always looked so tired?

Wayne seemed to notice her shift in mood too; a soft sigh escaped him.

"You're worried about him." It wasn't a question.

"I'm worried about a lot of things." It wasn't an answer.

"Whatever it is that we have to do, we'll do it," Wayne offered after another brief pause, and though the words were meant to be a comfort, they only left Jo feeling oddly heavier. "We've been through hell before and made it out alive, haven't we?"

Jo swallowed thickly. "Most of us anyway."

"Nico, he—" Wayne paused, running a hand over his face, suddenly looking as tired as Jo felt. "In a way, he gave us this chance too, you know? He's part of the reason we're here at all right now."

"And I'm the reason he's not." It was painful, to bring Wayne's old words back out, but this time, unexpectedly, Wayne only shook his head.

"We all could have done something different for Nico. We all could have tried harder. But in the end, he did what any of us would have done. He gave us his time to keep fighting and surviving. So all we can do is take that sacrifice and keep doing exactly that. Fighting and surviving. Even if it means going up against Pan one more time to end this for good." A moment of quiet, and then Wayne asked, softer but with just as much seriousness, "That *is* what we're going to have to do, isn't it? All of this about danger still lurking . . . You need us to find a way to snuff her out?"

Jo wasn't sure *what* they were going to have to do, but Wayne definitely had the right idea. Pan was the only threat left. If they—and the whole world—wanted any hope of actual peace, it would mean making sure she was dealt with. And quickly. Jo wasn't sure what Pan was planning, or if she even knew that Jo had finally arrived in this new age, but Jo couldn't shake the feeling that they were running out of time.

Before she could even begin to explain the whirlwind of thoughts and emotions battering about inside her head, Wayne held up a hand to silence her.

"You know what? Don't worry about explaining anything now," he said, looking back out at the cityscape again. "You were right. We should wait for the rest of the team."

Jo wasn't sure if Wayne had seen the conflict on her face, or if he was just perceptive enough to know she needed more time to get her thoughts in order, but she was grateful nonetheless. This was going to be hard enough to explain; she might as well only have to do it once.

After another long minute of simply enjoying each other's silent company, Jo whispered a confession into the night air. "Thank you, Wayne. For taking the risk. You . . . I know you didn't have to," she said, realizing just how true the words were. He and the whole rest of the team could have simply denied her request for help and gone on living their own lives. The only one Pan was after was her. But instead, Wayne and the others had agreed. As if they were still a team.

"It's not like I have much of a choice, do I?" Wayne rolled his eyes, but there was something off in the dismissive tone of his voice, his smirk stiff. "I mean, knowing Pan . . . we're talking world domination or something here, right? What kind of man would I be if I said no when called on for something like that?"

Jo watched as he took another long drink of his scotch, followed the bob in his throat as he swallowed. She watched emotion flicker across his features as he did it again, knocking back the rest of it and then licking his lips. His eyes were distant as he ran a finger around the rim of his now empty glass.

"This team . . . They're the only family I have left, you know? The only one that matters anymore anyway. Hard to feel much toward a family I'm supposed to have in this world but have only known for a few months," he finally whispered, another confession drifting between them on the night air. The mention of family brought her mind back to her mother. But Jo's earlier decision was merely further reaffirmed. Some things were best for her not to pursue—at least not until the matter of a psychotic demigod was settled. "Even if it means going up against a power I frankly don't even *understand*, I would see this through for any one of the Society. I would do anything for my team."

He'd always been that way, hadn't he? Loyal to the team, placing them before anything else, even his own wants and opinions. "We're lucky to have you, Wayne . . . truly."

She heard a huff of amusement, but Jo couldn't bring herself to look at him. "You really think that?"

"I do."

"Good." A pause, a breath. "Because I would do anything for *you*, dollface."

Jo felt her breath catch in her throat as her eyes were pulled to his face, emotion welling up at the sincerity in his voice. She didn't have the words to say how much that meant to her. So instead, she held his gaze and reached her free hand out in his direction. After a moment of confusion, Wayne grabbed her hand, allowing her to link their fingers together. When she did, she held on tight, hoping that little bit of connection would show him just how grateful she was to have him by her side.

They stayed like that long after the cold had made its way beneath blanket and coat, not breaking the hold even when their fingers had gone numb.

3. VAMPIRE CREAM

JO COULDN'T SLEEP.

When Wayne had finally succumbed to his own exhaustion—since apparently members of the Society were once again beholden to the energetic constraints of being alive—Jo had settled herself in one of the guest rooms, expecting sleep to take her under swiftly after the day she'd had. But after an hour of tossing and turning, she began to realize the dawning approach of a new complication.

Jo found she lacked even a minimal *desire* to sleep now. Whether it was because of her newly awakened demigod status or genuine insomnia, she wasn't sure. But after one hour of restlessness became two, three, and finally four, Jo decided it wasn't worth trying to force herself into a state she clearly didn't want to be in.

So, keeping as quiet as possible, fully and enviously aware that Wayne was probably deep in his own slumber, Jo wandered the penthouse with her thoughts . . .

Which turned out to be more stressful and anxiety-inducing than anything. So instead she switched to distraction.

It took a few minutes for Jo to figure out how to use this world's version of a television, another obsidian device similar to the briefing room table—except this one was mounted on the wall. If the awkward hand waves, various thoughts, and magical pulses to figure out how to turn it on weren't bad enough, the blaring noise that emerged when it did flick to life had Jo certain she'd disturbed her host's slumber. Jo held her breath, but when she heard nothing, she turned to the projected image.

It was a sort of hologram-meets-augmented-reality, as the picture came alive around her in near life-like clarity. Wayne's living room was transformed. The furniture stayed the same, but now it was as if she were seated at the edge of a theater's stage. Jo watched as it displayed what looked like the telenovelas her abuelita used to watch. Except where the novelas she knew were Spanish-language soap operas spouting over-dramatic arguments between lovers, this one focused on two werewolf-looking creatures howling at each other—Jo honestly wasn't sure if she was supposed to know what they were saying or not.

For the rest of the night, Jo lost herself in the various news and entertainment channels this new world had to offer, marveling at the similarities and differences to the world she'd come from. One channel was airing a historical documentary about the war between their kingdom and the neighboring kingdom of Taristin;

another aired a colorful show about current social media trends, hosted by what looked to be a half-pixie, half-peacock hybrid creature. After who knew how long, Jo eventually settled on a news outlet, watching in awe as they covered current affairs.

Apparently there were weakening magical energy currents beneath the sea surrounding a kingdom named Zakon. Another kingdom, Hoña d'Plasar, was celebrating its five-hundredth year of independence. Also, the release of a new cream meant to return a vampire's skin to their pre-bio-death pallor had apparently been recalled due to increased sun sensitivity. Who knew?

Jo was so engrossed, she didn't even notice the sun had risen, her focus on the television only broken by a mug suddenly being shoved in her face. She startled, nearly knocking it out of Wayne's hands.

"Morning, dollface," he said through a laugh, voice made deep and rumbly from sleep. "No need to worry. It's just coffee."

"Thanks." Jo cleared her throat and picked up the mug from where Wayne had placed it on the table. A pang of loss hit her at the scent, Nico's memory wrapping around her as she took a hesitant sip. It hit her then, how long it had been since she'd allow herself to just savor the rich, caffeinated beverage without guilt, without sadness. But Wayne's words from the night before settled like a comforting weight against her chest; she owed it to Nico to keep going.

Wayne sat down next to her on the couch, crossing a leg over his knee as he sipped slowly at his own mug of coffee. "I didn't hear you get up," he said eventually.

"Sleep alright?"

Jo's initial reaction was to tell Wayne that she hadn't slept at all, that perpetual insomnia might be her new demigod normal, but then she remembered the desk at the police office, the look of fear and worry on his face. Wayne had only just started looking at her like he used to, speaking to her like he had the night before, with a familiarity and fondness she'd missed dearly. She didn't want to ruin that by reminding him again just how different she'd become.

There'd be time for that when everyone else arrived. "Yeah," she responded as casually as she could. "Just woke up early, that's all."

Wayne hummed around another sip of coffee before moving on. If he noticed anything amiss in her answer, he didn't say. "I sent a car to pick up Takako. She should be here any minute now."

As if on cue, the doorbell chose that moment to chime. Jo's eyes lit up at the promise of her friend's arrival. When she didn't automatically get off the couch to answer the door (it wasn't her home, after all), Wayne laughed, motioning with his chin in its direction as if to say, *Go ahead*.

Jo got up at once, rushing with probably enough eagerness to look a bit silly, but it didn't matter. Seeing Takako over a hologram screen was one thing. But seeing her in person? Knowing that she really was alive and safe? That was something Jo only just then realized how much she'd been craving.

The moment the door swung open, Jo couldn't stop herself; her arms were wrapped around Takako's shoulders in an embrace fierce enough to have her

22

stumbling back a step, bags clattering to the floor. She seemed stunned enough that she remained frozen in Jo's arms for a long moment, but then, with a soft chuckle that Jo could feel vibrating between them, Takako hugged her back just as fiercely.

"It's good to see you too, Jo," she said on a heartfelt breath into Jo's ear. Jo's heart soared, arms tightening for a split second before releasing Takako from her death grip—only releasing her to arm's length, where she could look her over with an awed smile.

Takako was wearing what appeared to be the casual version of a military uniform: a simple coat that ended at her waist and a well-tailored pair of pants, both in deep maroon. A badge was pinned over her left breast, little beads dangling from it. Her hair was noticeably longer than Jo remembered, enough to merit the ponytail it was currently wrapped up in, but in every way, she was still the same girl Jo had come to know and love.

"Are you going to stand in the foyer all day, or are you going to let Takako inside?" Wayne's voice echoed from back in the living room, once again startling Jo out of her thoughts. At the look of fond amusement on Takako's face, Jo decided not to fight back the blush that rose to her cheeks, smiling at her friend as she grabbed one of the bags off the floor and slung it over her shoulder.

"Right, sorry. Come on in."

"Thank you." Takako nodded, picking up the remaining two bags and heading inside. By the shape and size of one of them, Jo wouldn't have been surprised if it held some variety of firearms. It was with that realization and the full recognition of the military uniform that a new concern fell into place.

"Is it really alright for you to be wearing that here in Ameri—I mean, Aristonia?" Jo asked, gesturing with her free hand at Takako's uniform as she deposited the bag next to the couch with the other. For a moment, Takako only looked down at herself in confusion, and Jo quickly continued, trying to clarify, "It's only 2058. I saw in a documentary that there was still a war in this time right around my timeline's World War III . . ."

"Oh, right," Takako smirked. "Apparently in this version of the world, our kingdoms actually *like* each other. The Federal Isles even offered support to Aristonia during that war against Taristin."

"No kidding..." Jo grinned, putting her hands on her hips. She'd no doubt flipped the channel before the documentary had gotten to that bit. "Well, Aristonia appreciates your support, I guess?"

Takako laughed. "I guess."

After that, Wayne left the two of them alone to make lunch. Jo chose not to mention her lack of appetite and instead settled easily into a conversation with Takako. It was clear that the other members of the Society had been released from the bodily restrictions they'd experienced in the mansion—they now seemed to feel hunger and exhaustion as keenly as any other normal human. So where did that leave her? That was an answer Jo wasn't rushing to find.

"So where did the timeline spit you out?" Jo asked as she curled up into the corner of the couch, second cup of coffee balanced on her knees. Takako sat with her legs tucked beneath her, cradling her own mug in both hands.

"I'd apparently served long and successfully enough in Hajisha's Special Forces Unit to merit paid leave."

Jo whistled in appreciation. "Impressive."

Takako just chuckled softly to herself. "I'm sure it was. Can't remember any of it though."

"Me neither." Jo nodded in agreement. "Not the war, but . . . anything of the life I've supposedly been living." *If there'd been a life to live at all*, Jo added mentally. She still wasn't convinced there had ever been a Josephina in this world.

"I've been spending the last year since I woke up with my family," she continued, smiling down into her mug. "I requested that leave the second I realized they remembered who I was. No tragedy like Mt. Fuji, no war to fight, plus the added bonus of my family actually recognizing me when I showed up at their door? I mean, I sometimes wonder if I should feel guilty for reaping the benefits of a soldier when I don't remember actually fighting as one... But how could I not?"

The look of easy happiness on her face as she spoke about her family was unfamiliar to Jo, but beautiful to behold. Even if the love for their families had persisted in the Society, it had always been hampered by the knowledge that those family members no longer knew of their existence.

"I don't think you should feel bad at all." Jo rested a hand on Takako's. "I would've done the same in your shoes."

After getting up-to-date on each other's lives—a process that included Takako cursing impressively over a black disk until it showed some holo-images of her sister's twins—they settled in to wait for the rest of their team to arrive.

Except Samson didn't arrive for another two days. And when he finally did, he was alone.

Jo pulled Samson into as equally fierce a hug as she had Takako, though she could tell by his body language that it would be wise not to smother him too much. Still, Samson returned the hug eagerly, relaxing a bit into her embrace before pulling away and regaining an anxious sort of full-body tension.

Aside from the way he was slightly curled in on himself, his smile a bit forced, he looked good. His bright orange hair was shaved short on one side and styled in tight braids on the other, his outfit casual but new and fashionable. He had brought with him a rather impressive collection of bags, most of which Jo assumed contained his tools and projects worth traveling with.

Though it itched at her to ask about Eslar, instinct told her to let Samson settle in first, picking his brain about what he'd been up to since he "woke up." Though he seemed less willing to offer up detailed information than Takako had been, he talked enthusiastically enough about his new life.

He'd woken up in a kingdom called Riviah—what in Jo's world had been India—and had spent the last year in the far north of the Luanian Empire, near the western side of the Kingdom of Brulith, around what Jo knew to be Spain. When she asked him if Eslar had woken near him (since they were clinging to each other at the end of the Society), Samson mumbled something incomprehensible and changed the subject, rambling happily on about his current setup as an independent craftsman with an extensive list of loyal patrons.

It was Wayne who eventually brought up the elephant in the room.

"So what took you so long to get here?"

Jo threw a glare at Wayne over her shoulder, but he ignored her. As much as she wanted Samson to be at ease, they really did need to know where he'd been. And more than that, why Eslar hadn't shown up with him. That feeling that time was most certainly not on their side hadn't abated.

When Samson seemed overtly reluctant to answer, however, Jo tried a different tactic. She reached across the couch to grab Samson's hand. She gave it a comforting squeeze before speaking.

"Eslar's not coming, is he, Sam?" Samson looked at Jo first in surprise, then with a mix of exhaustion and something that looked painfully like guilt. When he shook his head, Jo squeezed his hand a bit tighter. Still, as much as it hurt her to pry, they deserved to know. "Did he say why?"

At that, Samson's hand twitched beneath hers, his back hunching further into the slouch he'd adopted. "He, um . . . No. He didn't... didn't say," Samson managed after a moment, the fingers of his free hand fussing with a loose thread on one of the couch's throw pillows. Jo could feel his magic stuttering out of him and recoiling as if he was physically preventing himself from altering the composition of the pillow into something easier to fidget with. "I tried to ask, but he . . . he just said he wasn't coming." He looked up at Jo with sad eyes and a strained half-smile. "I'm sorry.

That's all I could manage."

Something about the admission seemed off to Jo's ears, though whether he was stalling or hiding something or possibly just uncomfortable with the whole situation, she couldn't tell. All she knew was that any mention of Eslar was making Samson increasingly distressed. Unfortunately, or fortunately for Samson's sake, they didn't have time to dwell on that fact—something Wayne seemed to pick up on at much the same time as Jo.

"Well, if the elf's not coming, he's not coming," Wayne sighed. He'd taken to pacing, arms crossed over his chest and face stern in concentration. "We can't force him to help if he's determined to keep pretending we don't exist." Jo raised an eyebrow at that, but Wayne went on without explanation. "Nothing for it but to move on for now."

Samson let out a soft, sad sigh, one Jo was sure no one was meant to hear, as he nodded in quiet agreement. They may have been willing to move on out of necessity, but for Jo, the curiosity surrounding Eslar only grew.

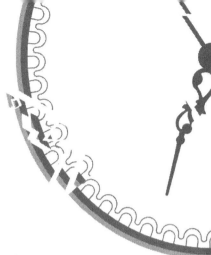

4. A BRIEF HISTORY

"THANK YOU ALL for coming," Jo started awkwardly. She felt like some half-baked manager at a company meeting, going through the motions while trying to hide her resentment for the situation. Pushing herself onto her feet, Jo crossed her arms over her chest and headed toward the large windows, speaking as she walked. "I know that we're all in the same spot—waking up to lives that we have no recollection of having. But at the same time, being given a second chance at life without the Society . . ."

"The Society *really* is gone, then?" Takako asked. "It's not going to come back?"

"I don't see a way it could've survived." Given the way she remembered dismantling it . . . She had every faith. "If it had, we would know by now, I think."

"Then why is Pan . . ." Samson started and trailed off, looking at Takako and Wayne to see if they had any insights he didn't. When neither moved to provide an explanation, he turned back to Jo. "Why is she still a threat?"

Jo paused, placing her hands on her hips, looking out the window as if she'd find some easy way to tell them everything somewhere within the city skyline. She didn't. "I realize that what I'm about to tell you is going to sound clinically insane."

"Doll, we existed for hundreds of years granting wishes in a Society outside of time," Wayne said, clearly amused as he slung one calf onto the other knee. "I doubt you're going to shock us."

Challenge accepted. "I'm a demigod."

Their faces would have been hilarious in any other situation. Samson's mouth dropped right open, his hands still for the first time. Takako squinted her eyes, as if trying to see proof of the claim, and tilted her head. Wayne kept opening and closing his mouth like a gaping fish, but no words came.

"See? I told you it'd sound crazy."

"I think you need to start at the beginning," Takako encouraged gently.

"Yeah, go back, way back, because I must've missed something since I was there at the start. And while you're one amazing broad, I'm not sure about godly . . ." Wayne added his unhelpful interjection.

"Well, I wasn't a demigod *then*—" Jo stopped herself, deciding to take Takako's advice. She looked to the Japanese woman. "You're right: start at the beginning. You have to believe me, first, when I say I have no memory of anything before my life as a human leading up to joining you all in 2057."

"Of course we believe you," Samson encouraged.

"Not exactly hard given how all of us just woke up this past year," Wayne muttered.

"I was working to put it together, at the end. I'd come to some conclusions on my own, and then most of what I know was confirmed by Snow . . . and Pan."

Jo took one more second to collect her thoughts, before launching into the explanation, deciding to over-share rather than under-shoot.

"We all know there was an Age of Gods, then Magic, then Man." Nods all around. "Well, apparently, just before the Age of Gods . . . There was a goddess, Oblivion. She heralded a sort-of unspoken first age—the Age of Oblivion, before life and light."

"I know that name," Samson whispered.

Jo nodded at him. "It was in one of Eslar's story books. You may have read it too . . . Like the lore of the Society itself, certain things carried throughout the ages and one of those things was mythology surrounding the story of Oblivion."

"Kind of how magic lingered in us even in the Age of Man," Takako reasoned.

"That's what I think, too," Jo continued with a nod. "Other gods came—and no, I don't know from where—formed the world, and Oblivion didn't like it. I'm paraphrasing, but I think you all get the idea. Needless to say, this created a rift among the gods, with Oblivion on one side and basically everyone else on the other."

"And Pan's Oblivion?" Wayne asked.

"Not quite . . ." This was the moment she'd been most apprehensive about. The moment they learned, truly, who and what she was. The moment when any of them would be well within their rights to hate her, to change their minds about helping her at all. "Demigods can be made two ways. One, they can be crafted by two greater gods—and that's how Snow came to be. The other is by splitting a greater god in two. In this case . . . Oblivion was split by the other gods to prevent her from destroying, well, the entire universe. The two demigods formed were Destruction and Chaos.

"From what I can tell . . . every divinity was just named after the thing they created and represented in the world—light, life, creation, what-have-you. Mortals gave them other names. Names that, like Eslar's story, continued to linger through the ages in different forms even when the gods themselves did not. Chaos's name is one such example."

"Well, don't hold us in suspense—what was it?" Wayne asked, though Jo could tell from the expression on his face, he already knew.

"Pandora."

"Pan," Takako whispered.

Wayne let out a groan that turned into an expletive. "We're so stupid."

"Destruction?" Samson was the only one still glued to the story. Jo held her breath for a moment, letting it out in a weary exhale.

"That . . . was me. Which is why my magic was—"

"Always breaking things." She couldn't tell by Wayne's interruption if he was upset or just eager to know more. Either way, Jo was too far down the rabbit hole to stop now.

"As long as Destruction and Chaos existed together in the same world, there was a chance for them to come together and become Oblivion once more. The pantheon wanted to avoid that, so they made a natural counterbalance to hide me, Creation . . . or Snow, as the mortals back then called him.

"It worked, for a while. But Pan was none too pleased about the situation and began wreaking havoc."

"Shocking," Wayne rolled his eyes. Jo almost smiled.

"Creation and I knew that for mankind to ever be free of Pan's terror, we needed to destroy her for good."

"How?"

"We came up with a plan . . . a demigod split is made mortal. The idea was that Snow would split my power once more and gain control of it once it was freed from my body. He'd use it to destroy the world as it was, but then use his power of creation to quickly rebuild it free of gods . . . and Pan."

"The Age of Gods to the Age of Magic," Samson seemed to realize, and when Jo and he shared a glance, there was something indescribable in his eyes.

"Clearly, it didn't work," Wayne remarked, ever helpful.

"Sadly no, it didn't. As long as I'm alive, she's alive. And since my magic was in Snow and my body was reborn as a mortal, Pan persisted. Snow was weak from the shift—"

"It takes a lot out of him to change an age," Samson said softly. Jo paused, briefly, taking note of the understanding tone in his voice. There was something more there, his eyes still alight with that indescribable expression, but she pressed on nonetheless; there would hopefully be time to pick his brain later.

"—and Pan seized the opportunity to bind him to her, forming the Society outside of time, so she could wait to try to find me. She knew Snow would have to grant wishes to skim magic for them both to survive, for the whole Society to survive. And eventually, she knew would have her chance to be whole again."

A heavy silence settled on the room as everyone processed. Jo felt like she'd just run a marathon and now, even though there was suddenly no more track, every muscle in her body was still cranked taut with tension.

"For better or for worse, I have my magic—all of my magic—back again. In destroying the Society, I've gone back to being a demigod. Pan and Snow are once again walking among mortals, and the world has been reverted back to when the Society was founded . . . sort of, at least. The year is different, I think. My money is on things resetting from square one, even if to us it seems like this world has only existed for a year—or a few days."

"And now that you're back, too, she's going to be on the hunt for you again," Takako added.

"Yes. The stalemate in a war that's been going on since the dawn of time has ended. Now, I want to finish the war for good."

"Why?" Wayne asked, looking at all of them with denial filling his eyes. "Why not just let her be? She hasn't done anything too bad over the past couple hundred years according to the history of this world. We have our lives back, we don't have to deal with time, and—"

"And there's a demigod who can gain the power to

destroy it all," Jo interrupted. "As long as Pan and I are both alive, mankind isn't safe."

"Couldn't you just stop her from joining with you?" Wayne asked.

"I can try, I *would* try . . . But there's something about her magic. It calls to me in ways I don't want to hear . . ." Her voice trailed off and none of them probed further. It was the darkest corner of her soul, the part that Jo was coming to accept as the lingering remnants of Oblivion. She wanted to vow that there was no way she could ever be tempted by it. However . . . "The best course of action is to destroy Pan and ensure that Oblivion is gone for good. That's the only way to be certain."

"I bet she's trapped Snow again," Takako mused, changing the topic and following a train of thought Jo hadn't even considered before. "If she trapped him once after a seismic shift of realities, I bet she did it again. I bet that's why he has her as his 'advisor'."

"It must be; he liked her no more than the rest of us," Samson agreed. "And she's been his advisor since the dawn of Aristonia, according to all records."

"We have to free him." Panic swelled with worry over all of the horrible things Snow could be enduring— possibly *had been* enduring for who knew how long.

"Sounds to me that freeing him and protecting the harmony of the world both hinge on the same thing: killing Pan," Takako pointed out.

"That's all well and good, but how do we get rid of a demigod?" Wayne heaved a somewhat dramatic sigh. "This isn't a point-and-shoot sort of situation."

Takako looked at him from the corners of her eyes,

clearly uncertain if she should take offense. "Let's think through it logically. What was she afraid of?"

"Pan wasn't afraid of anything," Wayne said quickly. "She chewed glass, spat it at us, and then asked for thank yous."

"Then what is a demigod afraid of in general?" Takako was undeterred, and looked to Jo.

She began to pace, mulling over every bit of information that had seemed so overwhelming even minutes ago, but now seemed like precious little to cull through. "It's not as if I have a handbook on how to be a demigod. I mean, I told you all everything I know and—"

Jo stopped. Memories: a book detailing an ancient battle, a mention of Pan being afraid, her room at the mansion . . . all muddled into a mismatched jigsaw puzzle that felt like the start of a good idea—maybe.

"When I was in her room," Jo started slowly, giving herself time to try to clarify the hazy vision as much as possible. "She showed me something . . ."

"What?" Wayne asked.

"I'm trying to remember." Jo held up a hand to one eye, as if physically trying to force some part of her to see back to the memory Pan had given her while staying rooted in the present. It was the first time she was actually trying to invoke the shadows that had come to haunt her at the end of the Society. But now that she had reclaimed her full powers and actually had need of them, they no longer seemed interested in tormenting her. "We were in a forest . . . there was darkness all around us . . ."

"Forest, darkness—that really narrows it down."

The sound of a hand striking firmly into another body.

"Quiet, Wayne," Takako hissed as Jo kept focus.

"There was . . . a spear of darkness? Something lodged into a tree. She said I was the only one who could destroy it. To destroy it before it destroyed us—I think?" Jo shook her head. "I'm sorry, that's all I have."

"It's something," Samson said softly, encouragingly. Jo gave him a tired smile in thanks.

"Why don't we take a break for the night?" Takako suggested, pulling out her obsidian disk and fumbling with it until numbers appeared. "It's getting late, and we'll all think with clearer heads after a good night's sleep. We can start first thing in the morning."

"Works for me." Wayne was the first to get to his feet, eager to flee the room. *Just when she thought they were getting on better footing he—*

Jo's thought was interrupted by his hand falling on her shoulder. "Thanks for trusting us with this, dollface," Wayne said softly. "We'll get you through this."

Jo raised a hand, clutching his fingers tightly for a moment. "Thank you." Her eyes shifted. "Thank you all."

Wayne departed and Samson was the next to stand. "He's right. We can do this."

"I know, Sam." They exchanged a brief hug, and then it was just her and Takako.

"It'll look better in the morning, I'm sure." Takako gave her a hug as well, tight and fierce. "Get some rest."

"Yeah . . ." Even if it was a front, Jo admired her teammates' hope. And perhaps they were right; perhaps everything would be clearer after a night of rest.

Unfortunately for Jo, she didn't feel the least bit tired.

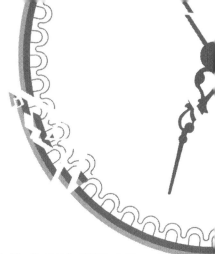

5. ALLEY ENCOUNTER

J O DIDN'T EVEN attempt sleep this time. After the last three days spent wasting the first few hours of night tossing and turning, she figured it was about time she got a jumpstart at this new life of twenty-four-hour wakefulness.

With Takako and Samson both occupying their own guest rooms downstairs, close enough to the living room to be easily disturbed, Jo forwent her usual TV binge. Instead, she grabbed a coat at random from the hall closet and bundled up for what would probably prove a lengthy nighttime walk.

The coat was a heavy thing, thick and too big for her, but warm; it smelled a bit like whatever cologne Wayne now wore. For a moment, it left Jo just standing in the foyer, wrapped up tight in the material and breathing. There was a spicy note to it, sharp enough that it triggered a heart-rending sense-memory of cloves and crisp winter air.

Every part of her ached for Snow, making the musky scent of the coat, though pleasantly similar, seem lackluster in comparison. Without a conscious command, something in her was reaching out blindly for him, longing in a way that could not be described. Somewhere, as though he were on the other end of an invisible tether, Jo could almost feel him. But she lost the sensation before she could grasp it fully.

The elevator descended smoothly and Jo watched as the numbers were illuminated in swift, decreasing succession. When the doors in front of her opened, a cool breath of night air gusted over her. The lobby was icy, and Jo drew the coat tighter around herself, bracing for the even colder temperatures that awaited her outside.

The security guard watched her closely for several seconds, his eyes shining golden in the darkness. The longer Jo stared, the more "not quite human" the creature began to look, until eventually she had to tear her eyes away. He turned his head down with a sniff, looking back at the tablet propped against his knee and muttering something about "humans." As Jo passed, she noticed long ears—much longer than even Eslar's and far more narrow—tucked under his cap.

Outside, her previous assessment about the chill was spot-on. But Jo relished every shoulder-trembling gust of wind, the night itself carrying the scents of the city and the faint spark of magic throughout. Yorkton and New York City were both large, and on a numbered grid, but the similarities stopped there. Sure, there were some things found in every city, like the steam billowing up from its underbelly. But now Jo wondered what lurked in those depths: Subway cars? Giant worms? A whole different city? The possibilities in this new Age of Magic seemed endless.

As she wandered down the first block, Jo's mind turned from the city to wondering what the others were dreaming about. Nineteen years of experience, and she already couldn't quite remember what it felt like to dream. She could recall images and feelings, but the distinct sensation of dreaming had left her, a misplaced sort of energy taking its place. There was so much time here in the after-hours where most of the world slept and Jo didn't quite know what to do with herself.

She shoved her hands in the pockets of Wayne's coat as her mind whirred with countless possible failures to their as-yet-unformulated plans. Pan was crazy and unpredictable, but she was also powerful and terrifying, and those things combined left a metallic tang of panic at the back of Jo's throat. If they didn't come up with a good enough plan, they'd be playing victim to whatever world Chaos—or worse, Oblivion— might determine.

The thought carried Jo's mind in a different direction. Pan versus Chaos. If Jo had reclaimed her demigod status with the destruction of the Society, then any tethers holding Pan back must have been broken as well. Was Chaos similar to Pan? Or would her new personality be different entirely?

A solid block away from Wayne's building, Jo felt it.

To call it a sensation was too simple, the prickling beneath her skin and at the back of her neck tantamount to the faint itching of a forgotten memory. Without

41

really knowing why, Jo picked up the pace, splitting her focus between the growing itch and the length of sidewalk in front of her.

It took about another block for her to identify the itch as a physical thing, a magical presence probably a dozen feet behind her.

There was a creeping, crawling feeling to the magic. Invisible tendrils attempted to sink into her lungs like a heavy smoke and weight her down. Every sensation was physical, though any casual observer would see nothing more than two people walking down the street.

Jo stopped suddenly, and felt the presence stop as well. Swallowing, she braced herself for what she might find when she turned. Even with that, she was caught off-guard. She'd been half-expecting, perhaps even half-hoping for, the candy-haired woman-child to be standing there.

Fortunately or unfortunately—Jo couldn't decide which—it was a fairly unassuming-looking man. Average build, human as far as she could tell, generally speaking not someone she'd be too worried about if it weren't for his face. His eyes were completely blackened and oozing down his face, like melting charcoal.

"You've finally awoken," the man spoke. *Well, not quite.* He opened his mouth and the words came from his lips, but it was not whatever the man's voice had been. Instead, it was an eerie echo of a voice Jo knew well.

"Go away." She didn't think the command would work, but it didn't hurt to try.

"Aren't you already tired of the hunt?" Pan

continued through the man as if Jo hadn't said anything at all. Every time his spoke, his lips chapped, peeling away like paint chips to reveal a new, nearly glowing color underneath. "We're right back where we started." The man tilted his head. The movement was awkward and unnatural, as if the rest of his body were limp, held upright and commanded by invisible strings. "Not quite. I have something here you want."

Snow. The thought cracked through her mind like lightning and, as if she'd said it aloud, the man smirked in the most uncomfortably familiar way.

"Yes." The man took a lurching step forward. "Him. The one who was made for you. But he was only made, Destruction." Jo shuddered at the sound of her old name rolling off his lips in Pan's voice. Wrong, the whole situation was wrong. "I was part of you—I *was* you, long before he ever even existed."

The street had darkened around her. It was as if she now stood in a tunnel with no exits, only darkness. The man was before her with his haunted eyes and glowing mouth spewing Pan's words. And somewhere behind him, somewhere far but almost close enough to touch if Jo took one mighty lunge forward, was the ghostly outline of Pan.

"Come back to me."

"Free him." Jo kept her eyes on the man and not the wisps of color condensing further into the shape of Pan by the moment. "Free this man. He's not part of this game."

"It's too late for that." A giggle echoed off more corners than the not-quite reality should have. "I've already turned his intestines to gummy worms and his heart to lead."

It was true. The closer the man got, the clearer she could see it. Chaos had done her work on him—nothing was in its right place.

"There's only one route out for him now." *Destruction*, Jo heard the word left unsaid. "Put him out of his misery and come to me. Snow and I are merely sustaining in this castle. There's not much energy left now. Come to me and save others from suffering his fate."

Jo took a small step back. She could see just what thread to pull on to make the whole knotted mess of a man unravel. This was not the first time she'd been confronted with this decision. The shadows clouded her eyes—*a forest, running, Chaos hunting her*. Jo blinked the memories of her past life and Pan's games away.

The man was right before her now, a horror to behold. His skin was turning scaly, nose flattening into that of a kitten, or hog. Though his eyes were still the same void that bled down his face in rivulets.

"Kill him, Jo." With Pan's voice, the man commanded his own death.

She'd killed people before, like this, back then. Jo's mind was twisting in on itself with every flash of memory. She'd put an end to their suffering when she had to. So why couldn't she now?

"Destroy him. Let it out. Feel how good it is to further the world to its natural state of oblivion once more."

Jo opened her mouth to object, but the words never left. His hands were around her throat, compressing. *Could she even be killed by strangling as a demigod?*

Jo didn't know; all she felt was her mind swirling with the panic of knowing she would have to undo a life.

"Do it!" Pan screeched. Jo's eyes pressed shut against the sharpness of the noise.

Another forest, another man—men—warped by Chaos's magic chasing her. It was a time of gods and the great war for the future of it all. She was Destruction. Creation came for her then. He told her . . . Told her . . .

A gunshot shattered the trance.

Jo's eyes opened wide and she took a gasping breath of air as the man's hands slid from around her neck. He fell to the ground with a dull thud, illuminated by the lights and sounds of the city once more. Jo blinked rapidly, trying to adjust her eyes to the nighttime brightness of the city lights that suddenly seemed blinding.

"Are you okay?" Takako's voice had never sounded so concerned, and so welcome. With a click of the safety, she holstered her gun and rested her hand on Jo's upper arm.

"I think so." Jo rubbed her throbbing neck. The pain was already subsiding. If anything, it felt even better than before. Her eyes dropped to the body of the man—or, where the body should've been. Light was cracking through his skin from the inside out and, all at once, he burst with a series of sparks and flurry of confetti that faded to ash on the wind.

"Good, because I think we should move." Takako's eyes weren't on her, but the confused couple staring with slack jaws across the street. "I don't know what people are used to in this Age of Magic, but in our time, that would've looked a lot like a murder."

"You're right." Jo barely had time to finish her sentence before she was being tugged along by Takako. Within a few steps, she was keeping pace with the woman as they ran back to Wayne's building. "What were you doing out?"

"Following you." Takako glanced over her shoulder, though Jo had nearly caught up to her. "I was worried Pan might try something . . ."

Instinct told Jo to be offended, that she wasn't someone who needed to be coddled or protected—especially not now, as a demigod. But the thought of someone chasing after her. Of someone trying to protect her . . .

Creation. A forest. A plan.

Jo stopped so fast her momentum had her tripping over her own feet in a short series of hops.

"What is it?" Takako stopped as well, spinning in place, eyes scanning behind them for any further pursuers. Luckily, there were none.

"An arrow," Jo heard herself whisper on half-second delay, mouth catching up to her rampant thoughts.

Takako stared at her in confusion. "What?"

"It wasn't a spear of darkness."

"Spear? Are you talking about your vision in Pan's room?"

"It was an arrow." Jo straightened, closing her eyes and trying to sink into the memories of a time she barely remembered. "Hunt," she whispered, as if invoking the name of the ancient bow-wielding goddess could make it all clear. Jo's eyes snapped open. "Samson. We have to go to Samson."

6. CHAMPION

JO WASN'T SURE her feet even hit the floor until she landed in the elevator. "Bouncing from foot to foot won't make it go any faster," Takako panted softly. Jo didn't think they'd been running—well, *sprinting*—that fast. She was hardly out of breath, but Takako's lips were parted and her cheeks flushed slightly. "Care to share just what is going on?"

"I need to see if Samson has something." Jo hoped the feeling in her gut, that nagging one that was finally beginning to play connect-the-dots with all the odd experiences she'd had over the past few months, was one to be believed. She clung to the memory of being in his room at the Society, of a special arrow in the quiver hung on his wall. "If not, he can help give us clarity on the arrow."

The doors dinged just as Takako was going to ask another question. *Saved by the bell*, Jo thought. The second they were halfway open, Jo darted through, starting for the main entry to the penthouse and to Samson's room, Takako close behind.

A strong arm around her waist stopped Jo just short of the door. Jo twisted, looking back at Takako questioningly. The woman immediately eased her grip.

"I don't think Samson's the type to like people just barging into his room. Especially not when they're likely going to startle him from sleep in the process."

"You're right." Jo took a deep breath, regaining her composure. The last thing Jo wanted to do was offend or distress their crafter.

So, with a much more restrained step, Jo crossed over to his door, lifted her hand, and knocked gently. She leaned in toward the wooden door—Wayne, and all his love for expensive things, had huge carved slabs of wood for doors, so thick that Jo wouldn't be surprised if her knock hadn't transferred at all. She listened, and heard nothing. Jo tried again with another knock and a soft "Samson?"

That was when she heard muffled noises from within and eased away. Takako was leaning on the wall opposite, arms crossed over her chest and seemingly content to watch the whole scene unfold before her. The door cracked open, revealing a sliver of a face and a tuft of orange fuzz that had escaped his tight braids.

"Jo? Is everything all right?"

"Yes, everything is fine," Jo assured him. "I'm sorry to wake you, but it seemed . . . We just . . . We were—"

"Jo has something she needs to ask you." Takako stepped in to assist in guiding Jo's frantic thoughts.

"I know it's late, but may we please come in, Samson?"

"Oh, um . . ." Samson disappeared and some more prominent shuffling could be heard.

Jo and Takako exchanged a look after it continued for several seconds with still no Samson back at the door. Jo leaned forward. "Sa—"

The door opened in full, startling her. As Jo straightened, she bumped into Takako and would've lost her balance were it not for the woman's strong grip on her arm.

"Sorry, I wasn't trying—"

"You can come in now." Samson smiled, and stepped aside.

"This is where Wayne put you up?" Jo frowned. She hadn't done that much exploring of the two-story penthouse. There were as many doors as there were windows—and Wayne loved his windows. She expected there to have been rooms on rooms on rooms.

But while Jo had assumed Samson would follow in Takako's footsteps and claim a guest room, this room in particular looked more fitting for the company below than the private home of its CEO above. It had a long oval table, carved of the same rich wood as the doors but inlaid with the obsidian that Jo had seen used for just about every other magical thing. However, none of it was visible due to the sheer mass of tinkering items that had been strewn about the makeshift workspace. The chairs that normally would have been occupied by executives had been pushed all to one side. Opposite was a small cot, barely enough room for one, piled with blankets and pillows.

"It's a bit sad as a workshop, isn't it?" Samson ducked his head.

Jo wasn't sure where she should start correcting him. That she hadn't been critiquing it as a workshop at all? That she'd been worried about his comfort? That she thought Wayne had put Samson in a corner initially and didn't think about the fact that Samson's most critical need was not his sleeping space, but his workspace?

"It's a fantastic workshop because it's filled with your creations, Sam." Samson blinked, then blushed, shaking his head. "Are they . . . working well for you?" Jo added hastily, thinking of how being tied closely with her destructive magic in the Society had begun to take its toll on his own powers.

"No issues." His tone assured her that he understood the underlying meaning of her question.

"Good, I'm glad to hear it." Jo wasn't sure if she could handle her magic breaking down another person after Nico.

Takako refocused them once more. "So, what did you need Samson for? Let's not dally. Who knows if the cops are coming."

"Cops? Why would—"

"Pan attacked Jo."

"What?" Samson's head whipped back and forth in confusion. "Are you all right?"

"I'm fine." Jo swallowed and forced herself to take an extra breath—forced an extra three seconds of thought into what she was about to say next. She had to get them—and keep them—on track. "Sam . . . Do you remember the first time I was in your room? When I helped you find weak points in the new seismograph machine you were working on?"

Samson nodded.

"You showed me your personal room too." It was a setup not unlike what he had now, Jo realized—a small bed shoved off to the right side of the entry and a much, much larger workspace. "In that room, you had some of your personal projects—arrows."

"Yes?"

"There was one arrow. An arrow you didn't want me to touch."

"I know the one you're talking about . . ." Samson seemed on guard. His hands began to twitch. The lack of tactile sensation caught up with him as he reached over to the table, grabbing the nearest bauble.

"That arrow—"

"Is special," Samson interrupted in rare form. "I still have it."

"What?" Jo and Takako seemed to say in unison.

"It survived the end of the Society?" Takako whispered, solo.

"Yes . . ." Samson gave a small nod. "Everything I made in the Society is gone. Perhaps because I didn't make it?" He went from nodding to shaking his head to shrugging. "It was in my room in the Society when I woke there, just as it was in the room where I woke up in this timeline. It seems to follow me."

"Can we see it? Just see it?" Jo's voice bordered on desperation, but she didn't care in the slightest. "Please?"

Samson's eyes darted between them for what seemed like forever, until he finally nodded. "Okay."

Jo's heart was in her ears as she watched him shuffle around the table. Along the wall of windows that overlooked Yorkton there sat a pile of heavy-looking crates, one of which Samson approached and opened. It was an odd contrast: the modern city illuminated behind the trunks that could have been from the set of an old fantasy film.

"It was a gift," Samson said, straightening, a quiver in both of his hands. His knuckles had gone pale with how tightly he was clutching it. "A gift . . . that's all I remember." When he returned to them, he placed the quiver on the table. Samson opened his mouth to speak, but was stunned into silence as Takako walked right up to it.

As if in a trance, Jo watched the woman move with precision and certainty. She had never seen Takako be half as bold as she was about to be. Even Samson stared, slack jawed, his words forgotten.

"This," Takako whispered, going right for the arrow Jo had been entranced by. It stood out from the others—slightly longer, with a slightly thicker shaft of pale wood, and a plume that seemed to sparkle with its own light.

"Taka—" Samson never finished whatever objection he was about to voice.

Right as he moved, Takako's fingers closed around the end of the shaft. Pure white light overtook the arrow, blindingly bright. As she lifted it from the quiver, the light seemed to drip off like molten, white hot metal, fizzling and disappearing as it met the table. In its wake, as though it was fresh from the forge, was an arrow made of pure gold.

At the same moment, all of Jo's past memories and discoveries finally clicked.

"A golden arrow," she whispered. "A golden arrow!" Her voice seemed to dislodge the other two from their trance, if only slightly, as both of them turned in her direction with yet-gaping mouths. Jo was quick to try to explain, though the thoughts seemed to whizz through her head as though they were arrows themselves, impossible to pluck from the air in any kind of order. "My research. Don't you remember, Takako?"

"You asked me about archer deities."

"Yes! It came up, across mythologies and timelines. It was even in Eslar's story book." At that, Samson gave a small nod of affirmation. "I remember . . . The Goddess of the Hunt, back in a time of gods. She was working with other gods to try to fight against Oblivion. But . . . it wasn't going their way. Pan killed her. That was when Snow and I—our past selves—decided to try to reboot the world to kill Chaos."

"Did a goddess give this to you?" Takako asked Samson.

"I think I'd remember." Samson shook his head almost violently.

"Can I see it?" Jo held out a hand.

Takako extended her arm, holding out the golden arrow toward Jo.

"Thanks." Jo reached for it, and the moment her fingertips brushed the gold, memories that did not belong to her flooded her sight.

Hunt, swathed in the furs of her kills and with dirt on her face, bestowing the arrow on a man she called Champion, so that none of the other gods would know of its whereabouts. The man was to kill Pan, but then . . .

The world shifted, and the man was without memory of the gods. As he lay dying, he passed it on to his son, who sold it to a collector. The collector's home was ransacked by thieves, who pawned everything off but the arrow. They held onto it, revering it for power and luck, before their hideout was burned down and the arrow was hidden in a bed of ash.

. . . Until a farmer discovered it while tilling the land. The farmer gave it to his daughter, and it was she who ultimately gave it to Samson as thanks for a night spent in his home during a storm.

"Josephina?" Takako asked. Instantly, Jo knew it wasn't the first time her friend had tried to get her attention.

The visions faded and Jo shook her head. She'd barely touched the weapon, but her hand fell from it. She felt heavy, weary from the onslaught of memories. "It's Hunt's arrow."

"You're sure?"

"No doubt," Jo affirmed.

"Let me see it?" Samson asked.

A brief look of uncertainty shadowed Takako's face but she quickly held it out to Samson. He ran his own fingers up and down the projectile.

"Please don't disassemble it," Takako cautioned uncertainly.

"I don't think I could if I tried. The craftsmanship is just . . ."

"Divine?" Jo finished with a small if tired grin.

"If it is something designed to bring down Pan— Oblivion—then why didn't Pan destroy it while she could in the Age of Magic, or the Society?" Takako

54

asked.

"I don't know." Jo thought aloud. "Perhaps she couldn't?"

"Or perhaps she didn't know what it was," Samson suggested. "You saw the protection slide off the arrow when Takako touched it. Which, why . . ."

"Because Takako is of the Champion's lineage," Jo whispered. "*That* was the magic that lingered within her through the ages." After the visions had seeped into her mind as if they'd been her own memories, it was impossible not to sense the similarities in magic between the original Champion and the young woman before her.

"So now what?" Samson asked. "If this is what takes down Pan, then what next?"

"We need a bow," Jo offered, and Takako nodded her own agreement.

"Samson, can you make one?"

On cue, the crafter lifted his head. "I can, but first I'll need something."

"What?"

"Not what," Samson corrected. "*Who*."

7. ON THE RUN

J O DIDN'T WASTE time knocking on Wayne's door, and instead barged in without warning, much to the man's startled and flailing dismay.

"D-Dollface?" Wayne blinked as much of the sleep from his eyes as he could, though he was clearly disoriented. "Is everything jake? Are we under attack?"

"Sorry to bust in like this," Jo apologized sincerely, even as she made a quick route to the nightstand to turn on a light. His room instantly filled with a painful brightness. At first, Wayne just continued to blink, letting his eyes adjust, but eventually, he noticed that Jo wasn't the only one in his room. His face contorted first in confusion and then concern.

He forced his gaze back to Jo. "If we need to hightail it for a bit, I have a bunker."

"Might not be a bad idea," Takako muttered.

"Why?" Wayne asked before Jo could get a word in.

"Jo was attacked."

"I'm fine." She tried to stop the concern from sprouting before it could take root. "More importantly, we have a plan."

"A plan?" Wayne quirked an eyebrow at her and on reflex, she glanced over her shoulder towards Takako. The golden arrow, the best clue they had to defeating Pan, was still nestled in the palms of her hands, as if the Japanese woman were cradling it like a child. Wayne looked from Jo to the arrow and back before taking in and letting out a deep, weary breath. "I think you have a lot more to explain than just this plan. But maybe first, you could let me put on some clothes?"

Before Jo could agree that was the best course, the phone at Wayne's bedside table rang.

"Who . . . no one ever calls that line," he muttered, reaching for it. Jo's heart began to race as he ran a finger over the obsidian backing.

A voice appeared to emit from thin air. "Mister Davis, there are some of the King's Guardians here."

"King's Guardians?" Wayne glanced back to them. Jo had no idea what "King's Guardians" were but she could guess it wasn't going to be anything good.

"Yes, they want to ask your guests a few questions."

"Go ahead and send them up."

"Wayne, no—" Takako hissed, stopping short when he held up a hand.

"Yes, sir."

"Give me a minute or two, however. I need to dress."

"Understood." The obsidian disk went dark and the sensation that filled the air along with the voice vanished.

"What did you all do?" Wayne turned slowly back

to them.

"Pan's after Jo. You can't let them in."

"We're not going to be here by the time the elevator arrives. Go, pack your things. We have a minute, maybe."

Jo wasn't sure if it was the panic of the situation, or the fact that Wayne gave them no warning before moving to throw off his covers, that had them scurrying from his room. Pack their things? Takako hadn't really unpacked and Jo didn't have anything, which fortunately left their hands free to help keep Samson as he worried away everything he wouldn't be able to take in such a short period of time.

In the back of her mind, a timer ticked down. Every second seemed to fly by and every movement seemed to crawl.

"Are you ready?" Wayne said, breathless, a backpack over his shoulder.

"Just where are we going?" Takako asked, lifting one of Samson's boxes as though it were filled with air and not pounds of tools. She clearly wasn't too hung up on the "where" since she was already following him out of the room.

"Remember that bunker I mentioned? There's a secret elevator that leads to it in the basement . . . It also has its own exit to the street le—"

"Myrth!" Samson interrupted suddenly. "We're going to Myrth!"

"What?" Everyone paused, stopping in lock-step.

"I have a workshop there. It can be a hiding spot. If you can get us out." He looked to Wayne.

"I don't know if trying to leave the country is the

best idea . . ." Takako muttered.

"Money finds a way," Wayne insisted. "And it's out of reach of Pan."

"Yes, but—"

Jo's head jerked away from the conversation. She could have sworn she'd just heard the soft *ding* of the elevator. Her hands went slick with perspiration, forcing her to adjust her grip on Samson's trunk.

"There's no time to argue," she interrupted. "Myrth is fine. Samson will have his workshop; he can make the bow."

"Bow?" Wayne looked for an explanation there wasn't time to give.

"Not quite . . ." Samson's fingers curled over the box he was holding. "I'll need—"

Banging on the door interrupted them all.

"To work it out later!" Jo hissed.

"This way!" Wayne started forward hastily. They all but sprinted through his penthouse to a far back room where he revealed a secret panel. With the sounds of shouting and more banging in the background, he moved his hands over the magical device to reveal a secret elevator.

The four stepped in, watching as the doors closed behind them, and feeling their stomachs rise up into their chests as the elevator descended away from the safety of Wayne's penthouse and toward the unknown.

8. READY TO JUMP

MYRTH SPREAD OUT before them like an exotic tapestry unfurled.

As the tiny airship began its descent into the city proper, Jo stared in wonder at what would have been, in her time, a coastal city on the Strait of Gibraltar. It was still that, she supposed, a coastal city bordering a narrow sea between one continent and another. But that was where the similarities ended.

The city was a towering landscape of spires with domed and slanted roofs. Lush foliage created emerald contrast as they sprouted from between the white and cream buildings, topped with not red (as she would expect of Spanish Mediterranean architecture in her time) but bright cerulean clay tiles. Great birds with silver plumage and bright blue heads stood out against it all, flying from place to place and dropping off messages.

Jo stood at the edge of the airship railing, taking it all in. As they continued descending, she could see the flecks of white in the birds' feathers, and the splashes of rainbow color in the various flags suspended over doors and balconies. She was so engrossed, she didn't hear Samson approaching until he was at her side, elbows on the railing next to her.

"What do you think?" he asked.

"It's hard to think." Jo laughed softly. "It all seems so magnificent and so . . . impossible."

"A far cry from the Spain you knew."

"A few thousand years of alternate magical history will do that." The first few days of the trip were spent cramped together in a small hold as they waited to clear Aristonian customs and be smuggled out of the kingdom. Jo had spent much of that time reading, per Takako's suggestion. It passed the time and, after all, there was so much to catch up on. Be it her age or newfound interest, she found herself much more invested in this world than she had been in her high school history classes. It was like finding where she was always meant to be.

"They call those skywings." Samson pointed. "The way the elves tell the tale, the early families were gifted the birds by the goddess." *The* Goddess. Jo remembered reading about that. Interestingly enough, the elves had evolved into a monotheistic religion. She couldn't help but wonder what they'd think when they found a demigod on their doorstep. "These birds were made for them, to suit their long life spans. They live as long as a member of a certain lineage draws breath, acting both as spirit guardians . . . and convenient messengers."

"I see." Jo's eyes continued to scan the cityscape. As the airship turned, they got a glimpse of the sea. "That's . . ." Her words trailed off at the splendor of what she beheld.

At the edge of the city, stretching into the water, was an arc-shaped building. From either end, a walkway stretched, joining together to form a single road. This road, lined by giant sapphire statues that glinted as though they were moving in the sunlight, led across the strait—The Sapphire Strait, as it was known in this time—to what Jo knew as Africa, but was now the Luanian Empire. She was trying as much as possible to expunge the past names she knew in exchange for what was before her: a completely different world that just happened to share some similar continental shapes to the world she'd been born into.

"That's the Sapphire Bridge," Samson finished for her. "And the only way into the Luanian Empire. The other wards around the continent are virtually impenetrable."

"How do they ward a whole continent?"

"The magic of the elves." Samson shrugged. "They've been around centuries longer than the second oldest race—the fae."

"And the fae are said to be an off-shoot of elves," Jo recalled reading. Samson looked somewhat surprised that she knew the fact, so Jo added, playfully defensive, "Takako's not the only one who can do a bit of research, Sam."

His eyes wandered back out toward the city and the Sapphire Bridge, the massive structure quickly disappearing from view as the airship turned yet again.

Samson rummaged through his pocket for one of his preferred cubes of wires and screws.

Jo watched as he fussed with it, eyes focused on something else entirely. She felt his magic radiating in unsettled waves, but Jo didn't inquire. If he didn't want to say, she wouldn't force him to. Instead, she opted for another distraction.

"Where's your workshop? Can we see it from here?"

Samson seemed startled, but quickly answered. "Not quite. It's a bit off in that direction." He raised a finger and pointed just diagonally beyond the bow of the airship. "It's small, but we should all be able to fit."

Their conversation was cut short by one of the smugglers poking his head out of the narrow door that led on deck. "We're gonna be dockin' soon. You should get under till we sort out customs."

"Customs? Again?" Jo mused as they stepped into the equally narrow passageway through the ship.

"It's nothing difficult. Should only take a moment on a vessel this small," Samson assured her. "I'm sure the crew has done it a thousand times."

Takako and Wayne were already curled up in the small cargo space positioned between cabins and the bridge—low in the hull of the ship. The few feet between them managed to look as wide as an arena as they sat squared off against each other like two fighters about to take the ring. Wayne curled his fingers into fists, where Takako gripped at the strap of the single-arrow quiver Samson had made her (a quiver that now never left her back).

"What did we miss?" Jo asked as she settled into her own space, Samson closing the hatch securely behind them.

Wayne opened his mouth to speak but Takako managed the first word.

"He wanted to pass us off as passengers and get off promptly. I insisted it was better to stick with the plan."

"*Crew*. I said pass ourselves off as crew."

"Takako is right." Jo sighed softly. "They said we'd just have to wait until nightfall and then they'll unload."

"I am not made to be shoved in a corner. I travel first class or not at all," Wayne huffed.

"Clearly not, Mr. Bigshot." Jo enjoyed the way he contorted to avoid her gaze. The trip had been the hardest on him. At first, he'd seemed thrilled to exercise some of his less-than-savory connections to get out of Aristonia. But that also meant stepping out of the comfort zone he'd settled into; this was the first time Jo had ever met a version of Wayne not surrounded by luxury.

They passed the rest of the descent in silence, rocking back and forth with the other illicit goods as the ship slipped into port. *Was it even called a port when dealing with airships?*

Jo pulled her knees to her chest, rested her forearms on them, forehead on her forearms, and closed her eyes. She was now an ocean away from Snow. An ache sank into her chest, flowing through her limbs with every slow beat of her heart. It solidified in every corner of her body, weighing her down.

I'll come for you soon, she wanted to say. But kept her mouth shut as the sounds of heavy boots ascending the gangplank rattled the side of the airship. Muffled voices could be heard over the sounds of feet shifting and boards creaking.

". . . on behalf of the Elvish government, we're going to need to see your papers."

A sudden jerk of movement grabbed Jo's attention.

Samson looked intently up at the floorboards, narrowing his eyes as if trying to peer through them. Jo wasn't the only one who'd made note of the odd expression and uncharacteristic mannerism. Takako glanced between her and Wayne, who merely shrugged.

". . . afraid your documents are out of order."

"Those documents should be fine."

"You don't seem to have the new papers. No matter, we should be able to assist you in procuring them."

Samson leaned forward with an agonizingly slow movement that the rest of them mirrored so they didn't make a sound. When they were almost nose to nose, he whispered, "Those aren't elvish customs."

"How do you know?" Takako breathed in reply.

"Wrong accent. All wrong."

"Are you sure?" Wayne asked.

Samson nearly loosened a braid with the furious nodding of his head. "I . . . I know the accent. I lived here before I—I—"

"We believe you." Jo placed her hand on his. The man's stuttering forced the volume of his voice to rise. Samson's throat clenched as if he was trying to swallow down his anxiety.

"Now what?" Wayne asked.

"Nothing changes. The safest thing is still to wait here until—"

Takako was interrupted by the sounds of a struggle. The interior of the ship rumbled as the unmistakable sound of a body being slammed into something above reverberated down the walls.

"What? Who—" The man's question was cut short by a gurgle, and another scream was suppressed.

One of the earlier voices of the "customs" officers finally spoke. "Search the ship. They're smugglers. There's a secret hold here somewhere. Find them."

"Still safest to wait?" Wayne asked Takako sharply.

"Now what?" Samson began to pat around him, no doubt looking for something to occupy his hands. They came up to his chest, where he began to mess roughly with his own fingers, lacking a bauble to fidget with.

Without a word, Takako reached up to remove the tie from her hair, letting the dark, pin-straight strands fall around her shoulders. Careful not to startle him, she held the hair tie out in front of Samson's hands, waiting for him to take it. Samson let out a soft breath, taking the hair tie eagerly, and began to fuss with it.

"Can we fight?" Wayne asked, again pitching his question to Takako.

"I can, but I can't guarantee I can keep all of you safe," she murmured, no doubt trying to calculate the odds in her head. "Sounds like there are four of them."

Jo closed her eyes, trying to block out the panic surrounding her and the sounds of what were no doubt Pan's men closing in on them. They'd followed her across the sea. Pan knew where they were. Or, perhaps, Pan's influence was so wide she'd merely covered all of her bases in every port she could. Who knew what Pan knew, what she was capable of, how far she would go.

All Jo could focus on now was the feeling of the

ship around her, and deal with the immediate threat of the four—Takako had been right—pursuing them.

Destroy them, her magic seemed to whisper. It was the same feeling she'd had in Yorkton. But these men were different; they weren't like the chaotic, twisted version of a person. These were willing servants with only mere traces of Pan's corruption. In theory, they weren't beyond redemption.

Did she care? They'd sided with Pan. She should have no issues killing them on the spot and yet . . . something about giving into thoughtless murder felt like letting Pan win—*like letting Oblivion win*.

There also wasn't time for her to have an ethical conundrum.

"I can break us a way out," Jo said hastily, opening her eyes once more.

"Break us a way out?"

"Then they find us," Wayne hissed.

"Not if I break enough in the process that we can slip away in the chaos that follows."

"Can't say I'm following, doll."

A loud crack interrupted their conversation. The sound of wood splintering, breaking, and giving in was worse than an alarm clock on the first day of school. It grated against Jo's magic, as if some part of her was upset that something had been broken and it wasn't her doing.

"I think we're out of time. Just hold on."

Controlled demolition was the singular thought that ran through Jo's mind. Her magic surrounded every corner of the vessel. Like a sixth sense, Jo understood its construction, every support and load-bearing wall.

Such a little flex of her magic reaped such big destruction.

The airship's sides popped like popcorn, bolts flying off. A large crack ran down the length of the ship. Boards splintered away and whole sections collapsed.

"A hole is going to open there." Jo thrust out a hand, beginning to move in the same motion. "Get ready to jump. I have no idea how high up we're docked."

To her team's credit, they didn't hesitate.

The front of the ship cracked and fell away before them like a hatch opening. Takako was the first one out, followed shortly by Samson. Wayne stalled, but only briefly, before leaping awkwardly down to a pile of boards that had fallen like a ramp before him.

Debris fell around them like confetti as they tumbled to the ground that was—thankfully—not too far away. Shouting rose from within the airship and outside, but dulled briefly the moment Jo felt her body hit the ground, hard. She sprang back into action, expecting the pain to linger but feeling better than before.

The rest of her team didn't quite bounce back in the same way, but they pulled themselves together nonetheless.

"We need to go." Jo tugged on Samson's elbow.

"My supplies . . ." Samson swallowed, looking back toward the crumbling ship. With one more brief glance, he shook his head and ran forward, toward where Wayne and Jo had already begun pressing along the hull of another airship.

"Stand back, stand back!" someone with a thick accent was saying—an accent Jo now assumed to be Elvish.

"There's people trapped. Call healers!"

The four kept moving in the tight space between the hulls of airships and the ledge at their side. With the ruckus behind them, they went unnoticed, slipping around the hull of the fourth ship and up onto the platform where passengers, crew, and staff were running.

"This way," Samson said, keeping his head down.

Just like that, he led them though the lavish terminal with a flash of something Jo guessed was akin to a visa in her time, and a quick exchange of some words in what must have been Elvish. The real customs guard was more focused on the commotion at the platform than inspecting things too closely, and he waved them through to the busy central receiving area for the airship port. Beyond that was a giant cul-de-sac filled with vehicles, birds, and even a horse or two (if you count rainbow colored, equine-looking creatures with chicken feet as horses).

That was where they all stopped and seemed to take a collective breath of fresh air.

"It's only about an hour walk from here," Samson said, starting for the exit.

"I'm done walking, and sneaking, and being smuggled. It'll be faster if we get a car."

Before any of them could object, Wayne gave a confident wave and heralded what must pass for a taxi here in Myrth. Albeit, the nicest taxi she'd ever had the pleasure of riding in. The interior was made of a strange leather, one she'd only ever seen in the Society in Snow's room, and Jo wondered if she'd now find out what animal it came from.

The driver donned a pair of gloves, dotted in obsidian and sapphire, and gave a nod after Samson finished speaking. The second they came into contact with the wheel, both his digits and the dashboard glowed and the car began to move—powered entirely by the man's magic.

Jo tilted her head back, sighing again, letting the sights and sounds of the city wash over her as if she weren't still on the run. Men and women of all shapes and sizes went about their business. She realized she had assumed that all elves were dark skinned like Eslar, but that proved categorically untrue. She saw every skin tone imaginable, coupled with every hair color.

As they passed an outdoor theater, Jo witnessed a man orating a story, casting bright illusions that swept over the crowd. They drove through an upscale area where the men and women seemed to wear endless strings of sapphire and silver. And, for just a second, Jo got a glimpse of the long road that led to the Sapphire Bridge.

"Like this, it should only be about ten more minutes." Samson twisted around his front seat to tell them.

"Good, the sooner we can get inside the better," Takako muttered.

"Agreed," Jo mumbled, closing her eyes and letting the rumbling of the car fill her mind. It served as a poor distraction. All she could think of was the feel of the leather under her palms, and the memories of Snow's room.

9. IF YOU DON'T, I WILL

IN NO TIME, they were parked in front of a decent sized and homey looking building, cerulean tiles dotting the roof to complement the terracotta and Cherrywood of the facade. The door was painted a vibrant teal and boasted a sign that said, "Commissioned Craftswork, Enquire Within." Jo's heart clenched when she saw the small attempt at a painted bird in the corner.

"Here we are," Samson mumbled, getting out of the car as Wayne took the liberty of paying the driver. "It's not very large inside . . ."

"I'm sure it's great, Sam," Jo assured.

"And, if not, we can get a hotel," Wayne muttered as they stepped into the cluttered work room.

"Not very large" may have been a slight understatement.

The workshop had one clear space that Jo could only assume was Samson's equivalent of a front desk, and even that was threatened by a litany of screws and baubles at its edges. Every other space was overflowing, lost beneath a mix of trinkets and unfinished projects. It left a pang in her heart, how similar every space Samson occupied tended to be, as if he was holding on to something too tightly, trying to keep a part of himself liminal and unchanging. An indirect kind of stability.

"You three can stay in the loft. I have a bed over here."

"Or a hotel."

"We're not getting a hotel," Takako insisted. "We need to fly under the radar."

"Yeah? Just like Jo's demolition was under the radar?"

"We were out of options." Jo didn't spare him a long side-eye. "Hand-to-hand combat wasn't going to be less conspicuous."

"It doesn't matter now." Takako sighed, running a hand through her hair. "Look, it was a long journey to get here." She was right about that; four days of travel had never felt so long. "We're here, in one piece, and hopefully out of Pan's reach."

"You said the Luanian government doesn't much like working with Aristonia?" Jo asked Samson.

"Not with anyone. They like to stay out of things. And I don't go by Samson here. We should be safe . . ." he said hastily, as if trying to predict their next concerns.

"Still, we shouldn't stay here for too long if we can avoid it." Takako walked over to one of the tables, resting her hand on it. "How long will it take you to make the bow?"

Samson hummed and grabbed for something off a nearby table. It wasn't sufficient, because he promptly reached for something else. In the span of about thirty seconds, he was in full-blown reorganization mode.

"You can't, can you?" Jo whispered as the fact dawned on her.

"I can!" Samson turned quickly as though she'd greatly offended him. "I can make it. I just need a special material to do it with."

"I can get you whatever you need. Money is no consequence." Wayne never passed up an opportunity to flaunt his wealth and the influence it gave him. "What do you need?"

Samson shook his head, deflating further into himself. "*You* can't get this material."

"Oh? Try me," Wayne challenged. Jo wondered if he was oblivious to the fact that Samson was on edge (and had been since they started on their way to Myrth), or didn't care. She didn't know which was worse.

"No. No, no, we . . . I—we *need* Eslar for this," Samson argued through a frown, not quite looking at anyone. His hands were clenched into tight fists at his sides, trembling just enough to be noticeable. His magic spiked and tensed, though Jo was certain she was the only one who felt it. It wasn't the reaction any of them had expected, the following breath of silence proof that they'd all been a tad caught off-guard by it. And that silence was enough for Samson to deflate a bit, looking up at Wayne with a tired but determined glint in his eye. "An arrow is worthless without a proper bow and the only design I can assume will be strong enough, and magically powerful enough to balance this arrow, will be made of a branch from the Life Tree on High Luana."

"High Luana? You never said anything about getting there." Wayne moved to storm over to Samson but Jo stopped him, and whatever he thought he was about to do, with a straight arm.

"Okay, I read about High Luana—down south, where the elf royalty lives." A nod from Samson prompted Jo to continue. "Why are we freaking out about it now?"

"Getting to Myrth is one thing, doll. Getting to High Luana as non-High Elves is downright impossible. It's where the most ancient elves live—the originals, as they claim. Even elves have a hard time getting there."

"This is why we *need* Eslar," Samson insisted once more.

"Let me guess . . . He's on High Luana?" A nod from Samson. "Of course."

"He would be," Wayne muttered.

Eslar's absence was beginning to make a lot more sense. "So if we can't get into High Luana, we get him to bring us what we need?"

"Great, everything hinges on a stubborn, stuck-up elf." Wayne threw his hands up and they promptly fell onto his hips. He turned away with a heavy sigh, as if unable to look at them any longer.

"Leave that to me. I'm sure I can get through to him," Samson pleaded.

"We trust you, Sam," Jo reassured. "Do what you need. But as quickly as possible, please." She didn't think she really needed the last bit, but was compelled to add it all the same.

He gave a small nod, lowering his eyes. "I'll do my best." Just once, she wanted him to channel Wayne's confidence to the point of arrogance. "In the meantime, just . . . make yourselves comfortable."

Comfortable proved to be an impossibility. The loft was packed to the brim with tools, crates, and supplies, leaving little room for them to exist—not to mention sleep. As a result, Jo, Takako, and Wayne had all taken to spending the majority of their time in an odd hybrid space nearby—part restaurant, part bookstore, part concert venue.

She and Wayne had already set up in what had become their corner couches. Takako was the last to join them, book in hand. She perched with a steaming mug of something thick, green, and earthy smelling—something Jo hadn't yet been brave enough to try.

"Samson says he'll need a few more days." It had been Takako's turn to ask today.

Jo's stomach dropped, her magic crackling beneath her skin in rebellion. Even though Samson wasn't here, she wanted to argue, wanted to tell him they didn't have a few *more* days, not when Snow was . . . when they didn't even know if he . . . But Jo pushed it all down.

It had only been three days since they arrived.

Jo took a breath, letting it out slowly, and then looked up at Wayne and Takako, startling a bit at the look of concern on their faces. She cleared her throat, taking another bite of what she'd come to think of as an Elvish empanada. It was a pasty sprinkled with what looked like glitter, but with a rich, savory, meaty flavor—a deviation from the candy-like appearance that she'd been pleased to discover the first time she'd tried it. "Fine. We can wait a few more days."

Takako and Wayne shared a look before nodding in agreement.

Except, two days later, there was still no word.

"What's he even doing?" Wayne huffed, sitting back in the booth of a fancy bar and lounge they'd splurged on a taxi to get to. The scotch he ordered, which had probably cost as much as their fare, sat untouched in front of him, his arms crossed firmly over his chest.

"Making contact with High Luana in general is no easy feat, let alone one specific individual," Takako reasoned, but even her voice held a sort of flat disbelief. She was drinking a bright purple cocktail out of a swirling martini glass, a cherry-looking fruit changing rapidly through various neon colors at the bottom.

"You had smartphones back in 2005 that could contact anyone across the globe," Jo fumed. "We had biobands in 2057. And these, whatever they are, can do the same thing, right?" She fished one of the obsidian disks Wayne had bought her to play with out of her pocket and placed it a bit roughly on the table in front of her. "So what makes contacting one elusive elf so goddamn difficult?"

"Might want to dial it down there, dollface," Wayne hissed under his breath, and it wasn't until that moment that Jo realized how loud her voice had gotten, how much she'd been inching forward in frustration.

Takako wasn't wrong; Jo had been reading as much as possible about High Luana at night (in-between trying to actually learn some Elvish). It was the farthest spot of land in the Luanian Empire from any other non-elf territory, literally separated by a continent and a sea. Still, her point about the phones should be valid . . . She let herself slump back down in her seat with a dejected huff, grabbing her own cocktail from the table and taking a long drink.

"And this is why we're not letting you ask him for updates anymore," Wayne muttered.

The liquid inside her glass was perfectly clear sans an iridescent slick on the top. Though no ice kept it cold, it was chilled to near biting perfection and slid cool and calming from throat to chest to stomach. Jo shivered at the sensation, licking the berry tang from her lips before speaking again, voice more restrained.

"If we don't have anything by end of day tomorrow, I'm demanding news."

"We have no choice but to give him more time," Takako tried. Jo couldn't identify the undercurrent in her voice, but it made her less willing to argue.

Still, she couldn't help mumbling under hear breath, "We don't *have* time."

One day became two. Two became four. And Jo's ability to give Samson the benefit of the doubt waned completely. Eslar, and by association Samson, were the only things currently standing between her and finding Snow, making sure he was alive, saving him from whatever torturous position Pan had left him in after the Society had been destroyed. The longer they lay in wait twiddling their thumbs, the more likely it was that Snow was suffering a fate Jo couldn't even bear to think of.

It was clear Samson knew something was up the moment Wayne and Takako left without Jo.

"Jo . . ." Samson whispered her name, and it killed her how nervous it sounded, especially after she'd worked so hard for so long to garner his trust. But she couldn't keep waiting like this, not without understanding *why* at least.

"What's going on with Eslar, Sam? Why haven't you been able to contact him, really?" Jo tried to ask gently.

As expected, Samson winced, a near full-body, knee-jerk reaction, though whether it was to Jo's questions or to the mention of the elf, she couldn't tell.

"I've t-tried, been trying, honest." Samson ran a shaking hand through his hair, the other hand reaching blindly for the nearest bauble, fingers trembling as they began to rearrange its varying pieces. "He's not . . . I can't get a hold of him."

"I'm sure you've tried." Jo walked up to him, placing a hand on his shoulder and hating the way it tensed beneath her touch. "But it feels like we're wasting so much time."

"He's very busy," he said, standing up straighter, and Jo could almost see a physical wall going up between them. "And very far, that's all. It takes time."

"But you've *had* time," Jo groaned, hearing the whine creeping into her own voice, unable to pull it back this time. Samson looked at her for a moment, face crestfallen and eyes holding something heavy in them that made Jo's heart ache.

"Give me one more day," Samson offered after a moment, and though Jo wanted to argue, wanted to demand right now, she could see something in Samson's posture, in the expression lining his young face, that said not to. "My last attempt to contact him was fruitless, but I have a plan for the next time." The words sounded forced, and she could tell he was already emotionally drained by this conversation.

"Get in touch with him, Sam, and get him here. Or just get the material you need, I don't care which." Jo paused, a dangerous idea crossing her mind. But desperate times called for desperate measures, and this felt like nothing if not desperate. She was done waiting. "If you don't, I will."

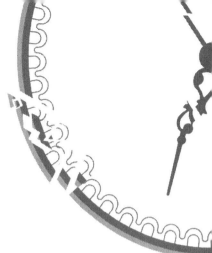

10. SAPPHIRE BRIDGE

J O SAT IN their usual café once more.

Today, the linens of the sofa were annoyingly bright and the dishware frustratingly brittle. Jo didn't know what she was putting in her mouth— some pastry slathered in a honey-like substance that left a bitter taste on the back of her tongue but she ate it diligently. All of her mental energy went to three simple ideas: chew, swallow, and don't immediately lash out the moment she heard the name Samson. Or worse: Eslar.

Wayne sat down heavily next to her. He took in a deep breath but no sound came out. His mouth just hung open for a long moment, until, finally, "Now listen, doll—"

"Out with it, Davis."

"Jo—" Takako started.

"*Now.*" She didn't want to be cajoled. She didn't want to be soothed. She wanted results.

"He says he needs—"

Jo set down her cup far too heavily, hearing fractures crack around its handle. She didn't even want to let him finish. "That's it, we've waited long enough." Magic crackled beneath Jo's fingers as she tightened her hands into fists against the table's surface. "If Eslar isn't going to play nicely, neither am I."

"Jo—" Wayne was on his feet as Jo started for the door, calling after her. "Don't do anything rash!"

"I'm *done* not doing anything rash." Jo threw her hands in the air. "I'd rather this blow up in my face than spend another minute not doing anything at all."

Takako rushed to catch up with her, stopping her on the sidewalk. "This, whatever it is you're about to pull, could alert *Pan*." Takako said the name as though it would act like a spell and instantly pull Jo back in line.

"Then let her be alerted. Let her come and face me here if she dares to risk the ire of the Elves after all. They already have no love for Aristonia thanks to Pan's own mischief, so I doubt they'll do anything to aide her or Snow.

"I'm done waiting," she declared. "I'm going to High Luana, *now*. Go tell Samson to let Eslar know, if he wants to prevent even a little of the destruction I'm about to bring."

Takako stared at her, mostly in disbelief, before finally letting her go. The woman turned, sprinting away in the direction of the workshop. Who knew if Samson could get to Eslar in time? Jo didn't really care. Nothing would change her mind.

Jo hadn't realized how tight the leash on her magic

was until she let it go.

There had been a subconscious dampening of her abilities, no doubt. Perhaps it was in part because she had woken up with expectations of humanity as her "natural state". But here, in Myrth, and with all that had transpired, Jo had cast off that expectation. She was *not* human, she was not even *mortal*. She was Destruction, and an Age of Magic was about to know what happened when a demigod was dropped among them.

Her time wandering the streets of Myrth in an endless holding pattern had given Jo an opportunity to learn the layout of the city some. More importantly, she remembered the brief glimpse of the Sapphire Bridge from her arrival. That was her destination. The point that connected the outpost of the Luanian Empire in which Myrth was seated—the only place that non-elves were allowed to tread—with the Empire proper.

It was simply a matter of crossing the bridge.

Though nothing would be simple about it, she was certain. In a way, she'd been planning for this moment from the second she broke the airship. It was as if, in the back of her mind, she'd known it would come to this: Jo was meant to destroy her path forward.

Before her was a large building that arched into the sea. Its four floors and massive windows shone in the sunlight. In front was a large wall and gate—a manned checkpoint. Men and women waited in a line that stretched along the length of the wall, all elves waiting to go home.

"Sorry to ruin your day," Jo whispered softly but sincerely. Even if she was prepared for what was about to happen, and even if she wouldn't regret it in the slightest, she had never truly wanted it to come to this.

Jo lifted a hand and felt her magic unravel like a fisherman's line. It spun out from the tight coil of her control and flew into the universe, ready to do what she had been born to do—destroy.

In a split second, Jo analyzed the gate before her. It broke down before her eyes, lifting its skirts and showing all its most delicate areas. And with a thought, she let her magic do as it willed with that knowledge.

The immaculately woven, wrought iron gate groaned and buckled. The hinges pulled loose from their bolts in the stone wall; the iron fell with a cacophony of clangs as it disjointed at each of its ornately designed connection points. It was as if Jo had her fingers on the hands of time and spun the watch forward until the gate arrived at its natural point of eventual collapse.

There was screaming. Somewhere behind her, she heard a, "The hell, Jo?!" but she couldn't be sure. The people in line ran, and the guards scrambled in confusion.

"Stop right there!" someone screamed at her.

Jo's eyes scanned the wall. Archers were taking their positions. Gunmen were crouched in a semi-circle around the opening.

All of them could be torn apart.

Mortals were such fragile beings.

Jo pushed the thought from her mind; even more than Pan's men, she did not want to kill innocents. They posed no genuine threat to her and, more than that, she didn't actually want to make enemies. Though she may have crossed that metaphorical bridge long before she had begun crossing the physical one.

"I'll give you one chance," she shouted back. "Drop your weapons and let me through. I could care less about the Luanian Empire; all I want is one man: Eslar Greentouch. Give me him and I'll be happy!"

Jo watched as the elf she assumed to be some kind of general took a breath, no doubt about to scream the order to shoot to kill. She still didn't exactly know if she could die, but she wasn't going to find out here.

They'd be far less deadly without their weapons.

With a thought, Jo watched as every weapon simultaneously self-destructed. Guns misfired, bows snapped, arrows splintered and fell harmlessly to the ground as the strings they were attached to gave out. One or two soldiers reeled, but there appeared to be no major damage and no loss of life. Jo continued forward.

There were the makings of chaos now, the makings of a situation she knew would make Pan dance in glee. As much as Jo loathed the thought, it was clear why, and how, they could join together. Destruction and chaos were the in-breath that would exhale total oblivion.

"Let me through!" Jo said again. "Give me Eslar Greentouch or passage to High Luana, that's all I ask."

"Stop her!" the general shouted once more.

Jo balled her hands into fists. She'd raze the whole thing to the ground if that's what it took. But that wasn't her objective or desire.

Leveraging the chaos to her advantage, she ran.

She pumped her legs like she never had before, in a sprint that turned the world into a blur. With a leap, Jo cleared the yet-crouched soldiers (all of whom were still trying to make sense of their broken weapons) and landed gently behind them. There was another gate in front of her, another checkpoint.

Jo lifted a hand—rinse and repeat.

This time, rather than falling harmlessly to the ground, the iron exploded. Jo watched as it flew from its origin and scattered across the wide paved courtyard between the outer wall and main building. Once again, people were rushing to stop her, but they weren't fast enough. That, or their weapons broke the moment she passed.

Through the gate, the arc she'd seen from the air was on full display. Right or left? *It didn't matter*, her magic told her, and Jo chose right on a whim, running toward the stairway that led toward the bridge directly in front of the gates she'd just destroyed.

Across the bridge was Luana. Across the bridge was Eslar. It didn't matter how far he was; she'd leave a wake of destruction on her path to get to him.

She should feel tired, Jo realized as she crested the top of the stairs. But she wasn't the slightest bit out of breath, or even fatigued. Pausing, Jo looked behind her. Everyone seemed so far away, so slow moving and stilled. They'd never catch her if she didn't want them to.

Not more than twenty bounding steps in, the first of the sapphire statues began to shift. Two giant elves, easily five stories tall, coming to life. One wielded a sword, the other a staff. The gem they were crafted of shone like starlight, glinting through the cracks in their bodies as they walked with ground-shaking steps onto the bridge itself.

This is old magic, Jo realized as the first raised its sword. It was far older than the magic of the gates.

Older than anything she'd ever felt before—save for Snow and Pan's rooms in the Society.

The sword screamed as it cut the air, the lumbering statue bringing it down onto the bridge. Miraculously, the surface didn't even crack, though Jo could feel the rumblings of the pressure down into the very foundations.

She leapt onto the sword's edge, sprinting upward. The sapphire golem was too slow to shake her, and by the time it tried, she was already on its shoulder. Jo scrambled toward its head—toward the shining point her magic sight had highlighted for her from her vantage point on the ground.

"So this is what holds you together." Jo stood poised on the crown of its head. Dropping to a crouch, she slammed her palm onto its forehead, magic pushing far beyond where flesh met sapphire. The stone cracked under her fingers, spider webs extending from crown to foot.

The golem crumbled like rain, and Jo was sent falling with it.

She felt the moment her body hit the stone of the bridge below. It was as if every organ exploded at once, every bone splintered and shattered into a thousand pieces, every inch of connective tissue pulverized. And yet, in the destruction of herself, she found life. Like a rubber band spread too wide, Jo felt herself expand and collapse, bouncing back stronger than she'd been before. There were no wounds to mend or limbs to regenerate, just the sudden flash of pain turned energy and power. A little giddy with the realization, she jumped to her feet, turning and sprinting toward the distant end of the bridge.

There was a whole sea of golems to cross.

One after the next, the guardians stepped forward to meet her. They attacked her with swords and staffs and daggers. The sixth had magic beams that made finding its creation point—its *weak point*—a little tricky.

By the seventh she was panting, but still had more than enough air in her lungs to scream, "End this, Luana. I don't want to destroy your history."

There was no response, just a sea of sapphire dust behind her, and more giants ahead.

After the eleventh, Jo screamed again, tilting her head to the heavens as if someone, somewhere, could hear her. "Are we really still going on with this, Luana? All this just for one man? How stubborn can you really be?"

Another sword swung for her.

Jo leapt, catching it on the broad side of the blade, clinging to the outer edge—dull from spending years in the rain and elements. The statue lifted the weapon, as if confused by her presence on the sword point. Jo used the opportunity to sprint up, landing her palm in the shoulder and feeling the same satisfying crunch from within.

She landed, hard. She felt her bones break and the air leave her body and was all the more alive for it. She rose to her knees, then her feet, and resumed her sprint.

At the fifteenth statue, Jo could see land in the distance, and a whole lot of bridge left to cross. Her mind had begun reorienting the purpose of this effort. Perhaps she wouldn't need to find Eslar after all; perhaps she could take on Pan herself with this much practice—hold the woman down while Takako just stabbed the arrow through her heart.

Jo clenched her hands into fists, ready for the next set of warriors, but they never came.

She lowered her eyes, looking not at the suddenly still sapphire giants, but at the bridge. There, in the distance, was a group of people. Ships—gilded in gold and bearing bright blue sails with the seal of the high elves on them—had been anchored.

"Does your offer to end this still stand?"

"It does," Jo shouted back.

"Then come, and let us parlay like two civilized parties. We hear you're looking for Eslar Greentouch."

11. SAMSON'S PAIN

THE WATER SPLASHED in waves against the boat's hull, sending sprays of mist up from beneath to tickle her face. It cooled instantly as the breeze whipped about the deck, a slight chill running down Jo's spine. They'd been on the ship to High Luana for a couple of hours now, and had taken to wandering the Elvish vessel with a frenetic sort of energy, the adrenaline still high in all of them. Eventually Jo had settled on the upper deck, willing her heart to slow, but she couldn't shake the itchy feeling of "hurry up and wait."

They'd finally managed to get a step forward, after much, much too much time wasted, but Jo couldn't find any success in it. Not when Snow's safety was still an unknown, not when Eslar's involvement was still uncertain, not when she may have just caused a diplomatic rift that could start a war, and most certainly not when Samson looked about a hair's breadth away from throwing himself overboard.

In fact, Samson had grown more and more reserved the longer they were on the ship. It was almost as though, the closer they got to High Luana, the more panicked their craftsman became. To Jo's magical eyes, it was as if he was shattering from the inside out, spider web cracks inching across his chest, shoulders, back, just waiting for a single strike. Though she still wasn't sure what was troubling him, Jo couldn't help feeling guilty for all the stress she'd put him through as a result of her antics.

She wanted to know Snow was all right, she wanted to put an end to Pan, but she also wanted to keep her team—her *family*—safe. Samson might be physically safe, but she was doing very little for his emotional and mental well-being.

"Sam?" Jo risked a soft whisper, and though she'd expected him to recoil in shock, it still hurt. He had clearly not seen her approaching from around the corner of the deck. "Sam, I'm sorry." She dove in before he could scramble away again—like he had when they'd first boarded—though the look in his eyes said he clearly wanted to. She made to reach for him, but held back at the look of anxiety marring his features, hugging her hand to her chest instead. "I'm sorry I've put you through so much."

He was silent for several long seconds, looking back out at the water. Heaving a deep breath, he let it out with precious few words. "I was trying to reach Eslar."

"I know you were," Jo said hastily. "I knew that. But I just . . ." And damnit, there was nothing she could do to stop the sudden tightness in her throat or the blurring of her eyes. "I need to know he's okay. We're so close, and we have a plan. But the waiting... And Eslar's stubbornness—it wasn't you Sam."

"You're worried about him." Samson saved her from herself by saying what she couldn't. There was no doubt as to who he meant. It certainly wasn't Eslar.

Jo lifted a hand to her face, shielding her eyes. She hadn't realized just how terrified she was for Snow until that moment. She'd been assuming the whole time that Samson was the crumbling one that she could see right through him. Jo had never bothered looking in the mirror. "I have no way of knowing, Sam. And I'm so . . . I'm scared that he's—That if we don't hurry, he'll be—"

It took the feel of arms wrapping around her in a loose embrace for her to realize she'd gone silent beneath the weight of unshed tears. Samson's arms were strong, if a bit hesitant, and Jo melted into them, willingly taking the offered comfort.

"You've gotten your wish, Jo," Samson whispered into her hair, holding her a bit tighter. She buried her face in his shirt, smelling motor oil and something sweet yet spicy, like hot chocolate spiked with cayenne. "We're on our way to save him. He'll be fine." Samson let go of her for a moment then, holding her out at arm's length. Though it was a bit awkward (he couldn't seem to figure out if he wanted to use his knuckles or fingertips), Samson lifted his hand to wipe a streak of tears from her cheek. "Snow is strong. After you destroyed the Society, he saved us all by making this world, didn't he? He'll survive long enough for us to save *him* too. Don't you worry."

There was something sad in Samson's voice; in it, Jo detected a level of defeat that was palpable, like a man walking to the guillotine. And as sickening as it was, Jo felt her magic leaching into that weakness, breaking apart exactly what was making Samson shatter, exactly what Samson had been so afraid of. It was as if she naturally wanted to level the field, make him as vulnerable as she felt.

"Sam," Jo whispered, "you know my worries . . . now, tell me yours. What happened between you and Eslar?"

Samson jerked back as if burned, pulling completely out of her touch. Jo wanted to follow him, wanted to pull him back in and soothe away the look of betrayal on his face, but she knew these words were important. And a part of her, somewhere deep where the shadows hid, told her Samson needed to talk about it. He'd been needing to put it out in the open for a while and they were running out of time before he was confronted with Eslar's presence once more.

"You don't . . ." Jo paused, letting her magic formulate the words she needed to say, but likewise letting her desire for Samson's trust and comfort guide them. "You don't have to tell me, if you can't, but I can see that something happened. And I wanted you to know you can talk to me if you want to and need to before we get to High Luana." Then, reaching forward with a cautious and steady hand, Jo grabbed Samson's wrist, sliding down to link their fingers together with a gentle squeeze.

Samson looked from their joined hands back to

Jo, conflict clear on his face. He seemed near tears. Keeping this secret was destroying him, Jo realized, the sensation potent and buzzing beneath her own skin. Talking about it may be its own form of breaking down, but part of her knew that if he got it out, it would destroy him less. So she held fast, silently luring him in.

Eventually, Samson seemed to relent. With a breath, he squeezed her hand back tight.

"He doesn't want anything to do with me now that he doesn't *have* to have anything to do with me," he said, so soft that Jo could barely hear it. His fingers were already trembling in her grip. "With . . . W-With us. With the Society and . . . and all this. With Pan. I tried, but—" Samson took a shaky breath, looking a little like he was about to pass out. As carefully as she could, Jo led Samson to one of the comfy chairs spread about the deck, kneeling at his side to keep their hands together.

"There's no rush, Sam," Jo offered, settling in to wait, her free hand resting against his knee. "The elves say we have at least two more days until we reach High Luana anyway. You have time. Just go slow."

Samson took another breath, a deep inhale that seemed wet with brimming tears, and a quiet, grounding exhale through his nose. When he looked at Jo, he seemed less anxious, and older than she'd ever seen him. Suddenly, she thought she could see every year of the countless hundreds he had lived.

"Why doesn't he want anything to do with us?"

"He's afraid."

"Afraid of what?" As far as Jo was concerned, the only thing anyone should fear was Pan.

"Afraid of losing his world again, his people, his culture. He sees the Society as the catalyst for . . . for the last time he lost it all."

Jo pressed her lips together, mulling over her next question. "When you say 'lost it all,' you mean his wish?"

"No, that was the first time he lost it all—his wish that brought him to the Society," Samson whispered, never breaking eye contact with Jo. "The last time was my wish." Her blood ran cold, even as anticipation and intrigue licked beneath her skin. "My wish caused the end of the original Age of Magic."

Jo . . . hadn't been expecting that. Luckily, once the floodgates had opened, Samson wasted no time elaborating.

"There was a war," he said, and then laughed dejectedly to himself. "There's always a war, isn't there? But I . . . I wasn't a soldier. I was a fletcher, watching my fellow countrymen die, watching villages burn, and I . . ." Samson shivered, no doubt remembering the sights and sounds of death, the stench and pain of a war he'd never wanted to be a part of. "The war was between those who had magic and those who did not. And I thought that maybe, if I begged, if I wished hard enough, I could—" His words failed him for a moment. But with a harsh exhale and a tightening of his jaw, he finished. "I wished to remove all magic from the world. I thought if I wished for it all to be gone, every last trace of it from everyone and everything, there'd be nothing to fight over anymore."

"It didn't just take the magic away, did it?" Bile rose at the back of Jo's throat, her stomach twisting violently. "It also removed the magical peoples and creatures, too, right?"

"I didn't know that I'd . . . I didn't mean for it to *do* what it *did*. I hadn't realized that—" Samson babbled, burying his face in the free hand not linked fiercely and painfully with Jo's. "I had never meant for something like that to happen, but I . . . I couldn't take it back. S-Snow said the deed had been done—it was when we learned about the dangers of forcing a transition without closing the Severity of Exchange. He'd forced the jump and it completely made a new age. Maybe if he'd hadn't? But the damage was done. Eslar blamed me for the erasure of his people from the first moment I woke in the Society."

Jo remembered her first week at the Society, and Eslar's passing comment about a time when Elves had existed. There were also the comments about Snow, how shifts with wide Severities of Exchange could be . . . violent. She'd been too new, too green to catch any subtleties between Eslar and Samson at the time, but now every remembered interaction between them seemed weighted.

What must that have been like for Eslar, watching a wish decimate his entire race? To have to live with the one at the root of such genocide for decades, generations? But to find the cause not to be a wretched soul, but a good-hearted man who made a scared and hasty choice that too many paid for?

"You and Eslar though . . ." Jo paused, trying to find the right words. "You always seemed so close."

"That took years and *years* of apologies." Samson sniffled through tears that seemed determined to fall even through his fingers. "It was a century before I could even get him to pass the salt. Eventually . . . Yes, we found a quiet peace and I thought it may have been enough. But how could have it had been?

"Now, the elves have returned—he's got people back. He's got his *home* back now. And . . . I thought that maybe, maybe he'd l-let me apologize once more, g-give me a chance to finally s-settle this so that we could move forward and put it all behind us for good." With a quick swipe at his eyes that did nothing for the snot and tears streaking his dark features, Samson looked at Jo with a weary smile. "I know I don't deserve closure, but I had hoped for it. We spent so many years together . . . there was so much time and he seemed like he . . . Not that you ever get over something like that. Perhaps, if I hadn't been the one to ask him for help, he'd have listened to your plea. Perhaps if I hadn't been selfish, if I hadn't wanted it to be me to bridge the gap, he would have offered his assistance in all of this far sooner. And for that . . . For that, Jo, I am sorry."

His words were filled with guilt and longing and pain, and Jo felt her own magic mingle with his, taking in the despair and destruction as if she could remove it from deep within him, spare him from it all. She eased him into another hug, allowing tears to soak into the fabric of her tunic as she rubbed soothing circles into his back.

It was obvious now, where all Samson's anxieties about contacting Eslar had originated. Still, he'd tried. For the team and for the mission and for Snow, he had tried and tried and tried. And while much was still left unsaid, that had to count for something.

If nothing else, Samson's pain and guilt counted for Jo, and she would find a way to make them count for Eslar, too.

12. A ROYAL AUDIENCE

TWO MORE DAYS on the ship to get to High Luana were proving to be two too long.

Wayne and Takako had spent the first portion of the trip gambling with the elves and then the second portion avoiding the elves due to Wayne's cheating. After Sam had confessed his secret to Jo, they'd spent the better part of the evening together, doing nothing at all. Jo appreciated the quiet companionship and she had a feeling Samson felt much the same, because he sought her out the day after, and the day after that.

Finally, High Luana came into view.

Mountains stretched up from the sea, and above them towered a giant spire. It stood offset from the main island, connected by an arching bridge made of two colossal sculpted elves linking outstretched hands, palms upturned, as though they were holding the bridge itself between their loving arms.

"Is that—"

"The castle where the king sits? Yes." The tall elf cut her off. "The bridge to it has stood even longer than the Sapphire Bridge." He gave her a long side-eye.

"My assurances still stand. Bring me to Eslar Greentouch and I won't destroy another thing of elvish make. Despite what you and your men may think, I am no enemy of the elves."

A curt nod was his only response.

Jo allowed herself be distracted by the swiftly growing scenery. The more she thought of divinity, the more she thought of Snow. And that was a dangerous path to let her mind go down. Despite herself, her hands balled into fists.

Hang on. Just hang on, her heart pleaded into the universe, as though he could somehow hear her. He'd sacrificed enough. Now it was her turn.

The brilliantly blue sea was cut off by a strip of white, and the beaches turned into emerald foliage or jewel-bespeckled towns. The waters became crowded as they neared closer and closer to the island. Fishermen stopped their work to watch the Imperial vessel speed by. They stared in fascination and . . . worry. Jo wondered just how much word of her had gotten to the rest of Luana, or perhaps more importantly, what words were said when it had.

Their ship sailed right under the massive bridge she'd seen from the distance. Jo twisted, looking up till her neck hurt and then some as they passed beneath. It was truly a marvel to behold and she wondered if Samson saw the same thing she did: utter perfection in craftsmanship. The only thing that was going to bring the bridge down was if she attacked it with the brute force of her magic. It was as if the very land had been coerced into shaping itself into the foundation for the bridge and the giant castle on the other side.

Past the bridge, they began to slow, pulling into a sheltered inlet of docks. The four of them gathered at the end of the gangway before a group of elvish guards in suits of armor that nearly covered them from head to toe. The man whom Jo presumed to be the leader was the only one to speak.

"If you'll follow me this way."

They wound up stairways on stairways, working their way up from the sea to the towering bridge. They were about halfway when Wayne stopped on one of the terraces, hands on his knees.

"Just go on ahead, I'll catch up," he panted, breathless.

"We can't leave you behind," the leader elf said, matter-of-fact. "We can wait for you to catch your breath."

"Or leave me where I fall," Wayne muttered.

"What was that?"

"Nothing." Wayne straightened, wiping the sweat from his brow.

"I could carry you," Jo offered. After the physical feats she'd accomplished on the Sapphire Bridge, Jo didn't think Wayne on her back would slow her down one bit.

"I'm not that out of shape, dollface. Wouldn't want to crush you." He motioned toward the next set of stairs. "Carry on, then."

They had to stop two more times, but Jo's offer to

carry Wayne seemed to keep pushing him all the way to the top. Even Samson and Takako had requested a small break each, though Takako's training as a soldier seemed to give her the greatest stamina, after Jo and their Elvish guides in ranked order. Jo couldn't help feeling oddly proud on the woman's behalf. It was late in the afternoon by the time they crossed the last stair. Wayne was the first one to mutter "Oh thank god" the second both of his feet were at the top.

This high up, the wind blew unimpeded, almost violently tossing Jo's hair. She raised a hand, pulling it back from where it whipped her face to get a better look at the city compacted into a basin of sheer cliffs. From the sea, it looked as if the bridge to the Luanian castle ended at a forested ridge. But the trees and ridgetop concealed a whole city within—a city of shallow pools, domed gazebos, hanging gardens, and all the lushness of a high society that had thrived uninterrupted for thousands of years.

Seeing High Luana, remembering Eslar's room, knowing what Samson had told her, all came together in an odd form of guilt. He finally had what he wanted— what he'd witnessed being blotted out from existence— his home. And now they were going to demand he remove himself from it and risk his life.

No.

Jo turned, looking up at the giant spire that loomed over it all, as though it were a watchtower for the whole world. They were coming to demand he remove himself from this home and risk his life *for* it, to protect it. She was no more pleased than he was about the situation, but that didn't give any of them the ability to ignore it, either.

"Think the elves are compensating for anything?" Wayne leaned in and whispered, motioning upward at the spire.

"You're going to get us in trouble," Jo hissed back.

"More trouble than a demigod bent on destroying the world and the thing you did to their bridge?" he said, deadpan.

Jo looked forward, determined to ignore any further remarks, and focused instead on the two giant silver doors that swung open soundlessly. Samson looked at them in awe as they passed through. The hallway was wide enough for everyone to walk side-by-side if they wanted and still have enough room. The roof was taller than any she'd ever seen before, tall enough that it was cast in shadow, tiny floating motes of light the only thing guiding their way forward. Especially once the doors closed behind them and plunged the hall into darkness. The lights descended one by one, falling to the floor, outlining the path for them to continue on. It was as beautiful as it was pointless, since there was only one way to go.

The hall dumped them into an even larger room. The floor was inlaid with silver, and made of stone fitted so perfectly that it was impossible to see the grooves with the naked eye. Thousands upon thousands of lines of elvish script traversed from one wall to the next, though Jo could only pick out a few words and one or two simple sentences with her elvish study so far.

Six columns, fat and reminiscent of the strange-looking trees she'd seen on their arrival along the beach, supported a vaulted roof. At the end of them, seated on simple thrones made of silver, was an Elvish man wearing an ornate headdress of silver. Next to him was a woman, and two younger looking boys sat on either side of them.

Their group was marched right up to the throne, stopping only when their leader dropped into a low bow. Jo didn't know what elvish custom dictated, but a little bit of decorum couldn't hurt, she decided. So she gave a small bow of her head, rising when the elf did. He spoke in the lifting tones of the elvish language and the king gave a nod.

Closer, Jo got her first good look at the elvish royal family; it wasn't what she had expected. These were ancient creatures, bent on the survival of their species and cultivation of their history before all other things. But they looked almost . . . modest.

Nothing like the storybook elves from Jo's history, the king had short, almost messy hair that was black as coal. His ruddy skin, clearly inherited by his sons, almost matched Samson's. He wore a simple silver tunic, cinched low with a wide sapphire belt. It complemented the blouse the queen wore with silver trousers. Jo hadn't been expecting trousers; she was used to cultures modeled on ancient times harboring an unnecessary obsession with gender roles and expectations. But perhaps the gender roles and norms Jo knew, and the ones here, were different.

"Which of you is the one they call Josephina?" The king spoke nearly without any accent at all, his English practically flawless.

"That'd be me." Jo took a step forward.

"Word has reached us that to a . . . vehement degree,

you have demanded to speak with our Grand Healer."

That's certainly a way to put it. Jo kept the remark to herself, opting instead for a simpler, "It is a matter of dire importance."

"I would hope so," the queen said softly, crossing her legs and leaning back in her chair, looking bemused about the situation. "It will take a century to repair the Sapphire Bridge."

Jo should feel guilty. But she didn't. If anything, she just felt slightly angrier at Eslar for forcing them all into this mess with his stubbornness. Then again, she didn't *have* to start destroying the bridge . . . Her head hurt if she tried to tally up the scores for "who messed up more".

"Tell me, why should I not just strike you down here and now for waging war against the elves?"

"Because I am not waging war," Jo insisted.

"It certainly appears that way."

"I was given no other choice to get the attention of your—" *How did he phrase it?* "—Grand Healer. We had made every attempt to contact him through conventional means."

"So you expect to go unpunished?"

That was something Jo hadn't considered. Punishment was likely fair. But Jo didn't find it very threatening. She bit back a sigh.

"You want to 'punish' me? Be my guest. Let's see how well that works for you." Jo shrugged. "Could be interesting, I suppose, because I've found there's very little that harms me. Locking me up would just give me a fun puzzle to break apart. And the longer you keep me here, the more at risk you all are." *Be it from Pan finally catching up, or the end of the world*—Jo kept the thought to herself.

The king gripped and let go of his arm rests as if he were giving them a massage. "I am willing to forgive your transgressions." Spoken like a man already backed into a corner, making it sound like it was his idea to be there all along. "On one condition."

"I didn't come here for conditions." Jo put her hands on her hips. "I was hoping we could have a productive working relationship."

"I hope for that as well." The king stood. "But to achieve that, you must tell us what strange magic you used to break our wards and level the work of our people as though it were a mere initiate's exercise. This information will be valuable to us in rebuilding and could perhaps expunge the damage you've done." *And give him an opportunity to write her off as a sort of test, or human wrecking ball making way for new improvement, to his people.*

Jo frowned. It wasn't that she didn't want to work with him... "There's not enough time for that."

"I have lived for over five hundred years. I am very patient."

"Even if I told you, you wouldn't believe me. There wouldn't be enough time for you to understand, and unfortunately we don't have five hundred more years for you to let it sink in." Her hands fell from her hips, as though pulled by the weight of disbelief at yet another hoop before her. How hard was it to just give her some time to talk to one elf?

"You presume too much to speak to the king that way," their tall escort cautioned.

"Fine. I presume a demonstration of my powers will be good enough? Maybe then you'll see why you should've just taken my word?" Jo cracked her knuckles, mostly for show.

"Don't do anything rash," Takako whispered as their escort quickly said something in elvish to his king.

But the conversation was interrupted by the loud shutting of a door echoing through the hall, followed by a simple statement in an all-too-familiar voice.

"You should know better, Takako. Our Josephina has yet to master the art of not being rash." All eyes turned. Eslar gave a small frown at seeing them. "You never knew when to quit, did you?"

13. IMPATIENT

FOR AS MUCH as Eslar's tone betrayed annoyance, Jo liked to think the exasperation didn't quite meet his eyes. He looked much the same as she remembered, though no longer wearing casual 2050s fashion.

Now, as he approached their stunned little group, a long robe flowed behind him, lined and accented in the oceanic tones that Jo was now learning to be the particular color scheme of those with import in Luanian society. His long black hair had been braided back from his dark face in intricate weaves, making the silver and sapphire jewelry lining his pointed ears and pinned throughout seem more prominent.

They had called him their Grand Healer, but to Jo, he looked equally as royal as their king.

"You've certainly put in a surprising amount of effort to get here." Eslar broke the stalemate that had followed his arrival. "Clearly my silence had not been answer enough to whatever request you plan to make."

Jo winced, not liking the way his tone shifted from indifferent to cold, though she held hope in the way his eyes took each of them in one at a time. Surely, despite his self-induced isolation from his former team, he would have missed them, *right?* Even just a little bit?

"We had hoped you would change your mind once you actually heard the request. And since you wouldn't give us the time of day over the phone—or disk—we had to come here to deliver it in person," Jo threw back, though Eslar's wandering gaze had finally shifted down the line of their group and onto Samson. Jo couldn't even be sure Eslar had heard her, not for the way his focus narrowed down to the craftsman as if he were the only one in the room.

At first, Jo's skin prickled at the attention, a need to protect Samson from any backlash rising like static electricity across her skin, especially after learning his truths on the ship. But the more she looked between them—the unspoken words on Eslar's tongue and a cocktail of emotions on Samson's face—the less protective she felt. In fact, the longer they stared at each other in silent communication, the more she just felt like a voyeur.

A couple of times, Samson opened his mouth to speak, but at each attempt he found himself losing the courage. He seemed relieved to see Eslar, maybe even antsy with nervous excitement, hands twitching against the hem of his shirt. But he also looked a little like he was going to throw up.

"Master Greentouch?" It was the king who finally sought to bring an end to the lingering quiet, the authority in his voice making Jo tense. And she wasn't the only one.

She wouldn't have noticed had she not been paying such close attention to the two men, but at the sound of the king's interruption, she saw both of their shoulders tighten, Eslar's back straightening as Samson hunched into himself more fully. She took solace in the fact that, at least for a moment, they must have been relaxing in each other's presences.

"Yes, my liege?" Eslar finally cleared his throat. Though the tension had fizzled some, it hadn't broken, and the Grand Healer and the Craftsman continued to lock eyes, a line of weighted communication passing like a tangible thing between them.

"Perhaps it would be best if you lead your *friends* somewhere where you can speak more privately and no longer trouble the crown with personal matters." The king emphasized the word *friends* in a way that left Jo more than a little miffed. This was clearly not the first time he'd had a conversation with Eslar about them, and it left Jo wondering how much of their initial interaction was for show. Eslar didn't comment, his back still to the rest of the group, but the tension had in no way left his shoulders.

"We have rooms prepared for you all in the East Wing," the queen added, this time addressing Jo directly. "We do hope they'll be to your liking." There was kindness behind the queen's eyes that Jo found comforting, even if her words still glistened with ice.

"I'm sure they'll be more than sufficient, your highness," Jo replied with another minute bow of her head. "We appreciate your continued generosity." She tried not to let sarcasm drip into the sentiment, but the slight rise of the queen's eyebrow suggested Jo hadn't succeeded.

"Our request has not been overlooked, Josephina Espinosa. We will allow you an audience with our Grand Healer—" The king's gaze shifted to Eslar, probably commenting on his interruption before any deal could be struck. "And in return for all the forgiveness and hospitality which we have shown you, we expect an eventual explanation of your rather . . . devastating magic."

A weight sank in Jo's stomach as she held the king's stare, her eyes narrowing into a glare. If she had to give them another "example" of her power, she would. But she also couldn't sacrifice their plan further by being hot headed, even in the face of the king's poorly veiled animosity. She'd known what she was risking when she destroyed the bridge, after all. As if to emphasize her thoughts, Jo felt Takako reach over, a subtle shift of her hand, to rest her fingers against Jo's wrist. Not a warning or a plea, but a reminder. They had Eslar, they would have their chance to appeal to him; no need to be rash.

Jo took a breath and closed her eyes for a moment before looking back to the king. "We'll see," she said, offering him what she hoped was more smile than grimace. The king didn't comment, finally shifting his focus back to Eslar.

"If you would, Master Greentouch."

Eslar bowed his head with a monotone, "Of course, sire," and began to lead the group out of the throne room. Wayne, Takako, and Samson followed without a word, Samson trailing a bit behind, but Jo spared one more glance at the royal family before following suit.

Through the doors on the right-hand side of the throne room, the group entered into a narrow but no less luxe hallway. Eslar didn't look back and his shoulders were so rigid, they formed an impenetrable wall.

"Your rooms will be in here," Eslar said when they arrived at a set of double doors at the far corner of the courtyard they'd been traversing. He opened both doors and led them rank and file into a common area.

It was an incredibly spacious setup, the windows along the far wall—bordered in swirling, branch-like patterns—only adding to the inviting openness. In the center of the room, flanked by two more open doors to the left and right, was a sitting area that boasted three couches, a chaise, and a long table that stretched toward the windows. The furniture was intricately carved in deep mahogany and covered in blue velvet.

Through the doors, Jo could see more furniture, including a four-poster bed. The bedding looked immensely plush, a pristine white duvet accented with embroidered swirls of green and no doubt filled with some type of feathers. The pillows looked equally as soft and inviting, if not more so. All in all, a very impressive place to rest.

Takako would certainly enjoy it.

Jo, on the other hand, took solace in the fact that the living room had an entire wall dedicated to shelves upon shelves of books (hopefully with some in English). She wouldn't have been surprised to count somewhere near a thousand or more on the floor-to-ceiling spread. Jo could already feel herself unconsciously dragging her eyes over each title, waiting for something of use to stick out to her.

The book that had helped lead them here had belonged to Eslar, after all. If they needed more information, more insight into their ever-changing plan, Jo's best bet would be this wall. At the least it'd stave off the boredom.

The elf stood behind them, still hovering in the doorframe as if he couldn't decide if he was really going to go through with talking to them, or if he was going to try locking them away and running. As if sensing her train of thought, Eslar crossed his arms over his chest and walked up to her, only barely breaching her personal space but looming over her nonetheless.

"You all wanted my attention so desperately," he said, voice cool and aggravatingly unemotional. "Well now you have it. After all that's transpired, what could you possibly need me for?"

Jo was struck with the sudden desire to tangle a fist into the collar of his tunic, to drag him down to her line of sight and demand that he stop being so indifferent about their arrival. Sure, the Society hadn't been kind to them, but they'd survived together. They'd bonded and grown and loved and lost. *Together*. Did that mean nothing to him? Now that he had his people and his status and his world back, did their trials mean nothing? Her magic was practically yelling at her to dismantle Eslar's truth, to rip deep into his mind and heart and find proof that he had cared.

But as much as it probably showed in her eyes, Jo said nothing. Not without taking a deep breath, willing her magic to settle back into her core. Arguing right off the bat would do no one any good.

"The Society itself might be gone, but we're not done fighting." Jo dove right in, willing herself not to mirror Eslar's dismissive pose. "I know having magic back, having your *people* back, is important to you. As it should be. But as long as Pan lives, none of it is safe."

As if it were involuntary, Eslar's gaze shifted over Jo's shoulder to where she knew Samson stood. She hoped she hadn't thrown the poor guy under the bus in some way, but Jo knew it was something Eslar needed to hear.

"We've come up with a plan to stop her, but we need your help to do it."

Eslar looked back at her for a long moment before speaking. "What makes you think, after a year of silence, that she intends anything so grandly malicious?"

"Because . . ." Jo hesitated, trying to figure out the best way to phrase it that didn't condemn her to the already reluctant elf, but really, there was no way to skirt blame on this one, was there? "Because I'm back. She's looking for me and will do anything to get me. And if she finds me before we have the means to defeat her, that's the end for us all."

Eslar raised an eyebrow at that. "And how, exactly, is that?"

"If she gets her hands on me and forces us to return to one being . . . Oblivion walks the earth once more."

By the look on Eslar's face, Jo knew he understood; knowledge of the Age of Magic, of the old gods and their demigod counterparts, had been scattered throughout his stories. Now it was come to life. She was one half of the monster from his people's fairytales.

"Then you are—"

"Destruction. Yes," Jo said, biting back a cringe. "And Pan is Chaos."

"And how much of this is actually about Snow?" Eslar's expression had resumed its look of careful stoicism, but Jo could see the judgment behind it regardless. So she swallowed back her defensive response and instead bared her soul.

"I won't deny that . . . that part of me wants to see him safe. Just as much as you no doubt want to see this world and your people's place in it safe. Snow is my counterpart in every sense. I was—" Jo felt the words lodge in her throat. The thought of Snow, still trapped, still so far out of reach, made her heart clench. "He was literally made to be with me. And being apart, not knowing if he's safe under Pan's constant presence— *hurts*. It's terrifying and painful and I've never wanted anything more than to know he is safe.

"But I need to know that all of you will be safe too. That this world will be safe. And none of you—none of us—will be, so long as Pan lives."

Once the words were out, Jo felt oddly exhausted, her chest aching and her throat sore. She could feel that tell-tale sting at the back of her eyes, the corners blurring with unshed tears, and she forced herself to look away. It was Wayne's attention that fell into her line of sight then, and she hoped the plea in her eyes was enough for him to pick up where she had left off.

Wayne nodded once, focusing on Eslar; the ache in Jo's chest eased.

"We have a weapon we think will work against her," he said. "An arrow Samson's been carrying through the ages. We have reason to believe it's the arrow that once belonged to the Goddess of the Hunt."

Recognition flickered across Eslar's face.

"All we need is a bow," Takako chimed in.

Eslar eyed Wayne and Takako each in turn, still somehow managing to look unconvinced. "And you expect to find such a bow here in High Luana?"

Though it sounded like it physically pained him to do so, Samson was the one who answered Eslar this time. "I can c-craft one, I think, that will be strong enough. I may need help. I don't know yet. But I do know that I will need a special material that can only . . . that can only be found here."

Instead of looking at anyone in particular, Samson's head was down, eyes locked on his shoes. He wasn't fidgeting with anything, but his hands shook at his sides, as if the simple act of talking was dragging him closer and closer to the edge of panic. Jo was overwhelmed with the desire to reach forward and hold one of those trembling hands, but to her surprise, Wayne beat her to it. He stepped easily into Samson's space until their shoulders were pressed together, just enough physical contact to know Wayne was there but not enough to crowd. It seemed to calm Samson down some, though his voice still shook as he went on.

"I know th-that it is unfair of us to ask this of you, Eslar. It is unfair of *me* to ask *anything* of you, and for that, I am sorry. I am so, s-so sorry." Here, despite the way his eyes filled with tears, despite the trembling plea in his voice, Samson looked up, capturing Eslar's gaze with a determination Jo could never remember seeing on the man's face. "But we can't do this without you, Eslar. Please. We need your help to get them to say yes and help us."

Jo looked from Samson to Eslar just in time to watch the look of surprise fade from Eslar's eyes. There was something beneath his expression that Jo couldn't quite identify, a loose thread he was unable to tuck away, and though part of her knew she could use her magic to pick at that thread until the elf unraveled before her, she held back. This was between them.

For a long and agonizing moment, Eslar simply continued to hold Samson's gaze, a silent battle warring between them much like it had when they'd first arrived. But unlike then, it didn't take the crude clearing of Wayne's throat for Eslar to break their connection. As if finally seeing something on Samson's face, Eslar blinked, back straightening in what Jo would almost define as disappointment.

"I will need . . . time," he said, already heading towards the door. "Someone will be along shortly with dinner." He didn't bother turning to face anyone as he said it, his voice as expressionless as Jo had ever heard it. The look on Samson's face was utterly heartbreaking. Despite the urge crawling like fire-ants beneath Jo's skin, she didn't follow Eslar out.

No one did.

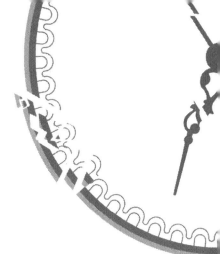

14. BROKEN TABLE LEG

"TIME?" WAYNE BALKED. "Time? He's had a whole—"

Jo caught Wayne's wrist before he could bolt out of the room. Wayne spun, his momentum redirected. But Jo didn't let go.

"Leave him be," she cautioned. "At least for now."

"We came all this way and you just want to let him act like this?"

"I think we have to." Jo's attention shifted to the door. Two soldiers had positioned themselves on either sides of the double doors leading to their chambers, pulling them closed. There was the sound of a heavy lock clanking, engaged from the outside.

"The hell is this?" Wayne reeled back to the door. "Now we're locked in like prisoners? So much for being honored guests." He wrenched his hand from Jo's grip.

"Calm down. It's not like we can blame them for being skeptical of us and, beyond that, I don't think we can be locked anywhere." Jo started for the bookshelves. "Given that we have a man who can make any bet happen with the guards, a woman who could shoot for the vulnerable part of the locks and never miss, a crafter whom I'm sure could make a key or some other mechanism to open the door . . ." She paused, just for emphasis. "Oh, and the demigod of Destruction."

"Takako doesn't have a gun right now to shoot with," Wayne muttered, but it was obvious in his posture that he was just clinging to his tantrum.

Jo turned to roll her eyes at him, but stopped when she saw Takako reach into her coat, and deftly pull a small handgun from a harness Jo hadn't realized she'd been wearing.

"You think I go anywhere without a gun?"

Jo barely managed to bite back her laugh, an awkward cough taking its place.

"Fine, you can all be relaxed with this." Wayne threw his hands in the air, stomping over to a sofa that he proceeded to throw himself onto. "I'll be over here, being the voice of reason."

Takako snorted at the notion, crossing over to the windows.

"Seriously, where does Eslar get off being all high and mighty?" Despite appearances, Wayne was clearly not done.

"Well, he is a *high* elf." Takako's grin was apparent in her voice, and the burst of laughter Jo had originally attempted to smother broke free. Even if Takako was only resorting to bad jokes for the sake of lightening the mood, it was both unexpected and gratefully received.

"Puns? We've resorted to *puns* now?" Wayne

groaned, throwing an arm across his face in a way that reminded Jo of one of those heroines in her mother's favorite old movies, taken by the vapors and in desperate need of a lie-down.

With a final snort of her own, Jo left them to their banter, and looked instead to Samson, who still hovered as though completely lost. "Sam, can you help me with something?" Jo asked, loud enough to call him from his stupor, but soft enough that it wouldn't earn Wayne's and Takako's attention.

"Wh— *oh*, yes." Samson hurried over, shaking his head. "What can I help you with?"

"What do you think of Eslar?" she whispered, now working to keep the conversation entirely between them, purely because she had no interest in garnering any further remarks from Wayne.

"Me?"

"You know him better than any of us." Jo shot the man a small smile that had him looking promptly at his toes. She turned back to the shelves to give the illusion of scanning the books. The motion served a dual purpose: she could avoid both arousing Wayne and Takako's attention, and putting unnecessary pressure on Samson.

"I think . . ." Samson faltered. Then, in a sudden burst of energy, he took a step toward her. It was a little too wide, a little too hasty. He was suddenly close enough to be awkward but, for possibly the first time ever, he didn't seem to notice. "I *don't* think, Jo, I *know*. I know that I can convince him to help us. Now that I'm here. Now that I can speak to him, in-in person . . . I know—"

"I believe you," Jo soothed, covering his hand with her own as it clutched desperately at her sleeve. "I know you can, too."

"But with other people . . ." Samson's eyes drifted to Takako, Wayne, and ultimately landed on her. "He . . . I don't think he'll listen. He'll feel like we're ganging up on him. He always felt like the odd man out as the only non-human."

After their interactions today, Jo was inclined to believe it. To Eslar, she was sure they looked like a gang, here to bully him into submission. Even if Jo was willing to do that, everything would go much more smoothly if the elf was on their side of his own accord.

"Grab a book, Samson, and read with me," Jo said, reaching toward the shelf. She was forming a plan but didn't want to spook him. "And don't stop reading, not even when everyone else goes to bed."

Samson looked at her for a long moment, his lips parting around a question. But ultimately, it remained unasked; he gave a small nod. "I think I'd like that."

The two of them positioned themselves together on the couch, their noses in books. Jo had found a good primer on the elvish language and Samson had an unsurprisingly good command of it already.

Jo kept her head down as Wayne bemoaned how "she never used to be like this" and how bored he was and how she should, instead, go make trouble with him amidst the "easily connable" elves. Takako kept to herself, occasionally cleaning her firearms, but Jo could tell confinement made her antsy as well.

They broke only for dinner when it was brought to them, returning to their tomes as night filled the sky outside and a soft glow filled the lamps in their chamber. Takako and Wayne made an attempt at figuring out an elvish tile game they found on the bookshelf, but even that was eventually abandoned, and by the looks of it, without much progress.

Instead of books or games, Jo found herself distracted by the small obsidian disk Wayne had bought her back on Myrth, as Samson was fidgeting with an intricate gauntlet.

"This is the strangest thing . . ." she muttered, glancing over to Wayne and Takako as the former gave a mighty yawn.

"What about it?" Samson looked up from his work.

"I can't figure out how to break it, and it's driving me insane."

"It's likely because you can't see it."

"What?"

"Your restriction. You have to see something to use your magic on it, right?" She nodded. "Well, you can't actually see it like that."

"I still don't understand." She tapped the disk, as if to point out that she (obviously) could see it.

He held out his hand and Jo passed over the thin, oblong disk. He placed it in the palm of his left hand, holding it between them. With his right hand, he gestured upward from his palm, pulling his fingers together as if tugging something out from the stone itself. And, to Jo's amazement, an image did appear. It was multi-layered and composed of simple lines and interconnecting shapes that glowed faintly in the air. "This is the magical makeup of the item."

All at once, what had eluded Jo for days now fell

into place. She instantly knew how to break down every bit of magic the stone had to offer. "How did you do that?"

"You can do it with any obsidian—at least, any obsidian that isn't warded against intrusion. It's a sort of magic conductor in this world that can be impressed upon, not unlike a computer, I suppose." Samson closed his hands and compressed the image back into the disk. "Let me see your hands."

Jo obliged and Samson drew a few quick symbols with his fingers in the air over her palms. There was the faint outline of light as they seeped into her skin, and then nothing. "What was that?" she asked when he finished.

"It's a basic charm imprinted on you. It should allow you to pull apart obsidian workings as long as they're not warded . . . and even then, knowing your magic, you may not have a hard time of it. Why not give it a try?"

She did as told, and pulled out the same framework Samson had. "How do you know how to do this?" Jo whispered in wonder, looking at all the magical pathways at work inside the tiny disc.

"In my Age of Magic—which really wasn't *that* different from this one, just a few thousand years earlier—humans were the youngest race. Most had no naturally occurring magic within them. Other young races were similar, with very little or no magic." Jo recalled what he had said a few days earlier about the war of magic being between the haves and have-nots when it came to magic. "Those without had to develop charms and spells to draw magic from other sources, house it, and then give it a structure to do with what we wanted."

"What else is different between your Age of Magic and this one?"

Sadness flooded his eyes and before Samson could answer with what would no doubt be equally sad words, Wayne stood.

"Well, I think I'm going to go to bed. It's the only way to put an end to the longest, most tedious day ever. Of my many, many lives," Wayne announced dramatically. "Last chance to have some fun, doll."

"I can't tell if you're asking me to come to bed with you, or to stir the pot with the elves," Jo responded without looking up from the disk.

"Both, ideally?"

Jo just shook her head, and Wayne departed for the room to the left of the entry—designating it as the "men's dorm" with his choice.

Takako stayed with them a little longer, idly skimming a book selected seemingly at random. But eventually, she yawned more frequently than she flipped pages. Bidding them goodnight, she headed off herself.

Silence settled on the room.

After one more, long hour, Jo closed her book, set it to the side, and stretched. "Well, shall we, then?"

"What are you going to do?" Samson asked, looking tired but alert. Even though he questioned, he still followed her to the door without hesitation.

"I've been thinking about that a lot today . . ." Jo came to a stop at the door. "I know we could just break through and *demand* to be taken to him." She saw the objection on Samson's face and cut it off at the pass. "I don't want to do that either. I'd like to speak to him without a fuss."

"So, then . . ."

"I'm going to create a small diversion, send the guard over to investigate. Nothing serious . . . I just think one of those lovely tables holding those precious vases in the hall is going to lose a leg."

"You can do that from here?" he asked, awe apparent. "You don't need to see it anymore?"

"I think I have that covered. If I'm right, we'll move when the guards do. I'll destroy the locking mechanism on the door and we'll go through quickly. So, just stay close to me."

Samson gave a determined nod, one Jo mirrored back to him before she dropped down onto her hands and knees. She placed her cheek on the floor, peering through the slit she'd been watching the sun shine through for the better part of the day. One eye closed, and squinting, Jo could barely make out a table leg in the distance. But it was enough.

Taking a breath, Jo remembered what she'd seen of the tables earlier. Their make and design flooded her mind as her eyes narrowed on her target—a connection from the leg to the table, a point where the glue could be loosened—and just like that, pegs came free.

A crash echoed from the other side of the door, followed by the scampering of the guards positioned outside.

"Now!" Jo hissed and jumped to her feet, putting a hand on the door and feeling the inner mechanisms holding it closed crack and break. The door swung open and Jo immediately headed right, half-pulling Samson along with her.

They were down the hallway in a blink. With every step they took, her plan seemed to progress without a hitch.

Side-stepping into an alcove, Jo dared to look back.

The hallway was empty.

"I can't believe that worked," she breathed in relief.

"Let's not count our screws till they're tightened."

"You're right."

"Where to?" Samson asked, daring to look around himself.

"This way . . ." Jo started them down another hall, then quickly turned, ducking into a room that switched back, connecting to a stair.

"How do you know this?" Samson whispered.

"The elves were proud enough of their castle to include a book on its history in their library for guests. Even if I couldn't read it, I could look at the pictures." Jo paused only long enough to shoot him a grin.

Samson flashed her a broad smile, one that looked filled with relief and triumph. "I wondered why you picked up something entirely in Elvish."

"I think . . . it's one of these," Jo whispered as they finally came out on a landing high up in what she presumed to be the North Tower.

"Which one?" Samson asked.

"I don't—" Jo stopped in her tracks. She stood a little straighter, feeling a small amount of tension evaporate from her shoulders.

There, on one of the doors, in elegant script was the name "Eslar." It was not a perfect copy, but it was too perfectly reminiscent of another door to be pure chance. For a man who gave the impression of hating everything the Society had been, he had found an odd way to honor it.

Jo knew Samson saw it too by the look on his face. His eyes grew wide and glassy. His arms were limp at his sides.

"Well, go on . . ." Jo nudged him. He didn't move at first, but when he finally did, it was to look over at Jo with something akin to terror on his face.

"Will you wait here?" he asked, suddenly frantic.

"Yes, I will." Jo stepped down onto a lower stair, sitting low and close to the wall where she hoped she'd be out of sight.

Samson hovered alone in the hallway until his chest puffed and his back straightened. He balled his hands into fists and marched over to the door, muscles in his forearms tensing as he raised a hand. Then, with the lightest of touches, he gently rapped on the door.

A sliver of light appeared like a spotlight on Samson, and the door opened.

15. THE PERSON I LOVE

EVEN WITH HER eyes rooted firmly in front of her, Jo had no problem envisioning that initial exchange. Their breaths, their words, the slight shuffle of their feet—Jo could see it as if it were projected on the wall before her. It was Eslar who spoke first, as anyone would have expected. He muttered Samson's name in what sounded like surprise. The only response to reach Jo's ears was silence, a brutal heaviness that stretched long enough that Jo felt her own pulse speeding up, anxiety on Samson's behalf becoming not only palpable but almost suffocating.

"How did— What are you doing here, Samson?" Eslar spoke again, and Jo winced at the way the warmth leaking into his earlier surprise had vanished, replaced by a demanding cold. Samson must have heard it too, judging by his shaky inhale.

"I needed to see you," he said. There was a tremor beneath his words, but no stutter, a strength built upon the foundation of a newfound determination. Jo wished she could see it unfold instead of just listening in. "I need to speak with you in private. Can I come in?"

A beat of silence, then another; Jo's eyes staring straight ahead, unblinking, as if that might help her hear the words left unsaid. With the sound of the door shifting on its hinges, Jo exhaled a quiet breath of relief. A few seconds later, Eslar's door shut with an echoing click.

Jo crept forward, inching toward the door. She felt like a creep, but Samson had asked her to stay, so the least she could do was continue offering her silent and secret moral support. Not to mention, she wanted to be ready if Eslar decided he was going to turn on Samson, because Jo certainly wouldn't let that slide.

Inching up to the door, Jo prayed that Eslar felt safe enough this high up in the castle not to put any sort of wards on his room that would alert him to her presence. Pressing her ear to the door, by the crack on the floor, Jo could hear their conversation clearly.

"I told you I needed time to think this over," she could hear Eslar saying.

"We don't have time," Samson sighed. "We know of the dangers and we have a plan to go up against Pan, but . . . But without your help and the help of High Luana, we have nothing. And that means Pan wins."

"Would that be such a bad thing?"

Jo's eyes shot open, her jaw falling slack. Surely he didn't mean—

"For all intents, Pan has already won," Eslar continued, though his words did nothing to loosen the twist in Jo's gut. "But even so, the last year has been . .

. You can't expect me to risk a second chance like this, can you?"

"You know I would never ask anything of you if it wasn't important," Samson begged. "And you know I would never ask you—I would never ask you to give up everything, especially after losing so much already because . . . because of me. But this isn't about loss. This is about keeping everyone safe. You have to see that."

"I see a hot-headed demigod with a one-track mind leading you all down the path to ruin."

As much as she wanted to slam down Eslar's door and argue his comment, Jo swallowed back her spike of frustration and leaned more heavily forward, pressing her ear completely flush between the floor and the crack beneath the door.

"There's peace here, Samson. The Age of Magic *exists* again. It's not perfect, and it most certainly wasn't the culmination of anything ideal, but—" Here, Jo heard a quiet intake of breath, a shaky exhale. "We've been fighting for so long. How could you possibly want to step foot back in the arena?"

"Because I know it will keep this world safe," Samson replied easily, not even a waver to his voice. "Because I know it will keep *you* safe. Whether you want me around or not."

"Samson, please, you know I never—"

"Eslar, wait." Samson cut him off in a way that felt impressive for the mild-mannered craftsman. "I know my wish caused you centuries of heartache, something I can never attempt or expect forgiveness for. But I thought . . . I had *hoped* that, with the return of the Age of Magic, you might—*we* might—be able to set it all aside once and for all and focus on all that we found good between us..."

"Samson," Eslar whispered, and Jo almost startled at the intimacy laced into the syllables of Samson's name.

"It wasn't my doing, this second chance of yours," Samson continued, not waiting for Eslar to speak. "It was none of our doing but Jo's and Snow's. And now that Jo has returned to this reality, Pan's stasis of lying low won't last; she's already hunting us. I expect she'll find a way to come here too." A sharp inhale of breath from Eslar at that revelation. "Plus, we owe it to Jo, don't we? She broke the Society; she's the one who gave us this, after all."

"So now we are to risk someone's safety just to repay a debt we never asked for?"

"This is the best chance we have to *ensure* your people's safety, Eslar. This is the best chance we have of keeping *everyone*—"

"I wasn't talking about my people," Eslar interrupted this time, and Jo felt her throat catch. "I wasn't talking about the safety of everyone else. I was talking about *yours*."

This time, when the silence stretched, Jo couldn't help but hold her breath, wishing she could see their faces if only just to understand the silent communication they must have been sharing. Eventually, another sigh filled the emptiness.

"Forgiveness, in a sense, is something I never expected to give, Samson," Eslar went on, voice strained but filled with purpose. "But it was also impossible to maintain animosity towards you. Not just because of our close quarters and your guilt, but because of your kindness, your need to comfort." If Jo didn't know any better, she'd have said Eslar laughed a bit to himself at that, though it was a sound she'd never heard escape him before. "I wanted to hate you. And you know that I tried but . . . But I could only attempt to hate you for so long before I failed. Before I learned the nature of your wish and why it was made. Before I learned more about *you*."

"I wanted you to hate me too," Samson replied, sounding so, so small. "Part of me still does, even if I keep following after you like this. And . . . And I'm overjoyed, Eslar, beyond ecstatic to see the Age of Magic returned, even if it wasn't my doing. Even if it doesn't change what I did. So . . ." Jo imagined him squaring his shoulders, his voice coming out stronger, despite its pleading tone. "So I refuse to be the reason it gets taken away from you again."

"You wouldn't be the—"

"If I can help," Samson pushed, volume rising, "if there's something I can do to stop Pan and save everyone but I *don't* . . . Then I'm just as much at fault as I was the first time. If I have the chance to do something, if there's even a slight chance this might make the world safer for the . . . for person I . . . I l-love, then how can I—"

Samson's words cut off beneath a soft, muffled noise, and Jo felt heat rising to her cheeks. She'd known there was something between the two, something visceral and important to them both, but somehow, she hadn't stopped to consider love. Now that she did, however, she couldn't help but remember every moment they'd chosen to spend together instead of being alone, every moment they'd stood just shy of too close, every time they'd shared a private conversation as if no one else in the Society had been in the room.

But more than that, Jo found herself remembering those fragmented moments right before Snow had remade the Age of Magic, when she'd been pinned to the fractured Door, Snow held out of sight, the rest of the team in wounded shambles. She could see Samson's face as clearly as if she were witnessing it all over again, the look of anguish on his face as he cried over the unconscious form of their healer. How she'd never seen the love there before, she had no idea. It was so obvious it was almost painful to look at, especially with all they'd been through.

She'd seen herself in Samson's eyes then. If something were to happen to Snow . . . she couldn't even process such agony.

As slowly and quietly as she could, she got to hear feet, suddenly feeling much too much like a voyeur. Before she could turn back the way she came, however, Eslar's voice, deep and filled with a longing, made Jo's heart ache.

"That's what I've been trying to do, Sam," he whispered. "That's all I've ever been trying to do."

Jo hurried her steps after that, not wanting to eavesdrop any more than she already had. Whatever else needed saying, she had no doubt they would say it. And when the time came, Samson would surely be able to find his way back.

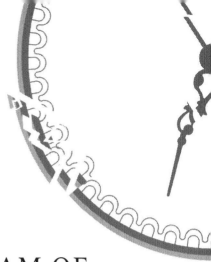

16. DAYDREAM OF LONGING

WHEN JO FINALLY made it back to their quarters, it was with an odd mix of pride, heartache, and happiness for her friend that left her somewhat distracted. The guards grumbled at her, but didn't look exactly surprised. Perhaps they'd received the memo that trying to keep her locked up was a bad idea.

"Welcome back, doll," Wayne said from where he sat near the wall of books. His voice was a bit hoarse and low, though whether it was from sleep or because he was trying to keep his voice down for Takako, Jo couldn't tell. She was too busy nearly jumping out of her skin. She managed to bite back her yell of surprise.

"What are you doing still awake?" she asked, trying to keep the accusation out of her voice. So much for a covert operation.

"I heard you guys leaving and got worried," he answered, no hint of judgment or even defensiveness.

Jo felt herself relax a bit beneath the words, a trickle of guilt crawling up her throat. "Thought about following you, but I didn't want to throw a wrench in any plans."

"That . . ." Jo said, clearing her throat as she walked up to him, rubbing a hand along the back of her neck. She felt tense all of a sudden, sore in a way she hadn't felt since waking up as a fully-fledged demigod. "That was probably a good idea, thank you."

"So?" Wayne raised an eyebrow before leaning back in his seat. He gestured to the one next to him and Jo didn't hesitate to take it. She felt like she'd just chugged three RAGE energies after being awake for three days straight; exhausted and yet wide-the-hell awake.

"So," Jo parroted, letting out a groan as she sank into the plush cushions.

"So what were you guys up to?" he elaborated. Though Jo had leaned her head back into the seat, closing her eyes against the warm, yellow light of the reading lamp, she could still hear the smirk in his voice. "I'm assuming you two played jail break so you could go see Eslar. How did it go?"

Jo couldn't help but replay their conversation, the emotions running heavily enough between the two of them to be nearly tangible even from the other side of the door. Then, without meaning to, Jo found herself remembering the sound of silence, what was clearly a muffled kiss bringing the conversation up short. The blush that Jo had managed to walk off as she'd snuck back to their quarters rose to her cheeks once again. She sat up, blinking away the image.

"I think it'll be fine by morning," Jo offered,

clearing her throat when she caught herself mumbling. She wasn't embarrassed, far from it, but she also didn't quite know how to process the information. She was happy Eslar and Samson had been reunited, but she was worried, too. If this whole ordeal, and by association Jo, somehow managed to come between them and what they'd just finally managed to act on after who-knew-how-many-hundreds of years, Jo wasn't sure she'd be able to forgive herself.

"Well," Wayne interrupted, "I'm glad you're all right. I'm assuming Samson is too?"

"Yeah." Jo let out a snort before she could stop herself; Wayne's eyes widened a fraction. She shook her head but couldn't keep the grin off her face. "He's all right."

This time, it was Wayne who cleared his throat, looking away with a blush that shone far more prominently on his pale skin than it probably did beneath her light brown tone. It was a small victory, but one that brought with it a familiar sense of camaraderie.

"Glad you two made progress then." Wayne sniffed when Jo only continued to grin at him; it was obvious he knew that she and Samson weren't the "two" who'd made progress at all.

When he got to his feet, Jo felt almost disappointed to see him go. Unlike her, he needed his sleep now. Being left alone with her thoughts every night was starting to become exhausting, especially when, more often than not, she found herself thinking about Snow and how far away he still was. They were getting closer by the day, but it still wasn't enough. It wasn't his touch or his embrace or his words of comfort whispered into her skin.

Once again, Jo felt the phantom pull of longing, like a physical rope binding the two of them together, making their separation a heavy, tangible thing.

"I'm going to bed, dollface." Wayne pulled her back to attention once more, and this time, when she looked up at him, his face was knowing, eyes a little sad. Jo felt something tug at the center of her chest. She smiled up at him, hoping to convey some of her gratitude for his company. Judging by the wink he threw her, the sentiment might have been lost in translation. Especially when he added a half-teasing, "If you get bored of reading, or doing whatever else it is you do... I'm a light sleeper."

Jo rolled her eyes, but the smile never left her face. "I'm sure I'll be well entertained," she said, gesturing broadly at the bookshelf behind her. Wayne just shook his head, shoving his hands into the pockets of his sweatpants.

"If you change your mind, you know where to find me," he added, turning towards his and Samson's empty room. "I'm sure we could both use a little stress relief."

Jo felt the laugh escape her before she heard it, leaning back into the chair and running a hand down her face. They both knew she wouldn't accept his offer; her relationship with Snow was something beyond even mortal comprehension now, a bond that Jo couldn't, and wouldn't, disrupt. Which made Wayne's offer all the more comforting. Like old times.

"Have fun with your hand, Wayne," she called to his back, softly enough for him to hear but not loud enough to wake Takako in the room over. She watched his shoulders shake with his own silent laughter, said hand coming up to wave at her from behind before he vanished into his own room.

In another life, maybe, things could have been different for them.

Bathed in the warm glow of the elvish lamp, Jo let her mind wander back to Paris. Where before, it had left a pang low in her belly, the memory now was mostly a comfort. He'd been there for her with Yuusuke and her re-formed family, and had taken her mind off of the stress of the Society in the best of ways.

They had fit well together.

Maybe, if she was just Jo, not Destruction, not one half of Oblivion, she would follow him to his room, ease herself into his offer for stress relief like she had in Paris. Maybe, if she had met him in another life not burdened by demigods and magic and their lives hanging in the balance of it all, they might have wound up finding each other, being together—no Society, just them. A sort of simple, playful relationship that could've happily extended across years.

Jo's heart clenched, a painful twist that had her sitting up in her chair, a hand already pressed firmly into her chest.

It had been the thought of being with anyone else, she realized with start. Just the thought alone of being with someone other than Snow had been physically painful.

In fact, Snow had settled so completely into her mind that she hadn't even realized how frequently she thought of him. That pull she felt, drawing her to him, was a near constant thing, dulled only by distraction and determination to breach that distance. Even now, with Wayne's joking offer still hanging in the air between them, all she could manage to think of was Snow.

All she *wanted* to think of was Snow.

Snow's hands on her face or in her hair or caressing her hip. Snow's lips against hers or pressed gently to her temple, her forehead. Snow's voice whispering comforts and moaning her name. The more she thought about him, the tighter that rope pulled, and as if it could somehow lead her to him, Jo let herself follow it.

It was hard to explain the sensation, like her magic was wandering freely, tracking the trail of breadcrumbs to where her other half might be. She imagined it was akin to astral projection—some true part of herself wandering while her physical form remained still. Jo's body grew lax as her mind took over; every thought became hot and desperate, a neediness spreading the closer her magic got to that other end of the rope.

She pictured Snow's fingers caressing her face, tracing the length of her body, tangling in her hair. She pictured herself beneath him or on top of him or just tucked in next to him, borrowing his warmth. She pictured—no. She *felt* the thrusting slide of him inside of her, the curl of his tongue between her thighs. She could taste the words of promise and love pressed humid and sticky to her collarbone and neck. She didn't even realize she'd slid a hand beneath the waistband of her pants, chasing the mounting pleasure.

Eventually—the closer she got to the end of the rope, the closer she got to a pleasure she'd been missing almost as much as the one who gave it to her so freely—

she felt the images blur. It was less vision and more sensation, like all of her memories coalescing around a singular path. The path that led to Snow.

If she could have spoken, she would have called out his name. If she could have touched, she would have tugged him in close and never let go. If she had been standing, she would have collapsed beneath the burst of all consuming pleasure she felt building, spreading, dragging her under.

Jo hardly knew what she was doing, her fingers wet and sticky, her magic spread thin in an attempt to stretch farther than should be possible, but she kept going, chasing and chasing and begging and reaching for—

All at once, the world collapsed, like a camera capturing two overexposed images at once. She could feel a hand inching atop hers where it lay trapped between the fabric of her jeans and the center of her own pleasure. She felt fingers join hers to rub slow, teasing circles. She thought she might be dreaming, maybe hallucinating, but something in the crackling magic around her told her otherwise.

Hot breaths tickled her ear, soft, wet lips dragging against her neck. Jo tilted her head back, exposing herself for him, for his touch, for Snow, Snow, *God, Snow I miss you, I need you, please—*

"My love," Snow's voice moaned against the dip of her jaw, his voice echoey and disjointed, real but somehow not real enough. His touch felt the same, a constant pressure but somehow not there at all. Jo could almost cry at the realization, at knowing that, the moment she opened her eyes, that touch would be gone,

Snow would be *gone*. If he was even really there at all.

But her pleasure was mounting regardless, her body and her magic and the very essence of her being longing for release, for Snow to wring ecstasy from her body and soul the way only he knew how.

Don't go. Even in silence, the words floating in the magical space between them, she could hear the heartache in them. *Please don't leave me again, Snow. Please.*

"I'm sorry, my love."

The words shivered in tandem with her body, a gasp escaping her throat.

At least let me know that you're safe. Has she hurt you? Are you alright? Snow, please tell me you're all right.

An arm wrapped tightly around her as long, familiar fingers dipped past her entrance with a deft curl.

Jo broke.

Please, Snow. Please I— I need— Are you— I can't— Snow . . .!

Jo was too busy drowning in waves of pleasure to worry about it. And yet, she still felt unsatisfied, her body and mind already lamenting the dwindling connection they'd somehow managed to make. Jo clung to it, riding the aftershocks and pulling at the rope between them with every ounce of strength still left in her. It wasn't enough.

I'll find you, Snow. I'll save you, I promise, she called into the remnants of their connection. If it had even, truly, existed.

Jo's eyes snapped open, burning and rimmed in the beginnings of tears. She was back in their quarters, chest still heaving and body still twitching beneath the shock of such a powerful release. Jo pulled her hands away from where they'd been white-knuckling the armrests of her chair, startled to find she hadn't even really been touching herself. She ran one of those shaking hands over her face.

Too quickly, the high faded, the desire to be held overshadowing any afterglow with a heavy ache, a desperate sadness. She wanted to *actually* be with Snow, not just in some liminal space their magic (or even her mind) might have created. She wanted to hold him, to know he was safe.

But the question of his safety was the one thing he hadn't answered in their interaction, and the fact had Jo on edge until dawn.

17. KING'S DEAL

J O STOOD AT the window, eyes closed, the morning sun breaking over the horizon and onto her face.

In her mind, she envisioned a book—the same book she'd been reading (or trying to) for the better part of the night. She'd known its every page and had her fingers on the parchment for hours.

Her brow knitted as she tried to recreate the book with exacting precision in her mind. Lines weaved together, forming the outline, then filled in with color as she tried to simulate an exact replica. She tried to ignore the feeling of the sunlight, the sensation of the breeze coming in salty and crisp off the ocean, and only pay attention to the book—without actually looking at it.

Inhaling through her nose, and out through her mouth, Jo imagined the first page tearing at the corner as if someone pulled on it too vigorously while flipping it. Not completely off, not the whole book, just the first page. She could almost hear the sounds of the fibrous paper pulling, stretching to the point of ripping. A bead of sweat rolled down her neck with the mental effort.

Doors opening behind her broke all concentration. Jo turned, looking not at the figure standing in the doorway, but down at the book on the table she'd turned her back to so that she'd avoid all temptation to peek. It was just as it had been. Hesitantly, Jo reached out, flipping open the cover to the first page.

It was pristine, unblemished, not a tear to be found. *Damn.*

So perhaps her restriction was something she couldn't "learn" her way around after all. Jo had been experimenting with her magic all night. After the *interaction* with Snow, she wanted to test the limits of what she could and couldn't do—further hone the abilities she had as a demigod so that when the time came she'd be ready.

The man in the doorway cleared his throat and Jo's eyes flicked upward. "Good morning," she said when it became apparent that he was waiting on her to make the first move.

"His supreme highness, King Silvus the Third, has generously extended an invitation for you to break fast this dawn with him and Master Greentouch," the man said, projecting his voice to a near shout.

"How generous," Jo said, wincing at the noise as it shattered the morning's quiet.

The door to the room the men were sharing opened and Wayne blearily poked out his nose, muttering, "Could you keep it down?"

"The king has most generously said we can go to breakfast this morning with him," Jo paraphrased before the herald could repeat another ear-splitting shout.

"The king?" Wayne looked to her.

"And Eslar." Jo couldn't help but notice that her use of Eslar's name in such a casual manner set the herald's eye to twitching.

"Okay, how about in an hour or, better yet, three?" Wayne gave a yawn.

"Eslar?" Samson pushed past Wayne, stepping into the room. Jo was surprised to see him up, given how late he'd been out.

He hadn't said anything when he returned to their suite of rooms. Jo had been perched on the couch, fumbling with her obsidian disk, trying to make sense of the layers of magic Samson had helped her see. Samson had given her a small smile, and a nod, but said nothing as he dragged his feet to bed. As much as Jo had wanted to ask then, she'd assumed there would be ample time for her questions this morning after Samson got a few hours of shut eye.

Then again, Eslar calling them for breakfast may well be answer enough.

"They expect your presence promptly." The way the elf said the last word left little room for misunderstanding. "Promptly" actually meant *now*. "I shall wait for you while you freshen up."

Takako emerged. "What's going on?"

"Do you sleep in your clothes?" Wayne asked from across the room.

Takako looked down at herself in a way that seemed

not just dismissive but annoyed. "No."

"Then, how?" He motioned to her meticulous attire.

"I heard noise. . . You didn't think I'd open a door without being ready to face whatever might be on the other side, did you?"

Jo didn't bother fighting back a smile. The way Takako handled this strange new world, taking everything in stride as though nothing would stop her. It was admirable, to say the least.

"Fine, I'll go get dressed," Wayne huffed, following behind Samson.

It took Wayne the longest to get ready. Jo had resorted to fumbling with her disk yet again while Takako and Samson made small talk. Samson didn't bring up their adventure the night before, so neither did Jo. And they both kept quiet about their interactions with their respective lovers.

When Wayne stepped out of the room once more, he was dressed impeccably from head to toe—tailored pants in a charcoal gray, vest to match overtop a crisp white shirt. His hair had been coiffed in its usual fashion, not a strand out of place.

"You know we're just going to breakfast, right? Not a gala." Jo stood, pocketing her magical trinket.

"Breakfast with a *king*." Wayne adjusted the knot of his narrow tie. "Gotta look the part, dollface."

Outwardly, Jo rolled her eyes. Inwardly, she assessed the clothes she wore. It was the same pair of cotton pants—the closest thing she'd found to denim in Myth—she'd been wearing for a day now. She had the sense in the night to change her shirt, but it was another plain tank top, much like the ones she'd always worn. Overtop was a flowing tunic—an evlish upgrade from her usual hoodie—that she'd discovered mixed in with her other clothes she'd brought. It was perhaps a not-so-subtle nudge by some persnickety elf that her clothes were sub-par.

She didn't know what part she looked, but it certainly wasn't demigod.

"I guess we're ready?" she said both to the group and the elf that had been sent to summon them.

"If you'll follow me."

For some reason, Jo had expected them to be going for a long walk through the castle. At the very least, she expected them to be going to some grand dining room. But the minute they left their rooms and turned the corner, they were practically at their destination.

The inner courtyard they had walked around the day before had been repurposed as a makeshift dining area. Set along a winding path to the center of the courtyard were posts that arched overhead like shepherd's hooks, fragrant white flowers strung atop them with ribbons of lilac. Elves stood with their heads bowed between the posts on either side—twelve in total—as if waiting for any reason to be of service.

"If this is the royal treatment he gets, I can see why he doesn't want to leave," Wayne muttered. And, judging from the small glance from a servant as they passed, she wasn't the only one to hear.

The path ended in the center of the courtyard. Pavers created a checkerboard circle of black and white, surrounded by low shrubs completely covered in the same tiny white blooms they'd seen on the makeshift pathway. At the center of the patio was a silver table, rectangular, set with six chairs.

The king stood in front of his chair at the far head of the table. Eslar stood at his right. They were both dressed in layers on layers of flowing fabrics in silvers and whites, with navy seaming and ribboning at their edges.

"Thank you for joining us," Eslar said. The king merely continued to stand, as though the world should sing praise for his mere existence. He certainly was not going to thank them for taking breakfast with him.

"Thank you for having us." Jo made it a point to speak to Eslar over the king. She had no issue with the noble, but she also felt no inclination to kiss the ground he walked on.

"Please, sit." Eslar motioned to the chair next to him, and the three on the opposite side of the table.

Samson went straight for the chair at Eslar's right. Since Jo had been leading the pack, she ended up seated to the left of the king, Takako beside her, and Wayne close to the opposite end of the table. They all sat when the king did, the servants that had been waiting along the path immediately stepping into motion to bring them a variety of foods. Unsurprisingly, Jo didn't find herself particularly hungry. But she picked out a few of the pastries and interesting-looking sliced fruits that intrigued her, doing her best to not offend the king beyond the affront her mere existence caused.

"Master Greentouch has informed me that it is of the utmost importance to assist you in your quest." Well, that sounded hopeful. "However, he was unable to give me a satisfactory reason why." Significantly less hopeful. The king turned to Jo. "Perhaps you can further illuminate why, *exactly*, you are here."

Jo wiped her mouth with her napkin, even though she'd only taken two bites and there was nothing on her lips. It gave her a second to figure out what to say. But all clever options left her, so Jo opted for the most original thing she could think of—the truth.

"It is difficult to explain. . . But I carry a—" How to word it that was both honest and not insane sounding? "Very ancient power. A power that only two others in this world carry."

"And those two are?" Well, he wasn't immediately writing her off, surely that was a good sign.

"You know them as King Snow and his Grand Advisor, Pan."

The king leaned back in his chair. "You are asking me to go to war with Aristonia?"

"Nothing of the sort," Jo insisted. *Though if he didn't help them, Pan may bring a war.* She managed to keep that thought to herself, continuing, "We merely require some aid and then will be on our way."

"And how do you think that aid will be perceived?"

"No one has to know."

The king let out a low chuckle. "If I give you a bough of the Life Tree, it will be known that the Luanian Empire has assisted you in what amounts to aiding a revolution."

"I don't want a revolution," Jo insisted, taking it as a good sign that Eslar had told the king that much already. "I don't want to see Aristonia and Luana fight. I don't want to see King Snow overthrown."

"Then what do you want?"

"To kill Pan." Jo didn't mince words, and she

could've sworn she saw the glimmer of appreciation in the king's eyes for it. He leaned back in his chair, looking only at her.

"Killing the main advisor to a ruler is as much a sign of war as anything."

"Not when the king hates that advisor." Jo bit back further commentary on Pan. She didn't want Snow to seem weak, even if the time jump at the end of the Society may have left him in a vulnerable position.

"How do you know this?"

Jo faltered. Should she explain that—

"Josephina was his consort," Eslar answered for her.

"Excuse me?" Jo didn't know which she disliked more—the term, or the carefree way Eslar had dropped it.

"Is this true?" The king looked to Jo.

"I. . ." She glanced down the table, as if one of the others could offer a response. They were silent. "We . . . have been intimate," she confessed, feeling like a teenager put on the spot about her boyfriend. "More than that, I love him, and he loves me. You could say we were meant for each other."

"Then how have I never heard of you before?"

Eslar cleared his throat, directing all attention to himself. "Do you remember, my lord, when I told you of the dreams I had of my past lives? Of the knowledge I gained there, and the companions?" The king nodded. "These are the reincarnations of those companions and, as a result, I believe her past relationship with King Snow still lingers in his heart."

Well, that was a way to explain it, Jo supposed. But Eslar had been around in this new Age of Magic longer than anyone, and had to reconcile being in a prominent position at that. Waking from a dream was as good an excuse as any.

The king brought his fingertips to his lips, tapping them in thought. He looked from Jo to Eslar and back. Finally, speaking to Jo, he said, "Where does your mysterious power come from?"

It all came back to that, didn't it? "The goddess," Jo answered, as honest as she could be. She knew the elves held firm to monotheistic faith, and trusted he wouldn't ask *which* goddess. When he didn't, Jo doubled down. "I'm sure it's unconventional for a non-elf to say. But you must believe me that it's by her will that I *must* destroy Pan. If she is left unchecked, a great misfortune will befall not just Luana but the entirety of this world."

For several seconds that felt like hours, the king considered this. It was long enough that Jo was left wondering if she'd stepped too far. If, in her attempt to secure his help, she'd merely guaranteed his ire.

"Then I shall grant you this boon as a personal measure of faith—not one of state. Should any ask, the fact will be perfectly clear that this is not an action on behalf of the Empire, and that the Life Tree is at the discretion of the royal family and our holy mission to guide the elves in our faith." Jo had no objections, and the king continued. "You may have two weeks. This centennial cutting will go to your work." He gave a nod to Samson and the man nearly jumped out of his seat, though whether it was at the attention or excitement at finally getting access to the material, Jo didn't know. "I will offer you a workshop and access to the knowledge of my expert bow makers.

"In two weeks, you shall return to Aristonia, and never speak again of what happened here on High Luana."

"That is more than fair." Far better than anything Jo had hoped for.

The king motioned for one of the servants. "Following breakfast, show the Master and his companion to the lower-level workshops."

"Well, isn't this berries," Wayne chimed in.

"Berries?" The king blinked in confusion.

"Don't ask," Jo said with a shake of her head and a smile that she couldn't hide.

"We have the craftsman, the material, the arrow, and the marksman. Now all we need is a plan," Wayne continued.

"I will leave you to that, as I have no interest in being a conspirator in whatever action you take with my boon." The king stood and Eslar stood with him. At a small hand gesture from Eslar, the rest of the group rose as well. King Silvus departed, pausing to speak to the herald who had initially summoned them. "See they are given free use of the workshops and other basic facilities. They are not permitted in the royal wing. Any other questions of permission come right to me."

"Yes, my lord." The man gave a low bow and with that the king departed, two servants scampering to be at his side.

"We shall be off, then?" Eslar said to Samson.

"Yes!" Samson nearly burst from his skin, quickly grabbing at Eslar's elbow to walk arm in arm like an eager child. Eslar, to his credit, did nothing to shrug him off. If anything, Jo caught the ghost of a smile as they passed.

"And where does that leave us?" Wayne asked, looking to Jo.

However, it was Takako who responded. "War tactics are my area of expertise . . . but there's something that's not."

"What?" Jo asked.

"Archery."

18. COMING OUT ALIVE

T HE ARCHERY RANGE was elaborate to say the least.

The area was broken off from one of the main courtyards, bordered not by fences or ropes, but by rows of interconnected trees, their trunks literally woven into each other in a crisscross pattern that nearly looked artificial for its near-perfection. It was as though, for the centuries this range had existed, the trees had simply chosen to grow that way in deference to the courtyard's purpose.

The border of woven trees permitted glimpses of the ocean beyond; targets were placed inside the range at varying distances. Some were close enough that Jo assumed they were for elvish children in their early stages of training, but some were so far away even she had a hard time making out the bullseye.

Takako had chosen to start with some of the middle targets, closer than she would have for shooting, but farther than one would expect of a novice. Even with Takako's precision magic, Jo was curious to see what her aim would be like with a weapon so far from her element—and timeline.

"For training purposes, you will acquaint yourself with a standard longbow," a female elf dressed in a form fitting pair of trousers and cinched tunic explained. She handed Takako a sleek looking bow, already strung, and curved on both ends. When they'd been deposited at the archery range, they were left in the care of the royal archer and her unmatched expertise. She seemed less than thrilled to be offering that care to them.

Still, unfazed, Takako grabbed the longbow at the grip and positioned it the way the archer instructed. It took some fumbling to get the arrow to stay nocked, but eventually Takako managed it and aimed.

Jo felt the buzz of magic in the air at once, could taste it like static electricity at the back of her tongue. Jo could almost imagine Takako's eyes layered over with crosshairs, her magic allowing her to envision her target with scope-like precision. If the archer felt it too, she made no move to interrupt, a look of boredom on her face. The elves, for whatever reason, seemed to be immune to sensing the magics of the Society's members. But Jo was far from bored, practically leaning forward to watch magic meet arrow meet target.

With a breath, Takako drew back her arm, bent at the elbow. Jo watched her muscles strain, pulling the bowstring to tension. Fingers rested briefly against her lower jaw-line at the anchoring point, and then, on the exhale, she fired.

The arrow released from the bow with a satisfying

twang, and though Jo shouldn't have been surprised, it easily found a home at the very dead center of the bullseye of Takako's choice.

"Still got it." Wayne whistled in appreciation as Jo clapped Takako on the back. When she glanced over at the royal archer, it was to find a look of barely veiled surprise. And maybe even something resembling appreciation.

"I will leave it to you, then," she said, gesturing to a booth with more arrows and bows in case they wanted to practice different distances, styles, and resistances. "If you require any more assistance, I'll be on the other end of the field."

Jo got the impression the archer hoped they wouldn't take her up on that.

Takako was already readying another arrow by the time Jo turned back around. "I'm not surprised you took to this so easy, but I'm relieved," Jo said, watching Takako experiment with different stances, sometimes aiming in an arch, sometimes keeping the arrow pointed straight forward.

"It's not easy," Takako replied bluntly, her eyes never leaving her target. "My magic is used to the mechanics of a firearm. These weapons are organic . . . it's like they're filled with their own power. It's as if I have to ask permission to hit the bullseye."

As if to accentuate her point, Takako closed her eyes. Her magic spiked in a way that had Jo pulling in a shocked breath, then, without opening her eyes at all, she released the second arrow. It flew in perfect form towards the target, then avoided it completely, embedding itself in a secondary target a good twenty feet behind the first.

Another bullseye.

"Whoa," Wayne blinked, shielding his eyes from the sun as if it would make them understand what they'd just seen any better. Jo could understand the sentiment.

"My magic. . . It's used to being in full control of the weapon, not sharing it," Takako explained. "It's not as easy to command precision, but it's manageable."

"Do you think it will be harder with whatever fancy wood the elves are giving us?" Wayne asked, and Jo turned to him to elaborate. He shrugged. "If a regular old bow has some sort of organic magic Takako's got to jive with, then the king's boon-bow-life-magic-tree-thing-that-Samson-makes will probably be wrought with it, don't you think?"

Jo had to admit she hadn't considered that. When she looked over at Takako, already aiming another arrow, this one a bit longer and with more elaborate fetching, the woman looked indifferent towards the notion of any added difficulty.

"I think Samson's arrow—the lost goddess's arrow—will help appease whatever magic the Life Tree imbues into the bow," she said, letting fly another perfect bullseye. "It wants me to be in control—I could feel it, and the projectile is far more important than the weapon. It never fights me in hitting my mark."

Jo took solace in the fact that Takako sounded confident enough for all of them.

After a few more practice shots, and one particularly hilarious attempt at archery by Wayne, they settled into more practical conversation, doing their best to pick apart the logistics of their plan.

"I wish I had access to a rooftop," Takako hummed, scratching at her temple with the arrow head, lost in thought.

"Why?" Wayne asked, leaning against one of the posts at the end of the field and munching on what could have been an apple were it not bright purple.

"I need to emulate a higher vantage point. My guess is I'll be acting as a sniper while you all make me an opening."

"Fair point." Wayne frowned, as if wondering exactly how they were going to be able to do that. "But first we need access to *her*. I doubt she's going to let us just waltz into Snow's castle and ask for a duel."

A thought began to form, slowly but with promise. "She might not let *us* in," Jo said, half to herself, half to the group. "But she'll let *me* in. It's what she's been seeking from the start, after all."

Takako loosened her tension on the arrow she'd been about to fire, looking to Jo with a start. "You can't go in there alone."

"I probably don't have a choice." Jo tried for a comforting smile, but even she could tell it came out defeated.

"And what do you plan to do when you get in there, huh?" Wayne crossed his arms over his chest, staring Jo down. His concern was almost sweet, but Jo held her ground. "You think she's going to let you out once you're in her trap? If Snow couldn't escape, what makes you think *you* can?"

All at once, that slowly forming thought solidified, a sense of rightness pulling the words from Jo's mouth.

"She will let me in without suspicion if I agree to rejoin with her."

"And recreate Oblivion?" Takako blinked, mouth falling slack. "But why? Isn't that what we're trying to prevent?"

"Because that's when she'll . . . *we'll* be most vulnerable. If you just shoot Pan, she keeps living. As long as I live, so does she. But if we're one being . . . you can take Oblivion out for good. I don't see why the arrow wouldn't work on a full-fledged god." Jo let her magic filter into her mind, testing her idea for cracks. "I'll get inside, find Snow, and the two of us will find you guys an opening. Then, once I rejoin with Pan. . ." Jo looked at Takako. "You shoot."

For a breath, Takako and Wayne exchanged a glance. Then, without a word, Takako nodded, picking her bow back up and taking aim once more. Wayne, however, was far from done.

"But that'll kill you too, dollface," he said, barely above a whisper. Jo shook her head, her next words simmering in that same sense of magical rightness.

"You can't kill destruction with destruction, Wayne." Jo remembered the sensation on the Sapphire Bridge. How every fall and scrape and bruise didn't yield death, but life. Ironically, the only person who may be able to kill her was Snow. "I'm sure my magic will still exist, set free again from Oblivion." She wasn't, but it sounded nice to say. "Snow can make anything, even worlds. I'm sure he can rebuild me, too."

"I don't like all this guesswork, doll. . . What if you're wrong about all this?" he pressed, brow creasing in worry. But when Jo opened her mouth to reassure him, she found that she couldn't.

What if she was wrong? Her magic affirmed that the plan would destroy Pan, but what if bringing back Oblivion meant Jo wouldn't exist anymore as her own magic? What if, in killing Oblivion, Jo died too? It was a small sacrifice to make for the sake of an entire world . . . and yet. . .

Jo realized then that she hadn't given much thought to the possibility of not coming out of this plan alive. She wanted to survive this. She wanted Snow and her *both* to survive this. But she hadn't stopped to think about what might happen if things didn't go according to plan. Or rather, if them going according to plan meant Jo had to make a very important decision, one that meant giving up everything and everyone she loved so that they'd be safe. So that Snow would be safe.

She wanted to be certain. She wanted to square her shoulders right now and tell them that, if it came down to it, they would follow the plan and that would be that. If it was a suicide mission, so be it. If it meant saving everyone, Jo would make that sacrifice.

But when she finally spoke, all she could manage was a strained, "We'll think about that when we come to it."

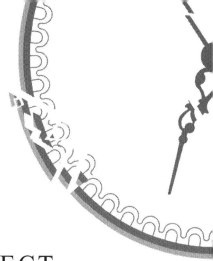

19. TO PROTECT

JO FOUND HERSELF torn between utter contentment and agony.

Physically, at least, she was content. High Luana was possibly the most comfortable place she had ever been. Her every need was accounted for. Better than accounted for, actually; the elves had a keen knack for predicting what her needs would be before she even knew them herself. And, if they were wrong, all she had to do was ask. It seemed like no request was too much, and it was hard not to have a sort of competition evolve to see if she could conceive something to ask of them that would be too difficult for them to procure.

But if it was a competition, Jo was losing.

Yes, High Luana was comfortable from a physical standpoint. And if she turned off her brain she could find herself content to reside in such a location for an extended period of time. The problem was when she was thinking.

Because when she was thinking, she found herself obsessing. If she wasn't obsessing about the plan to vanquish Pan, then she was obsessing about what it meant for her continued existence. And if she wasn't obsessing about *that*, she was obsessing about Snow's safety.

There was an agonizing sort of quiet that came out of Aristonia. For a kingdom that took up nearly a quarter of the world, news was slim, and it was the lack of information that led her mind to wander down every dark path, every sinister avenue of Pan's creation. Surely, after the incident at the Sapphire Bridge, it was safe to assume that Pan knew Jo was in High Luana, now? Yet, if she knew, she had made no moves since Jo's arrival. It was unnerving to think about, if Jo let her mind wander too far.

So Jo made every attempt to keep herself occupied.

In the mornings, she would go down to the shooting range with Takako—the woman was nothing if not determined to practice with every bow ever conceived. After she had worked through every specimen the elves could dredge up from their armory, she began to practice shooting in different positions, left-handed, right-handed, perched, crouched, from behind corners, and even hanging upside-down. She had yet to figure out how to simulate a snipers' vantage, though she pestered the elves daily to somehow devise one. Just watching the girl shoot until her fingertips bled and her arm guard was torn through filled Jo with both comfort and pride. If their plan failed, it would certainly not be because of Takako.

In the afternoon of the second and third day, Jo, Wayne, and Takako all went down to the main city of High Luana. Of course, they weren't permitted to go alone. A company of no less than four Elvish knights accompanied them through the city. Jo found it to be a little excessive, borderline paranoid, but she had to pick her battles, and so far she had won all of the important ones when it came to the elves.

The city was a sort of variant on Myrth. There were similar blue tiles on all of the rooftops—which led Jo to believe they were a synthesized material, rather than a naturally occurring one.

She dared to ask the elves that accompanied them about it. On the first day she was met with no success, but a new member of their crew on the second day seemed charmed by her interest in Elvish society and architecture. He ended up taking it upon himself to be their personal tour guide, and another day passed full of distractions to keep Jo's mind from dark places.

However, four days after their breakfast with the King, Takako announced that she was not going to the shooting range. She did not want to over-strain her body, and risk damaging it in some way in advance of their confrontation with Pan. It was a respectable decision, but after a particularly hard night—one during which every question Jo tried to ignore by day had returned to her mind with a fierce kind of insistence—it was not what she wanted to hear.

That was how Jo found herself, for the first time, in what had become Samson's new crafting room.

The room was positively massive. Jo suspected that Samson had never worked in a room quite so large before, judging from the fact that his tools only radiated in a small circle outward from his general work area, and there was still much open table space waiting to be cluttered. In fact, the crafter himself looked small in the room, his orange hair straining away from the braids he usually kept woven tight to his scalp, wafting like little flames atop his head.

He looked small, but Jo had never seen his shoulders quite so straight. She had never seen him stand so tall. Samson moved with deft confidence from table to table, material to material. Every now and then, he would walk over to the corner of the room, lift up a silver bell, and ring it. An elf would promptly come to attend him. They would flutter away on light feet, and returned with whatever it was Samson had requested. The crafting continued in an unbroken dance of magic and wood.

"Why does he have three bows?" Jo asked Eslar. They were sitting on the edge of the room, far away enough from Samson not to disturb him. The other man didn't so much as look up when Jo spoke.

"He's testing different design elements," Eslar answered. "He wants to be absolutely sure in his approach to the bow before he works on the branch from the Life Tree. There's no going back if he gets it wrong."

"What *is* the Life Tree, exactly?" Jo couldn't help but ask.

"Do you remember what I told you, back in the Society?" Eslar said without so much as looking up from his book.

"You told me a lot back in the Society."

"In my room," he clarified.

Jo thought back to that day. She had been coming off the grief of Nico's death and looking for any possible way to destroy the Society. While she had succeeded in that mission, it wasn't entirely because of the information Eslar had given her, and as a result she found herself struggling to recall the details.

"Regarding the pillars." Eslar helped her along.

"*Oh*," Jo said, the interaction coming back to her with clarity. She was reminded of the pillar the Society had rested on, the one she had destroyed. "Yes . . . yes, you said the elves fed magic into the pillars through rituals. Pillars . . . pillars of the earth?"

"Not quite, but you have the fundamental idea."

"So how does the Life Tree factor into this?"

"In this world, this Age of Magic, the Life Tree does not die. It only grows here, on High Luana, and is said to have been planted by the goddess herself. Every century, at Springtide, the elves cut a bough from the tree and offer it, not to a pillar, but upon an altar. They say this ritual is the reason why all elves may live their near-eternal lifespans. So that much seems to have remained the same."

"If we take this year's cutting, what happens to the elves?" Jo didn't feel the least bit guilty for their actions. After all, if they didn't stop Pan, it didn't matter how long the elves would live if the world was purged into oblivion.

"That was a matter of discussion." Eslar finally looked up from his book. "But the consensus seemed to be that we had not missed a ritual yet; perhaps it would be a good experiment. At worst, I imagine some of the older elves will die. But most, who are young, should have no trouble weathering another century. I do imagine though, that many will be praying to the goddess to help see us through this time."

Jo watched Samson as he measured out a new string of line and inspected how it fitted at the ends of the bow. He tried a new knot, one she had not seen him tie before. She spoke without taking her eyes off of him. "What do you believe?"

"Do I believe in the goddess?"

Jo nodded.

"As the Grand Healer of High Luana, I'm obligated to tell you that of course I do."

Jo snorted; she saw through him. "It's just us, you know. You don't have to put on an act for me."

"It's not an act," Eslar said defensively. "I do actually believe that at some point, there was a goddess. After all we've seen, how could I not?" After a moment, he added, "Looking at you, how could I not?"

Jo had no response.

"The tree is certainly magical, that much can't be denied. And the power is . . . great. I've never seen its like manifested in anyone other than Snow, Pan, you, and the arrow Samson has carried."

"So you knew about the arrow? In the Society?" Jo clarified.

"Do you mean I had seen it? Yes, I had. And, as I said, I knew it possessed great power. I had a suspicion that it might even be a relic from Snow's time. However, that was all it was—a suspicion. I could never find a way to affirm or deny, seeing as the truth was a mystery to Samson himself."

Samson continued on, none the wiser to all of their discussions. Every time she watched him work, she found herself in constant awe. The man was so unassuming, yet he did everything with unparalleled mastery.

"I'm lucky you're both on my side," Jo blurted out.

"Pardon?" Eslar had apparently gone back to his reading, as his head jerked up to look at her.

"I'm lucky to have you both on my side."

"Well. . ." He trailed off. Eslar didn't seem to know quite how to handle the praise. "I certainly think you are."

Jo gave a small laugh. "At least you teach me how to be modest."

"I've taught you far more than that."

The statement opened up a new pathway in Jo's mind. It was something she had never quite considered before, but seemed completely obvious on review. Eslar was the oldest among them; he was the first one to join the Society and saw the rise and fall of just about every age after. He was around even when Snow was still learning what the Society was.

"Did you know?"

"Did I know what? Really, Jo, you must get better about pronouns and ambiguous questions."

"Did you know who I was? Who Snow and Pan were? Did you know about the Age of Gods?"

"I knew about the Age of Gods, yes. Snow told me that much when I first joined. But everything else? No. Though, I had my theories." He leaned back in his chair, closing his book with only a slight huff of resignation. "Snow and Pan were always different—

as I said, their magic was unlike anything else. And when one is granted all the time in the world, one finds oneself learning . . . *a lot*. And not just through history books, but by bearing witness. There's a different sort of knowledge you gain from that."

In just the short time Jo had spent at the Society, that was a lesson she had easily learned.

"I noticed there were some things that persisted, no matter what was wished, no matter how the world was rebuilt, and no matter who or what was in power. I imagined those things to be somewhat like the arrow. Somewhat like all of the overarching stories of divinity that seem to overlap in impossible ways—impossible, unless they were all rooted in some kind of truth. Why I imagined only certain books followed me in identical copy into the Society and why I gave them particular value."

She had found herself following similar lines of logic in the final days of the Society. It was amusing to realize they were so close in their thinking when it seemed as if they had always been so far off in a fundamental way. "Was that why you gave me the book?"

"Yes," Eslar said with a nod. "It was more of an experiment than anything else. I was trying to draw conclusions, see what was there. While Snow certainly wasn't going to tell me anything, there is enough written on his face and in his actions for me to know that my senses about your magic were not off; you were different as well."

Snow. The name was its own arrow to her heart, an arrow fletched with longing and struck from pure want.

"I want to protect him," she whispered.

"As he wanted to protect you."

"He wanted to protect the world." She didn't know why she was trying to divert the topic away from herself. Snow had told her his motivations in forming the Society: to save the world from Oblivion, certainly, but that had not been the only reason. If that had been his only motivation, then he would have merely assisted the other gods in destroying both her and Pan in one fell swoop.

Eslar merely gave a low hum by way of response. Then Jo followed his gaze. No longer did he stare out over the room with a hazy, unfocused gaze. Now they had settled on one man.

"We will protect the world, this time," Jo said softly.

"We will," Eslar agreed without hesitation. "The world is finally as it should be, and I will not see it lost again. I will protect my people. . ." He was silent for a long moment, as if gathering courage. His voice dropped lower; he clearly didn't want to be heard by the room's other occupant. "And I will protect him."

It was there, in the mirror of Samson's words that she'd heard through the door days before, that Jo let the conversation die. There was no more to be said. Even though they had only talked for a few minutes, it was enough to give her mind information to chew on for hours. It seemed that with Eslar, there was always something to read between the lines.

One thing was clear: The root of all of this—all of the hardship they had endured, every wish that had ever been made—was the determination to protect the ones they loved.

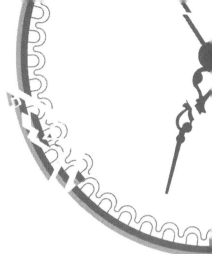

20. MISDIRECTED ASSASSIN

TWO MORE DAYS passed with relative ease—a week in total, and just long enough for them to be lulled into a false sense of security. Just long enough for them to believe that, somehow, they had actually gained the upper hand on Pan.

But that delusion came crashing down with the blast of warning bells sounding throughout the castle.

Jo had been sitting up, studying the Elvish tile game that neither Wayne nor Takako had figured out yet (she was determined to be the first). She'd spent the preceding hours trying and failing to use her magic on items outside her line of sight. Reading had also begun to grow boring. Sure, she was fascinated by her new world. But Jo had never really been much of a reader to begin with, and fascination alone could only take her so far.

As soon as the bells rang, she was on her feet. She didn't know what they meant, but she could safely assume it wasn't something positive by the frantic pace at which they echoed throughout the castle. A shift in the atmosphere set her on edge. The door to her left burst open, revealing Takako in its frame. She looked directly to Jo.

"What's going on?"

"I don't know," Jo answered honestly. "But I have a guess and I don't think it's good."

As if to underscore the assessment, at that moment, a figure appeared in the window. Jo felt it, as much as she heard the sound of two feet landing on the windowsill. She saw Takako's reaction as if in slow-motion. The woman was reaching for her gun as Jo turned to face whatever—or whoever—had put her in attack mode.

The creature—man, woman, or some other beast altogether—was lithe and spindly, unnaturally so. Its long gangly arms almost reminded Jo of spider's legs. Its actual legs were curled under its torso, but the length from hip to knee betrayed immense height. The creature seemed to be wrapped in shadow that mimicked Pan's in feeling. Jo squinted, trying to make out a solid figure beneath the shifting, almost anamorphic smoke that shrouded it.

The creature turned its head, looking directly at Jo. Its eyes glowed a faint vermilion, the light seeming to leave trails in the darkness like demonic fireflies. When it opened its mouth to speak, the shadows retreated, revealing two rows of jagged teeth.

"You," it hissed.

And without any further warning, it lunged for her.

Gunshots rang out, the bullets seeming to sheer

off of the creature's fog-like armor. The two shots sparked against the magical shield as though they had met metal, ricocheting away and falling to the ground as rose petals—removing all doubt for Jo that Pan's chaotic magic was in play. The creature threw back its hand, and with it the shadows retreated to unveil thin-looking skin and deep crimson veins pulsing beneath it.

Underneath the assassin's fingertips, magic formed. Jo could sense it before she saw it. Light drew under its palm and when it suddenly balled its hand into a taut, fist the light condensed into a spear-like beam, extending no more than a foot from its palm.

It lunged, slashing with its short-sword of power solidified.

Jo dodged with the same deftness she had used against the behemoths on the Sapphire Bridge. However, unlike that fight, her target was much smaller and more nimble. More shots rang out, and bullets whizzed past the side of her head. Were it anyone else shooting, Jo would have yelled at them for taking such reckless aim right over her shoulder. But Jo had nothing more than the utmost faith in Takako.

Jo spent the time Takako had bought her with her shots—a few seconds, *ample time*—seriously looking at the creature. She allowed her magic to work through her eyes, allowed her mental pathways to be charged by the power that seared every nerve in her body. Every synapse fired, each working with a singular goal—to understand the very essence of the magic she was witnessing.

It didn't *quite* work; Jo didn't actually understand what it was she was seeing, but she did have the very keen sense of how it could be undone. Jo reached out a hand before her. Her fingers uncurled as though she were letting a bird fly from her palm. Her magic took wing. She felt it as though it were a harpoon gun, shooting from her forearm and aimed from her fingertips, the rope of her magic unraveling from the tether at her elbow.

The spell, command, intent—whatever Jo could call it—hit its mark.

She saw the moment her magic sunk into the creature's shield. It struck it dead in the center of the chest, shooting outward along invisible fracture lines. Had it been wearing a physical piece of clothing, Jo would have sent her magic along the seams; instead, it ripped every invisible stitch in an extraordinary fashion.

The spell of protection sheared away, fading harmlessly into the air. And leaving the body of a bipedal, humanoid male behind.

He was left mostly naked, having not anticipated someone completely removing his entire spell of protection. He wore nothing more than a tight, black wrapping around his loins. The skin covering his entire body had the same deathly pallor as she had witnessed on his hand, spider-webbed veins pulsing shallowly underneath the surface. His eyes continued to glow, and his teeth were just as jagged.

He hissed, as though the cool night air burned his skin. It was the last sound he ever made as Takako's next bullet finally hit its mark. Whatever the creature was, it was not impervious without its chaotic shield, and it fell to the ground in a heavy slump.

Jo witnessed the man's demise on two levels. She

saw him physically oozing blood out of the wound in his chest. But she also saw him with her magic sight. She saw the frayed lines of his existence unraveling before her eyes. Without hesitation or remorse, Jo allowed her magic to help them along. She allowed herself to do what she couldn't back in Yorkton when Pan had first sent one of her agents. She helped this one be undone.

At that moment, the other door burst open. Wayne was standing at the ready.

"What's going on? What did I miss?"

Jo's eyes darted from the body to him; the scuffle had felt much longer to her but had no doubt only taken seconds. "Another one of Pan's men, from the looks of it."

Wayne looked down at the corpse on the floor for the first time, not even bothering to hide his cringe. "A man, or a monster? The hell *is* that?"

The final set of doors was thrown open and armored elves poured into the room. They had swords at the ready, though they quickly sheathed them when they saw the body. Behind them was a familiar face.

"Is everything all right?" Eslar asked.

"Yeah, though I'm going to need more bullets," Takako muttered. "Stupid magic shields."

"Are you all right?" Jo asked back, noticing a flush to his cheeks.

"Yes. There was one in my room as well, but I dispensed of him." For the first time, Jo wondered what Eslar could actually do in a fight. What did he fight with? Magic? Weapons? Some kind of weird reverse magical healing potion combination? She supposed that if everything with Pan transpired as they planned, she would eventually find out. Eslar crossed the room, kneeling by the corpse. "He is certainly dead."

"Thank you for that assessment," Wayne remarked dryly. "I can see why they made you their top healer."

Eslar gave him a nonplussed look but his eyes shifted to Samson, who now stood in the doorframe. The two shared a long look, and some kind of soundless communication. Because all Eslar said was, "Everything is fine."

"What even is that thing?" Wayne asked again.

"Dark elf," Eslar answered grimly. "Elves who have sold themselves to the dark arts. Usually, or rather unsurprisingly, under the tutelage of Pan. . . Or the great wizard of Taristin."

Jo made a mental note to ask—or read—about Taristin and their great wizard whenever she next found herself with free time.

"So it was another attempt to get Jo, then," Takako said.

Something didn't sit quite right with Jo and she spoke up about the nagging feeling, trying to put her finger on what, exactly, it was. "If this was about getting me, then why go after Eslar, too?"

"Maybe because she hates us all?" Wayne offered unhelpfully.

"Or hates that I'm aiding you," Eslar murmured.

"Why just send one? She knew we'd dispatch him quickly and it'd make no difference. . ." Uneasiness grew in her, but Jo couldn't tell if it was situational or a result of trying to get into Pan's headspace.

"Unless she wasn't trying to get you to come back

184

this time?" Samson's tone was confused, questioning. He was simply following the end of Jo's logic. But hearing someone else say it, hearing the words spoken aloud, gave her mind the clarity it needed.

"She wasn't trying to get me," Jo repeated in a horrified whisper. "This wasn't about me at all!" She bolted for the door.

"What's going on?" Wayne called from somewhere far behind, clearly struggling to keep up.

"It's a diversion!" Takako shouted back.

Jo looked at the woman at her side and gave a small nod, glad someone was both physically and mentally keeping up.

Pan knew she wouldn't be able to take Jo by force from the fortified and warded castle of High Luana. But if she had been able to infiltrate it in some way, then she already knew they were there to procure a weapon. With any luck, however, she didn't know about the arrow.

Her feet picked up faster underneath her as Jo rushed toward Samson's workshop, praying all the while that she was not already too late.

21. FINAL DEMAND

JO'S PRAYER WENT unanswered.

She made it to Samson's workshop first, all but breaking down the door in her attempt to get inside. Not that it mattered; the door was already practically knocked off its hinges. Jo's stomach dropped, her pulse quickening even before she'd managed a properly look at the room inside.

Or, rather . . . what was left of it.

Takako was right behind her, skidding to a stop just inside the door frame before walking up to Jo's right side. "Damn it," she hissed, and when Jo spared a glance at her out of the corner of her eye, it was to find the woman in full attack mode, ready and waiting for another attack. "Is the bow—?" She started to ask, eyes scanning the room, but Jo cut her off with a firm shake of her head.

"It's gone."

Takako's gun lowered a fraction from where it had

been raised to her shoulder, head bowing just slightly in pained frustration.

Jo shared her sentiment, her own rage near to boiling over at the sight of the wreckage before her. Samson's workshop had been completely ransacked, tables overturned and half-done projects destroyed, some nearly unrecognizable. Whoever had been given the task of demolishing Samson's work had not been picky, executing a full-scale obliteration instead of focusing on specificity.

Though it was obvious their objective had not been destruction, but theft.

Jo felt her blood run cold at the sight at the center of the room, a broken pile of all of Samson's other bows surrounded by a literal circle of debris that was obviously meant to draw their focus. The only solace was that fragments of the bow made from the Life Tree were nowhere to be found—it was the only thing that managed to escape the destruction. Jo could have laughed at the sick and twisted irony, but she was instantly distracted by the feel of a hand at her hip, her arm, the sensation of being shoved frantically aside.

Samson's momentum didn't stop in the doorway, his feet stumbling forward beneath him as he took in the state of his workshop, the littered remains of his work.

"N-No. . ." He gasped, face deathly pale and legs wobbling beneath him. Still, he dragged himself around the perimeter of the room, shaky hands picking up pieces of shredded material and broken tools. "No, no, no!" There was an aura of devastation around him, as if his magic were grieving just like he was, and it kept Jo rooted firmly in place—no matter how much she wanted to comfort him.

By the time Wayne and Eslar and a compliment of guards finally snuck in behind them, Samson was as much a wreck as the room. His whole body went slack the moment he saw the pile of broken bows, the most important part of their plan now missing—a literal circle of destruction left in its place.

It was no surprise that Samson collapsed then, falling hard enough to his knees that Jo winced in sympathy. Though Samson showed no physical pain, only the mental anguish of a promise of hope laid waste.

The moment Samson's knees hit the floor, Eslar was in the room and at his side, wrapping an arm around the crafter's shoulders. His grip on Samson's upper arm was tight enough that tips of his fingernails had gone light green, his hair falling into his face as he bowed his head.

Samson barely seemed to notice, clutching the remnants of the bows in both hands hard enough that Jo was certain he was giving himself splinters. "I sh should. . . I should have b-been here, I. . . I could have s-saved it, I would've never let—"

"If you'd been here when they attacked, you would have been killed for defending it," Eslar tried to reason, but Samson just jerked against his hold, looking at Eslar with wet, frantic eyes.

"I could have fought them off! I could have saved the bow! I could have. . . I c-could have—"

"We thought they were going after Jo," Takako said softly, her voice the only counterpart to the sound of Samson's labored breathing. "We had no way of knowing she knew about the bow."

"We sh-should have," Samson hiccupped as he clutched the broken bow to his chest. When he bowed his head, tears fell, soaking into the wood and feathers and painting them in splotches of darkened wet. "We should have assumed. Pan, she. . . Pan knows e-everything."

For some reason, Jo's magic recoiled at that, writhing somewhere deep at the back of her mind in rebellion. Pan had been one step ahead; she had foreseen the beginnings of their plan and cut them off at the pass. But she refused to believe the evil, candy-haired demigod knew *everything*. They couldn't afford to think that way.

"Can you make another one?" Wayne risked asking, a clear reluctance in his voice, as though he were afraid of interjecting. And rightfully so.

Samson's head shot up at the words, face stricken with guilt and fear. "I. . ." He started, but Jo could practically see the words lodging in his throat. "I don't. . . I . . ." Slowly, Samson held the pieces of various mismatched bows out in front of his chest, panicked eyes skating over every surface. Jo could feel tiny spurts of magic, but it was dim and withered; not even Samson's magic knew how to make this right. But as if he was too strangled by guilt to admit it, Samson just shook his head, eyes stuck wide. "I can. . . I could maybe. . . I don't know, I—" He swallowed, once, twice, before looking up at the elf all but cradling him in his arms. "E-Eslar, I—"

"It's okay, Sam," Jo said, taking a step forward only to be frozen still by the seething rasp of Eslar's voice.

"Another?" he bit out, pulling Samson in closer at the same time that he glared up at Wayne, a look so vicious it caused Wayne to physically startle backwards a step. "Of course not, you imbecile. There is only one. There could only ever *be* one, unless you want to wait another century and hope the elves will give us that bough too." Samson had bowed his head once more, though he rested further into Eslar's arms this time, wood and twine hanging loosely in his limp fingers. "Samson cannot make another," he added, and Jo almost scolded him when she noticed Samson tense. But Eslar pulled back then, just enough for Samson to look him in the eyes. "And we shouldn't expect him to."

It was surprise that flitted across Samson's features first, then relief. Eslar's eyes softened as they watched some of the panic ease out of his shoulders.

The relief was short lived, however.

"The bow wasn't the only thing Pan left behind," Takako interrupted, and Jo followed the sound of her voice to the far wall of the workshop, a piece of parchment literally stabbed into the table where the bow had been with an ornate, obsidian dagger. Because even Pan wasn't above the occasional cliché, apparently. Takako had chosen not to touch it, which was wise, but Jo held no qualms. If it was in some way warded or maybe even set to explode, Jo would be safe. Pan might have been overdramatic with the display, but she wasn't sloppy.

"Everyone take a step back," she said as she approached, just in case. Takako hesitated, but everyone else did as told. Jo smiled at her friend with as much confidence as she could muster. "It's just paper. I'm sure I'll be fine." Takako nodded, but she still kept her gun drawn, standing a bit closer than the rest of them.

Without wasting time, she reached out and ripped the parchment free.

When nothing happened, Jo turned back to face the group. She didn't have to tell them it was a letter from Pan, but she knew it was only fair to read it aloud; they all deserved to know what was about to happen next.

"'To my darling other half—'" Jo started, not even bothering to hide her cringe. "'As well as to all those who travel with you. Though I admire your resilience, I hope you can see now that your efforts are futile. As is your escape from any and all inevitable consequence. On this, I speak directly to King Silvus, to the elves of High Luana, and more specifically, to Grand Healer Eslar Greentouch.'"

Jo raised her eyes from the paper, first to spare a quick glance at Eslar, who was looking at where Samson had fiercely intertwined their fingers together, and then to the elvish guards by the door. They looked unsettled, though they did not make to leave. Jo cleared her throat before going on.

"'Your effort to aid the rebellion on the Aristonian Empire has not gone unnoticed. In offering your assistance, you have aligned High Luana with a known terrorist to our kingdom and have therefore administered a declaration of war. As such, the Kingdom of High Luana and all surrounding Elvish Kingdoms will be condemned to Chaos.'"

Jo could pretty much hear the King saying "I told you so," but she didn't let the thought fester, too distracted by the following line.

"'That being said, all may be forgiven on the grounds of one, simple request. An invitation of sorts.'" Jo had no problem hearing Pan's voice suddenly peek through in the letter, her sing-song cadence sardonic and twisted, even in writing. "'My dear, dear Destruction. If you wish to prevent this Chaos from befalling our dear friend and his people, then join me for an evening in Aristonia's Grand Castle.'" Jo's stomach soured at the thought, churning like curdled milk. Pan demanded their attention even from thousands of miles away.

Not that she had ever truly escaped Pan, Jo realized. With a single letter, Jo could feel their connection grow—Pan's magic was laced in the curved script like perfume soaked into the parchment. Unlike the rope pulling taut between her and Snow, this one she wished desperately to loosen. Ever since they had been first split from Oblivion, all those years ago, Jo had never been more than a half-step ahead of Pan.

"'A single evening is all I ask of you, Josephina Espinosa,'" Pan's final words declared, though it was obvious there was still much written between the lines. "'RSVP to my invitation and High Luana is safe, even protected by Aristonia should a future war arise.'" Jo didn't like the threat there, but nothing could be done to ameliorate it.

Finally, after it felt as though Jo's voice had gone raw from reading—though in reality it had been no more than a page of script—she brought the deranged announcement to a close.

"'My final demand is that you come alone,'" Pan had written, and though Jo had expected it, the implication still left her choking out the last word, requiring her to swallow once before continuing. "'Between the two of us, I'm sure we can work something out. Until then, my darling. Yours truly, Pan. Grand Advisor to the King.'"

22. NO OTHER OPTIONS

"THIS IS OBVIOUSLY a trap, right?" Wayne said what they were all thinking.

"Obviously," Eslar said, holding the letter. He'd stepped forward to take it from Jo after she'd finished reading it aloud. Now he inspected it as if some hidden meaning might be secreted away in the parchment itself.

They were all quiet, simply staring at the unassuming note, as if willing the words written on it to change. Well, all of them except for Samson. He was busy bustling about the workshop, trying to right things that had been toppled or tipped. It was a fruitless effort; no matter how hard he tried, he couldn't seem to get things just how he wanted them. It was as if the crafter could *feel* the invisible hands of the people who had ransacked his lab. But it gave the man something to do to keep his mind off his anxiety, so they let him bustle to his heart's content.

"So we're not actually considering just going back on her terms, right?" Wayne asked. When no one responded he repeated, "Team, we're not actually considering it, *right?*"

"What choice do we have?" If no one else was going to say it, then Jo would. "She has us between a rock and a hard place on this one. As Samson said, it's not like we can make another bow and we gave King Silvus our word Luana wouldn't get wrapped into this."

"But we also know that she isn't going to go after you, that she *can't* go after you while you're here. We have time and we still have the arrow—which maybe she doesn't know about yet. We still have the upper hand."

"He's not completely wrong." Takako almost grimaced as she said the words, as if the mere idea of agreeing with Wayne brought her some amount of physical pain. Jo stifled a laugh at the sight; this was certainly not a time for laughter. "We know she isn't going to make the first move."

"Or she already has," Eslar added. "And she will make good on her threats to Luana."

"Either way. . ." Takako motioned to the letter, unflinching at the mention of war. "She's at a stalemate when it comes to Jo. As long as we have the arrow we're a threat, and the bow is useless to her. Furthermore, as we already established, it's not in her best interest kill Jo. We can bide our time. We can think of a new plan."

Jo placed her hands on her hips, looking at the letter as though it were about to come to life and turn into something that she could actually fight. But there was no monster here for her to do battle with—only words scribbled down on a piece of paper by a madwoman. There would be no simple way out of this scenario.

"I can't imagine the elves will let us stay much longer after this." As if sensing the entirety of Jo's attention weighted on his hand, Eslar shoved the letter into an inner pocket of his robes.

"Rightfully so," he muttered. Jo didn't voice a disagreement.

"We could go to my home," Takako offered without hesitation. "My family would take us in. It's not much, but it's in the mountains and fairly off the radar. At the very least, it would give us a place to regroup without threatening Luana."

It was a good offer, but it only delayed the inevitable. "No," Jo said before anyone else could get an idea. "We're going back to Aristonia."

"What?" Everyone seemed to say all at once.

"Dollface, did you miss the part about this being a trap?" Wayne asked.

"I have no doubt it's a trap. But I also have no doubt that we have no other real options." Jo shook her head and every other possibility vanished, unviable. "If we go and hide somewhere else, she'll just find us again and wreak havoc there. I wouldn't be surprised if every time she'll find us faster and the devastation will get worse." Jo looked to Takako. "I'm not going to bring that on your family." And then to Eslar. "I'm not going to bring that on anyone's family. And you all know that's what she would do.

"Plus, it's not like we'll be able to make another bow. We'll just be delaying the inevitable."

Luckily, no one objected. Which was a relief; Jo

didn't have to bring up how Snow had told her of the chaos Pan had reaped during the Age of Gods in an attempt to find her.

"So, then, you're offering yourself up to her on a silver platter? After being on the run for weeks, you're giving her just what she wants, just how she wants it?" Wayne threw his arms in the air. "Then what was the point?"

"The point is what it's always been," Jo said sharply. "And the plan is as it's always been—for me to join with her and then for Takako to kill Oblivion. We're just changing the how and when a little bit." Her mind tried to account for all the variables at once. Jo was certain she came up short, but they had time (even if it was precious little now) to revise. She could count on Takako to smooth over the kinks.

"I go in and figure out where she has the bow. This won't be like the Society—I have all of my powers." Jo tapped her chest. "This isn't like when the box was opened and my magic was just set free. It's *in me* now; I have it here. She's not going to take it by force or wrench it from the ether. If she wants us to join, it still has to be on my terms."

"But even if she can't force you to join her. . ." Wayne's words trailed off. He looked at her with a sad, lost gaze, as though he could barely bring himself to think what was left unsaid, let alone say it.

"There's no way she's going to let you leave," Takako finished for him. "Once you're in, there will be no way out. She'll know she just has to keep you long enough to wear you down."

"I know that. Trust me when I say I'm no more

enthused by the idea of being Pan's prisoner than you are. But it's a risk I'm willing to take to get the bow back. Eventually we were going to her anyway; nothing has changed *that* significantly," she tried (and failed) to reassure them.

"How will you get the bow back?" Unsurprisingly, it was Samson who asked. The only thing that could draw him from the trance of cleaning his workshop was the desire for his lost work.

"I'll find a way. Trust me, Sam, I'll get your creation back," Jo swore to him, though it did little to quell the panic in his eyes.

"Let's say, hypothetically—and it is a big hypothetical—" Eslar started, ever the voice of optimism. "That you manage to get in unscathed, you're not forced in some way that we don't yet know about to join with her, she hasn't already destroyed the bow, *and* you can locate it . . . then what?"

"Then I'll find a way to let you all in."

"How?"

Jo shook her head. She wanted to throw her hands up in the air. She wanted to shake the elf and all of his questions until he rattled. Yet her voice remained level, and Jo remained calm.

"I don't know yet, but I know I won't find those answers standing here. We have to return to Aristonia before Pan makes good on her promises for Luana."

"For the record, I think this whole idea is insanity." Wayne made his final stand.

"So noted in the record," Jo replied, a tired smile on her lips.

"Well, at the very least, that means I get to say I told

you so right before the whole world is literally plunged into oblivion."

"Just once, you should try being optimistic," Jo called after him as he left.

"We'll figure out a plan." Takako grabbed Jo's shoulder and gave it an encouraging squeeze. "I'll go pack my things."

Then it was just Eslar, Jo, and Samson in the workroom, as it had been merely days before, the elvish guards long gone. Samson continued to titter about the state of his benches, otherwise oblivious to their presence. Jo started for the door, foolishly believing they were finished.

"Josephina." Eslar stopped her, always one to have the last word.

"Using my full name, *hmm*? Well, this must be serious." Jo folded her arms over her chest and turned.

"This plan is reckless."

"And I've already established I understand that risk."

"Do you? Because if you fail, we all lose."

"If we do nothing, we all lose as she plunges the world into chaos. There is no way out of this that doesn't end with Pan. It's always been that way." Jo stood her ground.

"I don't fundamentally disagree with you." He surprised her, because it certainly sounded like he disagreed with her.

"Then. . ."

"Make sure you're doing this for the right reasons. When the time comes, you can't be distracted." He leveled his emerald eyes against hers.

"Snow, you mean." Jo said outright. "You mean to say, 'don't be distracted by Snow.'"

"Are my concerns unfounded?"

Jo couldn't suppress a laugh, though it sounded cold even to her ears. "Eslar, this isn't a zero-sum game. Everyone else doesn't lose because I'm worried about Snow. And my not worrying about Snow doesn't mean everyone else will win. I'm about to walk into the lion's den, alone on terms that are far from my own. I don't think it's exactly the wisest choice to try to decrease the number of reasons that I'm invested in making sure I get out of there alive. . . Or, at the very least, see this thing through to the end for his safety *and* the world's."

Eslar opened his mouth to speak, but a hand on his elbow stopped him. Neither of them had noticed Samson walking over to Eslar's side.

"That's enough," Sampson said softly. He met Jo's startled eyes. "I believe in you. I believe you can get the bow back."

Jo knew better; blind faith on its own wasn't enough. But in that moment, with his faith in her, she too believed that it would be as simple as they all said. She too believed that the world still had a fighting chance.

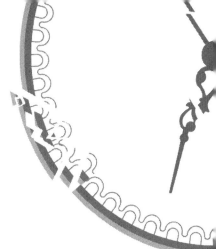

23. UNCONVENTIONAL TRANSPORT

"IT CANNOT BE denied that your time here has been . . . a hindrance on my kingdom." The king addressed Jo and the rest of her team—but mostly Jo. The royal family, as well as what must have been nearly two dozen royal guards, were there to see them off—the king's way of offering the last word before wiping his hands of the whole affair, Jo assumed.

Following the infiltration of his palace, the king had been all too eager to send them away. Now, they stood just outside of two large gates which led to the elvish carriage deck, and their ticket out of High Luana. While it had been explained to her in some detail, Jo had yet to fully comprehend what that ticket was.

"We appreciate all of your help," Jo said, instead of the multitude of sarcastic comments she wished to impart. Even if their help had been begrudging, the High Luanian royal family had stuck their necks out for them. "I'll do my best to make sure it isn't wasted."

"I trust you will," he sniffed, as if to say, *Better see to it that you do.* Jo barely managed to hold back her sigh, taking the king's words as their final interaction, motioning for Wayne, Takako, and Samson to follow her towards the gate.

"Before you depart—" The king's words cut her off mid-stride, and Jo looked over her shoulder at him with an eyebrow raised. He looked as indifferent as ever, though the corner of his lip twitched as if in protest of what he was about to say. "High Luana recognizes the risk you are taking on its behalf, on behalf of this world, should you be believed. As such, we also wish to allow our Grand Healer to accompany you. As an act of good faith."

At that, Jo actually turned to face them all in surprise. It had been touch and go as to whether or not Eslar was planning on joining them. On the one hand, he'd offered the assistance they'd requested, albeit with unfortunate results, and Jo could see him choosing then to stay behind, to be with his people and separate himself for good from all lingering memories of the Society—to leave the rest up to fate. But on the other hand, Jo could see him being reluctant to let Samson walk into imminent danger without him, even if he had the rest of the team to back him up.

When Eslar walked up to them, however, personal effects in hand, it was a wonder Jo had ever thought he'd stay behind at all.

"Wasn't sure we'd ever see you again, Doc," Wayne smirked, clapping Eslar on the arm, though the elf seemed none too pleased by the casual contact.

"Yes, well," Eslar sniffed, tightening the strap of his bag across his chest. "You came all this way to acquire my help. Who's to say, when situations get difficult, you won't require it once more? I'm simply cutting the burden of travel off at the pass, especially since my king has most graciously given you a fliorth as transport."

Jo bowed her head to hide the grin threatening to take over her face. It was obvious in the way he situated himself next to Samson and in the looks they shared that his reasons had nothing to do with logical efficiency. His real motivations were far simpler. And more selfish.

Not that Jo blamed him. Though she did resist pointing out the irony of him almost outright criticizing her for the same thing when it came to Snow.

"I'm glad you're coming," Jo said. Even with their hardships and differences, they were part of the same team. They all wanted to see this danger come to an end. Pan was their problem to solve—*all* of them.

"I promise to take good care of your Grand Healer, King Silvus," Samson spoke up, to the unmasked shock of everyone present, including Eslar. In fact, if Jo didn't know any better, she could have sworn she saw a slight tint darkening the elf's cheeks. Samson had said *I*, not *we*, and Jo had no doubt it was not by accident.

The king cleared his throat and made a motion toward one of his guards, clearly unsure what, if anything, would be a fitting response.

"To account for outside variables, we've arranged for a day's worth of supplies for your trip as well as travel arrangements," one of the king's royal guard spoke up at last, everyone gathering up their personal effects to follow him to the gated entryway. "When you arrive at the Aristonian capitol, there will be representatives of High Luana there for a final customs check. They have already informed me that the Aristonian Crown has permitted your visit." The last three words were said with a twinge of suspicion, but the guard continued. "From then on, we will consider interactions between our Kingdom and your group at an end."

Jo held back a shudder at the mere mention of customs following their last interaction, choosing instead to offer the king one final bow.

"Fair enough, your highness." Then, straightening her back and squaring her shoulders, she added, "Should this plan of ours succeed, know that you will have placed yourself in the favor of King Snow himself."

King Silvus did no more than raise an eyebrow at the proclamation, but Jo could see genuine intrigue behind his eyes. Despite her feelings toward the elvish king, Jo figured she may as well try her hand at diplomacy—so she didn't make things worse for Snow, at the very least, when everything ended. That was the note she left on, finally making her way towards the gate that led out toward their departure platform.

The carriage deck was massive, taking up the entire rooftop of one of the largest castle-towers. She imagined it to be at least the diameter of one of the super aircraft carriers from her time. In a way, it reminded Jo of a gigantic helicopter pad, though instead of any aerial methods of transport she might have expected in this world (planes, airships, maybe even dragons), it was filled with what appeared to be grand and spacious-looking carriages.

Each had a different color scheme, but adhered to a very particular design—swirls of metal arching in patterns along the roof and doors. In a way, they almost reminded Jo of the storybook depictions of Cinderella's carriage she'd seen as a girl. Most seemed to be empty, mechanics and maintenance workers bustling about and fine tuning. But one, a ways down the dock, was currently in the process of being hooked to the creature that would actually bear the burden of transporting them across a continent and an ocean.

The beast was twice the size of the carriage in both length and width, its back stretching in a long, spiked slope that extended a good few feet above the carriage's elegant rooftop. Its build reminded Jo of a lion, feline in body and face, but sturdier and with a muscular girth that seemed almost elephantine. Along with leathery, black skin and long, translucent wings, it had bright blue scales shifting along the length of its back and legs. At first, Jo assumed it was armor, but the closer they got, the more she could see its organic makeup. Add that to the large, opalescent claws and the protruding fangs, and it was truly an intimidating sight.

This beast was clearly an evolutionary predator playing at being domesticated in the way it regarded the elves checking its hookups . . . and the way the elves warily regarded it right back. Jo wondered what type of symbiotic relationship had to form to make such an unlikely alliance possible.

"Right this way, please." One of the elves on the carriage deck stepped forward to escort them over to the beast and carriage. This elf was wearing a long robe with buttons fashioned down both sides, a hat perched atop his head in matching accents of blue and green. Either he was their bellboy or the captain, Jo couldn't be sure. "Please leave any large belongings here and we'll have them stowed for you," he said, pulling a level that lowered a large panel from the bottom of the carriage. "I would like to stress that under no circumstances should you leave your carriage at any point in the flight. A fliroth has never failed to bring its passengers safely to their destination."

They finally reached the carriage and, as if knowing they had been speaking about it, the beast turned and its nostrils flared, as if getting in a long smell of them. Jo hoped it didn't think they smelled good, because its claws were even larger up close. "Now, if you please. . ." The man pulled open the door to the carriage, pulling out a stair from within for them to ascend.

"Well this is . . . something," Wayne mumbled under his breath as he placed his briefcase on the floor by his seat.

The inside was as elaborate as the outside, designed in a way that resembled a fancy, ovular train car. Small couches were set up along the side walls on either side with tables in between. Lamps hung above the long sweep of curtained windows, casting the car in a warm, orange glow. A spread of drinks and snacks were stacked at the far end on the top of what appeared to be a well-stocked bar. She should have been accustomed to the opulence after spending nearly two weeks with the elves, but Jo couldn't help suddenly feeling kind of. . . under dressed.

"Fliroth carriage is the most ancient form of

transportation in Luana. A true honor to be traveling as such." Eslar puffed his chest, as though *he* had been the one to bestow this upon them.

"So the king said," Takako murmured as she sat, clearly in apparent awe of the surroundings.

"We'll be taking off in five minutes," their elvish guide announced suddenly, barely giving them time to respond before he was collapsing the stairs and sliding the carriage door shut.

"Might as well get comfy, I guess," Jo said, still staring at the door.

Wayne wasted no time, moving from his seat to one of the lush couches and plopping down with a groan. "At least we can guarantee a good thirteen hours of peace before all hell breaks loose," he said, leaning his head back and kicking his feet up onto a table.

Jo walked up to the couch opposite Wayne and took her own seat. She rested her elbow at the armrest, looking out the window at the other carriages and elves that bustled around them.

"Don't jinx us," Jo said, folding her legs underneath her and willing herself to get comfortable. "For all we know, Pan could be waiting to shoot us out of the sky."

"Seems counterproductive," Takako said, turning to aim a smirk in Jo's direction. "But not unlikely. Knowing her, she'd do it just for laughs." She was already busying herself by unpacking a few of her guns onto a cloth she'd laid on her own table. Tools for dismantling and cleaning them soon followed. Samson and Eslar settled into their own set of couches, conversing in low voices that Jo would probably be able to hear if she tried, though she opted to give them their privacy. Though, given how their fingers had interlaced on the sofa between them, they may not care about privacy any longer.

"Either way—" Jo's thought was interrupted by a soft *oomph* as the carriage lurched forward. Her eyes turned as the world became a blur, trying to catch a glimpse of the beast at the helm taking long strides to get them airborne. "Either way . . . whether Pan attacks now or later, the plan is already set in motion."

Jo felt the moment the carriage became airborne, a hollow sensation deep in her stomach. It was just before the stone of the castle tower disappeared from under them and was replaced by the depths of the sea. High Luana's vast landscape blurred past, the whole carriage jerking violently for a moment as the creature turned before settling in a glide. In one solid lift-off from the carriage deck, they were making their way with impressive time up towards the clouds. What had felt like years of waiting and inaction to Jo had come to an end.

They were moving forward, back to Aristonia once more.

And finally back to Snow.

24. TOGETHER AGAIN

"**I**F IT CAN'T be taught in eight hours with a captive audience, then it can't be taught at all." Wayne threw his tile down, frustrated.

"You haven't been learning for eight hours," Eslar corrected, leaning back in his chair. "You slept for the first four, you drank for the next two, slept for an hour again, complained for an hour about how long our journey was taking, and then decided to sit down and learn tarith." Tarith, Jo had learned, was the name of the elvish tile game they had all been trying to pick up for the past two weeks. Naturally, Eslar seemed to be somewhat of a master at it. "And even then, you've only spent a collective two hours of the past four actively trying to *learn* the game."

"I've been trying," Wayne insisted, folding his arms over his chest and looking like a pouting child. "You're just not a very good teacher."

"Or you're not a very good student," Samson said

without missing a beat, not even looking up from the gun he and Takako had been working on.

"What was that?" Wayne turned in his seat. Jo couldn't stop herself from laughing. "What?" He turned to her. "Is something funny?"

"Yes, you."

"It's not like you've had any more luck than I have. You gave up an hour ago."

"I didn't give up," Jo insisted. "I just got bored and wasn't too proud to admit it."

"It looked like giving up to me," Wayne huffed.

Jo just rolled her eyes, no longer indulging the conversation. The truth was, she'd stopped being able to focus about an hour ago. She knew they were close to Aristonia, though how close was impossible to tell—traveling by fliorth was unsurprisingly low-tech; there were no in-flight maps. Instead, all she had was the vast ocean, and the eventuality of seeing land on the horizon.

"Wait, what are you doing?" Wayne turned back to find Eslar packing up the tiles and board.

"I assumed you were done."

"No, you and I are going another round. I'll get it this time."

Eslar looked skeptical, but before he could insist on putting away the game, the carriage dipped downward. Jo pressed herself to the window, looking for any sign of Aristonia.

"Look, there." It was Takako who spotted it first.

The Kingdom of Aristonia took up what had been North America and Greenland in Jo's time. She spent a few hours at the start of the flight looking at maps Eslar had found in a cabinet. For the most part, as Jo had first suspected, the continents and general layout of the world was familiar to her. However, there were some minor differences. Jo had no idea why they were there—what magical occurrence had led to what had been Canada and Greenland being connected by a land bridge, for example—but she took it in her stride as just another thing to accept with this new Age of Magic.

Getting up from her seat, Jo made her way over to Takako's window on the other side of the carriage. The woman quickly moved aside, giving her room to look. Jo squinted into the sunlight; sure enough, there was land on the horizon, quickly drawing closer.

The capital of Aristonia was near the southern tip of the land. Craggy bluffs reached upward from the ocean in the same color as the ancient blues of ice that one would find deep within a glacier. The landscape was coated in white: White snow on mountain peaks. White ice reaching out into that Arctic cobalt canvas.

The ice and water stretched tendril fingers into the mainland, as if reaching and trying to reclaim the land itself for the sea. They flew over capes and fjords, their shadow racing across land and sea below. Then, as if by the same magic that made its presence sustainable in such a harsh environment, civilization appeared.

"Do you think calling it Goddik was a little too on the nose?" Wayne murmured the name of the city under his breath.

"What?"

"*God*dik. As in, god. Gods. Demigods. I don't know, perhaps I'm reading into it."

"Would it really surprise us?" Takako asked. "Given who probably came up with the name?"

Jo gave a noncommittal hum, her mind and focus now completely consumed by the spiky black castle that reached upward, as though it were made of frozen black fire. Pan was somewhere in there, waiting for them, waiting for *her*. But more importantly, so was Snow.

Her heart seemed to skip a beat, as if to say, *I'll be there soon.*

The creature banked again, descending further. It seemed to know by instinct where it needed to go. Jo wondered if there was some sort of system that the elves had that only the beast could hear. Or did the beast have more sense than she had given it credit for, and this entire time it had carefully charted out their flightpath, fully understanding who it was carrying and where?

They were questions Jo would never get an answer to, for the Luanian customs elves seemed eager to wipe their hands of them the second they landed. She could ask Eslar, assuming he would tell her, but that would dedicate brainpower to something that wasn't finding her way to Snow. It was as if landing in Aristonia had given her a devoted sense of tunnel vision, her heart and mind stretching along that rope of magic and longing with renewed vigor.

They had just cleared the customs building when the fliorth took to the skies once more, carriage still attached. Jo paused, watching as it quickly ascended into the heavens, turned, and headed back the way it came.

"It really is incredible," she whispered.

"It is," Eslar said, equally as soft. His voice was

filled with longing and sorrow; mixed emotions were no doubt rampant in him at the sight of the last connection he had with his homeland leaving without him.

"How about that one?" Takako asked, pointing at the first hotel she saw.

"That'll work."

They checked in. Wayne paid for a room for him and Takako to share. Eslar paid for one on his own to share with Samson. The hotel clerk looked suspicious of his new patrons, but didn't question. Even though it was the capital of a major nation, Jo couldn't imagine people often made their way up here for pleasure. Especially not with Pan's reputation casting a pall over the landscape.

If she had been the owner of the hotel, she would've been thrilled for a walk-in.

They all crammed into Wayne's room. It was an extremely tight fit, but doable. This wasn't exactly a trip meant for leisure, and the likelihood of anyone spending significant time in the room was slim. Once everyone was seated—on beds, the chair, and even the desk—Jo decided to speak. It seemed like they were all waiting for her to anyway.

"Well, if she lets me go, I'll know where to find you all."

"She's not going to let you go," Wayne muttered. Just once, it would be nice to hear him as the voice of optimism. But under the present circumstances, pragmatism was likely far more valuable.

"I know. Which means you all need to look for my sign, for when I have the bow."

"What sort of a sign?" Takako asked.

The question had been in the back of Jo's mind as they were flying in, and Jo was pleased with the solution she'd come up with. "There are flags flying on almost every tower of the Castle, so no matter where I am, I should be able to see at least one. I'll go for the tallest one, break it clean off, shred the flag—something obviously unnatural. And if I can't get the tallest, I'll do one of the others."

"Then what?" Wayne asked.

"Then you guys will have to find a way in." Jo folded her arms over her chest. "I'm sorry I don't have much more of a plan than that, but at the very least, after the Sapphire Bridge, I think it's safe to say that I can break down any wards standing in your way."

"And then we'll find you in the castle," Takako continued. "Get the bow—if you don't have it already. And take out Pan."

"What if you're imprisoned?" Wayne asked. "Somewhere that you can't see these flags?"

"Then I'll break out. You know nothing can hold me back."

"Nothing except for whatever another demigod can concoct. She's done a good enough job of holding back Snow across time."

"Wayne," Eslar spoke up, using his best Team Mom voice. "We're all well aware of the flaws in this plan, but unless you have a better one, or even a useful suggestion, I think you should try to focus . . . *quietly*."

Wayne sighed heavily, hanging his head. "I'm sorry," he said to the group, scratching a hand through his hair before straightening back up. Then, looking directly at Jo, he added, "I'm just worried about you is all."

"I know," Jo said softly, meeting his eyes. "And I appreciate that Wayne, I really do. But we have no other choice. We have to do this."

He nodded, one sharp jerk of his head. Then, in front of everyone, he got to his feet, stepped forward, and pulled Jo in for a tight embrace. Whispering low, and directly in her ear, he said, "Be careful, and come back. Got it, dollface?"

There was a small waver to his words, or perhaps that was the hitch in her own breath, Jo couldn't tell. Either way, she hugged him back, fiercely. The moment he pulled away, he was replaced by Takako. And then Samson.

Eslar. . . wasn't really much of a hugger. But Jo took the firm handshake and long gaze, knowing they were just as good.

They ran over the details of their plan one more time, minimal as they were, and then Jo started out of the hotel alone.

The walk to the Castle couldn't have been more than ten minutes. Goddik was dense, but not large. However, with every step, time seemed to move more slowly. As the castle in the distance grew, so did Jo's nerves, and when the first ward pushed against her, Jo was already eager to break it. Anything to alleviate some of the pent-up anxiety coursing through her veins like its own form of magic.

The shattering of the magical barrier protecting the outer rim of the castle looked to Jo like a rainbow turned to dust—there was no doubt whose magic created it. Jo was ready to tear the whole building apart. She wanted the satisfaction of breaking everything brick by brick. Or magical obsidian shard by magical obsidian shard— she couldn't really tell exactly what the castle was made of. Whatever its makeup, it looked eerily similar to the obsidian disc in her pocket.

Two guards, swathed in the same shifting shadow as the assassin had been, came out to meet her. The shadows retreated from one of their mouths and a feminine voice spoke through rows of pointed teeth.

"She has been waiting for you."

Six words.

Six words summed up a millennia. They summed up a war that dated back to the Age of Gods. They summed up what would be the end of their world, either in the triumph of Pan's ultimate demise, or the failure of Oblivion being reborn.

Pan's shadow minions led Jo through the outer wall, across a narrow courtyard, and through another protective wall that led to a drawbridge. Wind howled over the iron spikes that reached up from the deep pit the drawbridge was suspended across, as if they were hungry for blood. The portcullis was raised, just for them, and was still clanking as Jo entered the final courtyard. As soon as they passed, it closed with a heavy *bang*, shutting out the outside world.

But Jo wasn't focused on what had been lost outside; she was too focused on the new sensations of magic seeping into her skin the moment she walked into this inner sanctum of her enemy. Across the courtyard, perched on a ledge next to a gargoyle, was the painstakingly familiar visage of a woman-child. Long hair, stick straight and bright orange, blazed like fire in the wind, striking a strong contrast to the black castle behind her.

Pan stood, and a scarf of bright yellow with pink polka dots unfurled. It fluttered behind her as she skipped over to Jo. With a wide grin, Pan grabbed both of Jo's hands, and before Jo could pull away, she began laughing, all but bouncing on the balls of her feet.

"It is so good to finally have you with me."

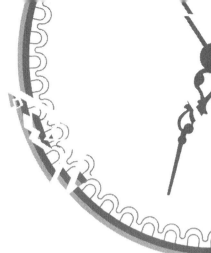

25.CHAOTIC CASTLE

"**I** CAN'T SAY the same." Jo pulled her fingers from Pan's; it took a massive amount of restraint not to wipe her hands on her shirt. But she wouldn't give Pan the pleasure of seeing her squirm.

"Don't be like that." Pan twirled in place and Jo watched as her dress went from short to long, changing color from a soft pink to a deep amber. In the same movement, she grabbed Jo's elbow. "It's good to be together again. Don't you feel it too?"

Jo wanted to say that she didn't. But there was an undeniable pulse between them that had never been there before. Every time Pan touched her, even in the lightest of ways, Jo felt the spark of magic crackle underneath her skin. It wasn't like the magic she felt with Snow—with him there was a deep sense of rightness, almost like sinking into a warm pool. With Pan, it was like lightning: sharp, fast, and terrifying for how powerful it felt. It was like the first drop in a roller coaster, or the rush of taking a life in self-defense—all adrenaline, all danger, all immense and thrilling power. It was something that she already knew would leave her wanting if she let it.

The taste, no matter how intoxicating, was something Jo did not want to acquire.

"I want to see Snow," Jo demanded.

Pan made a soft *tsk-tsk* sound and shook her head. "Not so hasty, darling. We just got together again! He doesn't get to hog you the whole time. . . I want to catch up. Come, walk with me."

Jo didn't really have much of a choice; Pan was already pulling her along.

With a wave of the woman-child's hand, a door in front of them opened. Pan led them into a narrow hallway lit only by ominous, green glowing orbs. The door closed behind them, plunging them into the dim twilight of Pan's castle.

"So, what do you think?"

"What do I think of what?" Beneath where Pan clung to her elbow, Jo's hand was clenched so tightly it shook. But if Pan felt it, she said nothing.

"This new Age of Magic."

Incredible, was the first word that came to Jo's mind. But Jo didn't share this assessment. She didn't want to betray any emotion to Pan. The more she said, the more ammunition she gave.

"It's certainly very different from my own time."

Pan puffed out her cheeks, making a noise that expressed her discontent. "You're acting so different from when you were in the Society. I think I might have liked you better as Josephina, Destruction."

A jolt ran up Jo's spine at the sound of her divine name. It was immediately followed by anger—anger at the notion that she was no longer considered Josephina. That, by gaining her power, she lost everything she had been.

"I am still Josephina," Jo insisted to them both.

Nothing could ever make her give up the memories of her mother and grandmother. She would never stop missing the feel of breaking *cascarones* over her friends' heads during Easter and watching the confetti spill into their hair and onto their clothes. She would never stop loving the sight of luminarios lining the walkway to her mother's house during the holidays or the perfume of rich foods and flowers lining her *abuelita*'s *ofrenda* during Dia de los Muertos.

Even after she'd grown and her *abuelita* had passed, Jo had clung to those memories. Even as she'd joined Yuusuke in a life of hacking and lawlessness, those days, those memories, had made her who she was. Every moment from Juarez to El Paso to Dallas to the Society had combined to make her the woman standing before Pan, here and now.

And regardless of past lives, that woman was still Josephina Espinosa.

"I'm not so sure about that," Pan said with a giggle as if she could hear Jo's thoughts. "Tell me, whose face do you remember better: your own father's, or the one the mortals called Odin?"

Jo refused to answer. At the mere name, Jo's mind brought forth a clear image of a king among gods. But her father's face? Hazy and shadowed.

Then again, she was never really that close to her father anyway. When was the last time he'd even come to visit? Her mother's face, her *abuelita*'s? Those were crystal clear. Pan wasn't getting into her head so easily.

"I'm not in the mood for games, Pan," Jo said dismissively, trying to convey her clear displeasure.

"Then what are you in the mood for?"

"I want to see Snow."

"Yes, yes." Pan rolled her eyes. "I will take you to your precious Creation. But before then—on the way to him," she corrected, with a placating smile, "there are things we should discuss."

The hallway ended at a door, and on the other side was a sitting area. The decoration was so mundane that Jo was almost surprised. For some reason she had expected the entire interior of the castle to be the equivalent of a carnival fun house designed by someone high on LSD and pixie sticks. Pan led them to the other side of the sitting area, and through another door. This one led to a spiraling staircase and then a hall lined with windows.

"What is it that you want to discuss?" Jo asked, simply to break the uncomfortable silence. Pan kept staring straight ahead, an unnerving smile on her face.

"Our future."

Jo barely bit back the remark that Pan had no future. Only she, or neither of them, would exist before the week was out—and the sooner the better. But for the time being, Jo tried to force herself to take a measured approach. There was no reason to arouse suspicion in Pan, or her ire.

"Well, go on." Jo looked out the windows.

From above, the castle looked as it was one solid structure. In actuality, there was an inner courtyard—a great room, more like. The castle zigged and zagged around it, and Jo was reminded once more of a ring of frozen, black fire. Giant archways supported a glass ceiling that was barely transparent from above. The floor looked like compressed pebble or stone, and there was no furniture, no décor, and no indicator as to what the room's function was.

"I'll start with a question," Pan said, smiling up at her like an excited child. "What age are we in?"

"The Age of Magic," Jo answered as if they hadn't talked about the fact already.

"Good!" Pan clapped her hands together. Jo enjoyed the brief reprieve of the woman-child's hands being off of her. It was short-lived as Pan quickly grabbed her elbow again, pulling her in close. "And what age did we come from?"

"I came from the Age of Man."

Pan huffed out her cheeks again. "You know that's not true! Well, your body may have . . . once," she clarified. "But what age did we *really* come from?"

"The Age of Gods." Jo put aside her need to defend the history she remembered as Josephina Espinosa for the sake of getting Pan to her point faster.

"Exactly. I think you can see the problem," Pan said. She opened another door, led them through a bedroom, into a closet, and behind a shelf that opened to a hallway eerily similar to the one they had first entered.

"Let's say I don't."

"This is no longer the Age of Gods."

"Yes, meaning?" Jo was more than ready for Pan

to arrive at her point, practically clenching her teeth to keep herself from demanding that she do.

"Meaning we are losing our power with every day that goes by."

"What?" Jo blurted the word. But she didn't know if it was more directed at Pan, or the room they now stood in.

It was a mirror image of the first sitting room they had walked through—mirror, literally. The ornate sofa Jo remembered being to the right, was on the left. The tapestry looked as though it had been flipped. Even the rug was oriented in the opposite way. Instinctively, Jo looked to the door across from her—were she standing from that vantage, the room would look as it had.

Or perhaps it was all in her head.

"I know, what a pity, don't you think? It makes one wonder what Snow's plan was when he ended the first Age of Gods. Would he have split himself, stored his magic, and joined you as a mortal? Or would he have joined *with* you, Creation and Destruction, to form a perfect god, strong enough to withstand and change the age around them back to one of gods? I'm not sure if he could do that, but maybe he would've tried?"

There was a long silence, long enough that Jo realized she was waiting for response. "I don't know."

"He didn't tell you?" Pan exclaimed with a whine. "He won't tell me either. I've asked him."

Pan led them through yet another door and up yet another staircase. At the top of the staircase there was a door again. Jo could feel herself getting dizzy from each transition, all of the doors and hallways starting to blend together, looking the same. Especially when, through another, Jo was faced with the same, near-identical sitting room.

"Either way, this is not a place—an Age—for demigods like us."

"You seemed to have no trouble existing in the Society."

"Of course we didn't—it was a place outside of time, our own little safe haven to wait for you. And you, you were born mortal, separated from your powers and immune." Pan paused, half-stepped in front of Jo, and raised up a hand to give her a condescending little pat on her cheek. "The Society was a reality without ages, fed by the power of destroyed worlds. But here we are now."

"So you're saying that even as demigods we will eventually—"

"Die," Pan finished for her. "Not really godly, is it?" She stopped in front of the tapestry in the sitting room, pulling it aside to reveal a mirror. Then, with a mighty squeal, Pan pulled open the mirror to reveal yet another hallway lit by the same green orbs. She stopped, mid-track, raising her hand to her chin in thought. "And you'll die faster. But it'll still take a while, long enough to have some fun."

"Why would I die faster?" If Pan was trying to confuse her both physically and mentally, she was succeeding.

"You see, after we ended up in this age, I decided not to make another Society. It was an interesting experience, but not something I would want to do again. It took far too long, and I think this route will be much more effective in convincing you to join me—or, doing it by force when you become weak enough."

Jo kept her mouth shut, following behind Pan on blind faith that they would eventually end up where Snow was.

"But I did manage to pull Creation into another little bubble of mine."

Jo stopped, her heart suddenly in her throat. "What did you do to him?" she whispered.

"Nothing major," came the no doubt false assurance. "I just tethered our magics together. Oh, goodness, I can see you don't understand. . . How should I put it?"

As Pan thought, Jo felt the rising need to punch her. It took everything she had to keep both hands, clenched and white-knuckled, at her sides.

"You see, Snow, as Creation, can continue sustaining these bodies of ours. If it were just him, he might even be able to survive off his own magic in this world. But sustaining two demigods. . ." Pan pointed to herself and then held up two fingers. "I don't think it will be enough. But maybe it will! I think, though, that eventually, both of us will die as well, just much *much* slower than you."

Jo was seeing red. She took a deep breath through her nose, and let it out through her mouth, trying to calm herself down. There was one sliver of hope here, Jo tried to reason: the knowledge that even if Jo was killed after joining with Pan, Snow would manage to live on.

"Don't look so upset." Pan motioned for Jo to follow again, and begrudgingly, Jo did. "I have a solution for you." Jo knew it was coming before Pan said it. "Join with me. If you do, then as a full-fledged god, we should be impervious to the fact that our structure was not meant for this world. And if I'm wrong in that, we'll just destroy it."

Jo opened her mouth to speak, but Pan cut her off with a small smile and a single finger pressed against her lips.

"I wasn't done," she said, almost tenderly. "Because I want you to know that if this is what you choose, we can let Snow live. We both get what we want: I get our ancient power once more. And you get the demigod you claim to love."

Jo's world went still. It almost sounded like a good option. For the briefest of moments, and against her behest, Jo's mind actually considered it. Could she live as Oblivion? What if she could control Pan's urges and not destroy everything in the process?

"Don't answer now," Pan said with a knowing smile. "Because now, I'll give you to your Snow. As a gesture of good faith."

She motioned to the door at their side. Jo hadn't even realized they'd stopped walking. She stared at the door, heart fluttering in her chest.

"This doesn't change—" Jo turned back, trying to get the final word, but Pan had vanished into thin air.

Opening the door, doing as Pan wanted, felt oddly like making a deal with the devil—a mistake Jo had made once in the recreation room and had vowed never to make again. She also had no proof that Snow was even on the other side. And yet—

Her hand fell on the door latch, pushing it open.

26. I'M HERE

LL AT ONCE, Jo was hit with a strong sense of déjà vu, strong enough that she had to grip the door frame against a wave of unexpected vertigo.

Whether it had been Pan's failed attempt at comfort or a twisted mind game (Jo assumed the latter), the room was set up to be a near-perfect replica of Snow's old room in the Society. In fact, if Jo allowed herself to pretend, she could almost be convinced that they were back there, that it still existed, that none of their trials since its destruction had happened at all, and what had once felt like prison was now a safe haven. But the small inconsistencies kept her in the present: the darkened floor beneath her feet, the black frames enclosing the art on the walls, the dim lighting and bright purple fire in the ostentatious fireplace at the center of the room.

Or the fact that, upon her first, frazzled sweep of the room, it appeared to be completely empty.

Jo instantly went on the defensive, magic pulsing in preparation for whatever mental war tactics Pan had intended to use this room for. Was it a distraction? Was she trying to use familiarity to get Jo to let her guard down? *Fat chance.* Even with distant memories of Snow clinging to the phantom image of this room, Jo would have no problem blowing the whole place to—

"If you have nothing to say to me, then I request you leave me to this prison in peace," a voice, achingly familiar in a way the room could never be, broke through the tense silence and pierced right through Jo's heart. She followed the sound to a window, just out of her line of sight, overlooking Aristonia. And standing in front of it, his back to the door and his eyes locked on the world outside, was Snow.

Jo's magic drained away in a rush, the need to attack replaced with the need to be near him, to comfort him, to be comforted, to touch, to hold, to feel. Every inch of her reached out with the overwhelming need for him, like her very essence was begging for him to turn around, to come to her. Even as she leaned heavily against the door in momentary shock, frozen in place by the sight of him (at last, *at last*), the rope between them tightened and pulled. If she tried hard enough, she could lasso him up and pull him close without moving so much as a muscle.

Even more than she could see it, her eyes dragging over his form without shame, she could *feel* the moment his magic sensed hers, the moment that rope pulled taut on his end too. She was reminded of their moment while she was in High Luana, the feeling of his presence all around her and within her, his hands over hers despite the distance. But this time, it was more potent. This time, there was no distance, and the sensation of their magics intertwining and mingling nearly took Jo's breath away.

Snow seemed to feel it too, his back tensing before all energy seemed to drain from his shoulders, his arms wrapping around himself in a desperate kind of embrace. He hung his head and let out a shaky breath, but didn't turn away from the window.

At first, Jo was confused, her feet finally pulling her away from the doorframe and forward, both her and her magic wondering why he wasn't holding her yet, why they weren't falling into each other yet, as they should be. But then Snow's hands tightened around himself, as if he could feel her worry and hear her concern.

"My love," Snow whispered, and his voice sounded so pained, filled with a longing that didn't make sense. She was right here, *right here*. Unless. . .

To prove it to them both, Jo crossed the room in an instant, arms wrapping around Snow's waist from behind. He felt so real under her hands, the smell of cloves and citrus and the crispness of winter filling her nose, the plane of his back sturdy against her cheek.

At first, she felt him stiffen, though whether in shock or confusion, she couldn't tell. She just held him tighter and whispered, "I'm here."

Snow remained quiet, though his arms loosened enough to fall to where Jo's had settled, fingers wrapping gently around her wrists. "You can't be," he said, barely a whisper and filled with so much doubt and pain that Jo felt it in her own chest like a physical ache.

"But I am," Jo insisted, pulling out of his slack grip to trace a hand up his chest and over his heart. "Can't you feel me?"

Snow didn't answer, one of his hands following hers and gripping tighter, more desperately at her fingers, digging his own nails into his chest. Jo let him cling, even if she could feel in the tension of his body and the weak thrum of his magic that he still didn't believe her, like he couldn't allow himself to, couldn't bear it if he was wrong.

Jo was struck instantly, and in a more agonizing rush than ever before, by the state of him. What had Pan done to him? What had he seen, been put through? Had she tortured his mind with images of Jo? Had she locked him in solitude with nothing but his own thoughts for company? How long had he been alone, waiting for her? Or had he assumed she would never come back, hoped for it even, taking solace in memories and expecting them to be all he would ever have.

No more, Jo thought, both as Josephina Espinosa, the girl from the Lone Star Republic who had fallen in love with a mysterious wish granter, and as Destruction, Creation's bonded and eternal love. Jo let the thought flow between them, hoping Snow could feel it. *You will suffer no more.*

Though she could feel Snow's reluctance beneath her hands, she pulled away from him, only just long enough to gently tug on his shoulder and turn him around to face her. Jo's breath caught in her throat at the sight of him, still so beautiful and ethereal despite the shadowed look in his eyes. He seemed to look through her, even as his gaze scanned her face, and

Jo swallowed back the agony and hatred for Pan that threatened to break her focus.

With as kind and gentle a smile as she could manage, Jo lifted a hand to cup Snow's face, thumb brushing against his cheekbone in soothing strokes. "I'm here, Snow," she said again, grabbing one of his hands to mimic the gesture against her own cheek. "I'm right here. For real this time."

Snow blinked once, twice, as if trying to clear his head, but the furrow of his brow never lessened and the clouded haze never left his eyes. When he tried to shake his head in disbelief, Jo trailed her hand to the back of his neck, fingers scratching at the shorter strands of his silver hair.

"This isn't like the last time, Snow," Jo whispered, pulling just enough to inch him down and closer, a request beneath her touch, her words. "I came for you. And I found you." She leaned into his space, lips barely centimeters apart. "This is real, I promise."

If she thought being in his presence had felt overwhelming, kissing him was like drowning in a sea of pure rightness, like her whole life had been in grayscale only to have watercolor bleed into every crevice at once. Even her magic seemed to rejoice, sparking both literally and metaphorically around them both as Snow's magic swirled and fluttered in graceful counterbalance. Jo wasn't sure how long the kiss lasted, but when she pulled away, the haze had finally lifted from Snow's eyes.

In fact, for a long moment, he didn't seem to know how to process the realization. Even as his other hand rose to her face, both hands cradling beneath her jaw in a reverent sort of awe, he didn't quite seem to allow himself to believe.

When he finally spoke, it was barely above a whisper, voice rough. "You. . . It's really you?" he asked, the last word getting caught in his throat. Jo nodded beneath his grasp, smiling as she lifted one of her hands to his own and leaned into his palm.

"It's really me."

"How?" Snow breathed, bottom lip trembling as much as his words. "Why?"

"You really thought she could keep me away?" Jo aimed for lightheartedness, but she could feel the sting behind her eyes, Snow's face blurring around the edges of her vision. The relief of seeing him, of feeling his cooling touch against her face, suddenly hit her in full force. Especially when Snow dropped his hands to pull her into a fierce hug, wrapping himself around her and pulling tight until every plane of their bodies touched.

"You shouldn't be here," he said into her hair, though the awe in his voice betrayed him.

"I know," Jo said, hugging him back just as fiercely. "But I am."

"It was foolish of you to come here."

"Probably," she said, knowing he could hear the joy in her voice too. "But I'd do it again."

"Why?" The word held more weight than any they'd shared so far, not just a question so much as a deep rooted need for confirmation, for four words Jo had no problem whispering into his ear.

"Because I love you."

A sigh of relief got lost in her hair, Snow's whole body relaxing against her as if the last shred of doubt had vanished, leaving him deflated. When he finally pulled away, his gaze was watery and his smile was formed of a new kind of disbelief, one Jo could tell her own mirrored.

"You're here." Snow huffed out a laugh, amazement overshadowing all other emotion. Jo breathed him in, feeling that rope between them go slack at last, its job finished.

"I'm—"

Jo didn't get a chance to finish parroting the mantra, Snow stealing it away with another kiss, this one deep and insistent, filled with a determination Jo hadn't felt in possibly literal ages. She gave in easily, slotting herself against him as close as she could and returning the kiss tenfold.

Snow moaned against her lips, one hand tangling in her hair as the other inched down to the small of her back, dragging her closer still, the hard length of his body molding against her like two puzzle pieces slotting into place—two lovers of godly design finally reunited

At first, Jo was certain the all-consuming sensation of his touch, his taste, was because of distance at last collapsed, because of time apart finally brought to an end. But the more they kissed—the more their touches lingered and traveled—the more Jo started to sense something intoxicatingly different.

This is the first time, Jo realized with a rush of anticipation, arousal pulling low in her gut and mixing with the warm glow of intimacy and love until it was an indeterminate cocktail of sensation and emotion.

This was the first time they had seen each other,

first time they had *touched*, since Jo had accepted her status as demigod and settled into her power and name. The first time being fully in the real world, as they were meant to be. This was not just Jo and Snow making love after tragedy had kept them apart. This was also their first time together as Destruction and Creation.

Jo's magic pulsed and thrummed at the realization, and if she focused, she swore she could feel it like a sentient lick of energy searching out to Snow's magic and tangling with it. As if Snow could feel it to, he looked down at Jo where he'd sprawled her out beneath him on his bed, and a cloud of lust filled his already half-lidded eyes. This time, when he dipped in to kiss her, it was as if his magic was tingling against her lips, waves of it washing over her naked body as her magic stroked along Snow's skin.

By the time Snow's hand reached between her thighs, she was already aching and desperate, back arching off the bed at the simplest touch. She wanted to beg for him to go faster, to give her more, but she also wanted this moment to last forever, for time outside this room to stop and allow them the taste and feel of each other for an uninterrupted eternity.

Still, she moaned in pleased approval as Snow crawled down her body, kissing and nipping at sensitive skin the whole way, until he could replace his hand with his mouth. Jo cried out, hands moving instinctively to tangle in his hair, not pulling but simply giving herself something to hold. Each swipe of his tongue was electric, her body bucking beneath his teasing ministrations until she felt herself teetering over the edge, her mind spinning at how soon he'd managed to bring her to this point.

"Snow," Jo panted, thighs trembling around his head with the need for release, heat coiled so tightly it was a hair trigger needing barely a touch more and she would—

Snow pulled away with a hot, shaking breath against her inner thigh, and Jo barely held back her whine of protest, instead opening her mouth to ask why he'd stopped. Before she could, however, he mumbled one word into her flesh, a shiver running up her spine at the sensation.

"Creation," he said, soft enough that Jo shouldn't have been able to hear it, though he might as well have yelled it for how firmly it settled in her ears. "Please," he kept going, kissing to the crook her knee, and back down. "After all this time, I just. . ." He looked up at her then, silver hair falling over one of his eyes, the other capturing her gaze with a ferocity that was almost tangible. Jo felt her breath catch, her heart stutter. "At least here, at least now. Would you call me by my name?"

Jo's tongue felt heavy in her mouth, her heart pounding with more than just strain and anticipation. She ran a shaking hand through his hair, keeping her eyes on his. Even before the word left her, it felt right. It felt *perfect*. "Creation," she sighed, smiling softly at the perfect image of him just inches away from where she wanted him most, where her whole body screamed for him almost as loudly as her heart did for him every minute of every day. "My Creation."

Snow's eyes fluttered closed as if the words alone had given him pleasure, an exhale leaving past parted lips that tickled Jo's skin and sent a fresh wave of need through her. But Snow stayed still a moment longer, seemingly basking in the echo of Jo's words. Then, he opened his eyes once again, looking up at her with more love than she'd ever seen written on his face. Jo was surprised her heart didn't stop at the sight.

"My love," he whispered with another kiss to her inner thigh. "My everything." A kiss lower, breath ghosting over the ache at her core. "My Destruction."

The feel of her name, her true name, on Snow's lips sent a burst of pleasure through her almost as powerful as the feel of his lips and tongue returning to their purpose. It took barely a single bit of pressure, a finger slipping past tight wetness, before ecstasy claimed her. It was a pleasure unlike any other, her body singing with it, her magic dancing with it. She could feel the rush of it all the way from the crown of her head to the tips of her curling toes.

By the time the pulses of pleasure died down enough for Jo to return to her senses, Snow was placing kisses to the inside of her neck. She could feel his own need pressing lightly against her as if in request, and even with the aftershocks of such an intense sensation still wracking her body, Jo felt her desperation for him double. She wasn't even sure if she formed words or simply reached for him with a begging whine, but all at once, he was sliding deep inside her, filling every inch of her that had longed for him since the moment she'd awoken in this new Age of Magic.

"Creation," she gasped as he began to thrust, first slow and deep, then with a harder, more demanding pace. When she called out his name, she felt his hips stutter, a groan of his own catching in his throat. So she said it again and again, reveling in how perfectly it rolled off her tongue, how deliciously it seemed to effect the man, no the *demigod* she loved. "Creation, my Creation, please—!"

"Destruction. . ." Snow groaned, lips dragging against the juncture of her neck and shoulder, teeth scraping against the sensitive skin there. It seemed as if every inch of her was sensitive and aching and desperate for him, needing him closer, needing him within her and around her for now and for always. When he sucked a bruise into her pulse point, Jo keened, wrapping her legs around him to get him deeper, wishing vaguely that his mark might last, that a part of her status as demigod didn't mean such easy healing. She wanted to feel him inside of her for days, wanted to look in the mirror and see where he'd marked her in the heat of the moment.

Jo wasn't sure what other words she might have laced around his name as his thrusts became sloppy and quick, or what she might have called out as his hand finally wormed between them to work her blissfully over the edge a second time. All she knew was that with their magic intertwined, even in the daze of her own release, Jo could feel Snow's pleasure, could feel the moment he'd fallen over his own precipice. She clung to him, held him through it, and whispered his name over and over again, "Creation, my love, my Creation, I'm here," until they both stopped trembling and she was certain he believed it.

27. THEIR PLAN

THEY'D FALLEN SILENT after that, content to simply enjoy the warmth and presence of finally being back in each other's arms. Jo snuggled into his side, head resting on his shoulder, and lifted a hand to his bare chest, fingers tracing loose patterns against his skin. When he hummed in contentment, she could feel the vibration of it all along her body.

"Just once," Jo whispered, stopping to splay her hand over one of his pecs, fingers lightly fanning out to brush against a still-hardened nipple. "I would like to have sex with you when the world isn't falling apart."

A deep chuckle vibrated beneath her hand. The bed shifted as Snow rolled over, his arm falling on her waist, pulling her closer to him and trapping her hand between their bodies. There wasn't much space left to begin with, so Jo appreciated the indents his body made on hers.

"What if you no longer desire me when the world

is not falling apart? How shall I find you in my bed if I cannot use desperation to have you running to me?"

She could hear the joke in his words and it brought out a laugh of her own. "Perhaps you won't be able to. Seems a poor reason though to leave the world in a near-constant state of worry and chaos."

"For you, it would be worth it." He kissed her forehead, her cheek, her jaw.

Jo's eyes fluttered closed and she sighed softly, feeling reality seep back into her. Despite the fact that it had been turned into something of a joke, she really did want to see how things would be between her and Snow without the weight of the world continually crashing down between them. She didn't think it'd ever be easy. Relationships, from what she'd seen, never were. Plus, Snow didn't really seem like the type to relax on a beach for the rest of his life—no matter how deserved it may be.

Her eyes opened again, the room coming into focus over Snow's shoulder. She had no idea what he would be like without living at the end of Pan's leash. But she wanted to know, and there was only one way to do that.

"Is it safe in here?" she asked delicately.

"Safe how?"

"Will she know what is said? Or are there wards like your room in the Society?" Jo clarified. Breathing under Pan's roof would likely never be safe.

"I've placed my own protections that I do not believe she can penetrate."

It wasn't an absolute like Jo had hoped for, but it was the best she was going to get. The feeling of sand slipping through the hourglass was beginning to creep up in the back of Jo's mind. Wriggling away, Jo sat, gripping the edge of the bed, as if bracing herself for what needed to happen next.

"She'll come for me soon."

"I have no doubt," he agreed, grimly. Jo felt Snow move behind her. He appeared at her side, fingers lacing with hers. "Why are you really here?" he asked, finally, rephrasing his earlier question. "You know it's not—"

"Let's not waste the precious time we have talking about what I should or shouldn't have done." Jo caught his gaze. "I'm here now. I've rolled the dice on this."

"What, exactly, did you roll the dice on?" he asked, simultaneously tucking a stray piece of hair behind her ear, his fingers brushing down her cheek as if he was still trapped in wonder at her mere presence. "You're not safe here."

"I know, but no one is safe if I do nothing. Pan said she's using your magic to keep existing." His expression told her everything, so Jo spared him an explanation and continued. "She also told me that if I join with her and form Oblivion, we can exist on our own, and she'll let you live with us." Snow pulled away from her as if burned.

"She's lying to you," he said quickly, rolling to sit up in bed before getting hastily to his feet. Jo fought to keep her focus on what Snow was saying when his naked backside loomed ahead of her. It became significantly easier when he wrapped a silken robe around his god-like form. "There is no way that once she gets what she wants, she will let me live. Beyond that, if you join to form Oblivion once more, then you will be something—someone—else. Who knows how your wants will change, if they are not lost entirely. And—"

Jo stopped him with a touch on his elbow. Snow blinked, clearly startled even though she hadn't exactly been quiet about getting up off the bed and walking over to him.

"I know all that," she said gently. "I know she's lying to get what she wants—that she'll do whatever it takes to get what she wants. Which is why I came here with a plan."

"What plan?"

It was Jo's turn to dress as she spoke. Snow returned to the bed, watching intently, a look of pure appreciation on his face with her every movement. Once more, she had to resist distraction, and not give in to the quickly refilling tank of molten need that sat low in her stomach.

"The Society is here."

Snow blinked, clearly taken aback. "*Here?*"

"Well, the team is outside, in Goddik."

"What do you hope to do?" The way he phrased the question told Jo he did not suspect that she was going into this blind—a fact she appreciated.

"We have the arrow from the Goddess of the Hunt."

Snow stared at her as though she had just grown several tails. Then there was a swift intake of breath, and a whispered "*What?*" Followed quickly by a "*How?*" that brought him from the bed back to his feet.

"Samson had it this whole time."

"Impossible. I would've been able to sense. . ." He came to a full stop, movement and speech. "She shielded it."

"I was hoping you could clarify how even Pan doesn't seem to know about it," Jo folded her arms, leaning against one of the pillars that surrounded the fireplace at the center of the room.

"When Hunt said she would make a weapon, she kept the details secluded from the other gods, afraid that the information would somehow get back to Pan—rightfully so, because it did. The only thing she assured us was that Pan would not, under any circumstances, know of the arrow's existence—it was to be shielded from her touch. But perhaps I. . . Perhaps it was shielded from her gaze as well."

Jo's eyes ping-ponged across the room, following Snow as he paced. "She gave it to her chosen champion. When I touched the arrow, I saw its history," Jo clarified at his immediate confusion. "He was going to take the arrow and slay Pan with it. Or, try to. But when the Age of Gods ended, he forgot this purpose . . . he only remembered that the arrow was important and passed it on to someone else. Who passed it on to someone else, from generation to generation. . ."

"Until Samson. And it followed him into the Society as the current champion," Snow pieced together, almost correctly.

"Not quite. It followed Samson into the Society, yes . . . but not because he was the champion."

"Then who?"

"Takako."

"Of course." Snow sat heavily on the bed, bringing a hand to his forehead. "Her ancient lineage of magic came from Hunt's champion. Why it persisted all this time. . ."

"And why her magic is what it is," Jo finished for him. "Takako is ready to be the champion, and we have the arrow. So—"

"You set out to make a bow," Snow interjected.

"Yes. How did you know?" A frown pulled on her cheeks. No matter what the reason, Jo didn't think it was a good one.

"Pan came to brag to me about thwarting your plans. Gloating about whatever chaos she's creating is a sort of pastime for her." The distant look that glossed over Snow's eyes told Jo that she didn't want to know what else Pan had done, or forced Snow to endure knowledge of. "She said she was going to bring you and that she'd taken what you were making—a weapon. Which I'm presuming to be a bow now that I know you have the arrow."

"It is. We went to High Luana and got a bough from the Life Tree to carve it."

"The elves agreed to that?" Snow said with equal measures of shock and pride.

"We convinced them it was in their best interest, and they had little choice." Jo pushed off the column, crossing over to take his hands in hers. "Snow, we can end this." She omitted the words her mind treacherously would not let her forget—that to end it could mean her death. Jo didn't want that weighing on Snow. She didn't want him trying to talk her out of the decision, or hesitating. He knew Pan could not die as long as she lived, so surely, somewhere, he also knew what was on the line. "But I need to find the bow. If she bragged to you about the bow then she likely didn't destroy it, right?"

He nodded. "I don't think she would destroy it. Pan is a hoarder. She enjoys the feeling of possessing too much."

That sounded about right. "Then, do you know where she might be keeping it? Once I get it, I'll bring down the walls and let in the team to finish her."

"I cannot cross the threshold of that door." Snow nodded toward the entrance Jo had come through. "At least not without Pan's invitation. Sometimes, it leads to throne rooms where I give messages to the people, maintaining the illusion of my rule—but never anything else."

Whatever frustration she felt toward not knowing the arrow's location paled in comparison to the visceral anger at Snow's treatment. "I will kill her," Jo muttered under her breath, never more resolved.

Snow squeezed her hands tightly. "But I have some ideas."

"You do?"

"I know enough from the Society and before. . . She usually likes to keep things squirreled away in a central treasure room." As he spoke, Jo's mind filled with images of Pan's room—the horde of treasures condensed at her innermost sanctum. After all the illusions had vanished, all there had been was Pan and her treasures.

"I think I have an idea. . ." Jo whispered, clarity dawning on her.

Just when she opened her mouth to speak, there was a knock on the door. Jo glared angrily at it, gripping Snow's hands even tighter, as though she could cling to him hard enough that she wouldn't be taken away. His hands went slack and Jo looked back in a panic she couldn't fight.

"You have to go," he said quickly. "Don't fight it, do what must be done, stay focused."

"I'll come back for you," Jo whispered hastily, as if everything they said could suddenly be heard.

"I'll be waiting," Snow said, as if there were anywhere else he could be. It made the words all the more sorrowful.

Jo's heart broke as she walked for the door, and rage filled the cracks. She gave the handle a mighty yank, feeling the whole thing strain under her touch. It was a satisfying reaffirmation that, yes, even Pan's magic could be broken. Jo had been ready to unleash her anger at Pan next, but she stopped short.

There was a man on the other side of the door.

He had skin that looked to be made of some kind of steel or alloy, and all-black obsidian eyes. He wore what could best be described as a child's interpretation of a butler's uniform, comedic in its ostentatious parts that didn't quite go together. His coat had capped sleeves that poofed up to his ears in a balloon of fabric. It was double-buttoned, a long silver tie running down the center and extending nearly to his knees. His shorts reminded Jo of what she'd seen boys wearing to prestigious private schools when she was a kid.

"She requests your presence for dinner." His lips barely moved when he spoke, like an automaton or a puppet, the jaw hinged at the corners of the mouth and sliding down from the chin rather than the ears.

"I am inclined to take dinner here," Jo protested. Even if she didn't have a choice, she didn't want to start a habit of going willingly. She would be trouble for Pan up until the end . . . whatever and whenever that ending was.

The butler looked at her blankly and then repeated in the same sort of hollow, echoing voice, "She requests your presence for dinner."

"I said I was inclined—"

"Jo," Snow stopped her with a deep utterance of her name. A hand slipped around her waist, tenderly, as if seeking one final embrace before she was pulled from him. He moved to kiss her shoulder and from the corners of her eyes Jo could see that his gaze never left the threshold of the door—the barrier that confined him to his room. With just one look of frustrated resignation from him, Jo wanted to say plans be damned and shatter it now. "Go on ahead. There's no point in fighting."

There's no point in fighting now, she mentally corrected. The time for fighting would be soon enough and when it came, Jo would not hesitate for a moment to unleash her full wrath on the world.

"Very well," Jo said finally. "Take me to her."

The man nodded. His head spun first, a full hundred and eighty degrees around to face the opposite direction. His body followed in an uncomfortable pivot. Without a word, he began walking away.

Jo gave Snow's hand one more squeeze, and then felt it fall from her waist.

By the time she looked back, his door had already shut, and unnatural shadows had begun to obscure it from view.

28. DRESS FOR DINNER

S HE FOLLOWED BEHIND the strange creature without question.

It wasn't that Jo didn't *have* any questions; she had quite a few, in fact, what it was and how it came to be in Pan's service, for starters. What kept Jo silent was the fact that she didn't think that asking her questions would actually get her anywhere. If the creature answered her, she was sure it would either be something vague and immaterial, or so specific as to be devoid of meaning for Jo—someone still learning the particulars about Age of Magic she now resided in.

But if she had to describe the man in her own terms, it would be a stone marionette. As she looked more closely at the grayish skin on the man's arms, she realized that it was not metal, as she previously thought, but some kind of dark, smoky quartz. It looked hard, and picked up the light as though it were mirror-polished.

She was so distracted by trying to pick it and its strange magic apart that Jo didn't notice she was now in a completely different hallway.

Gone were the halls she'd first walked through with Pan. There were no orbs to light the way, but glowing strips on either side of stone walkways where the floor met the walls. They looked like carved channels, some kind of luminescent liquid flowing down them. It cast an eerie reddish haze that caught on every bottom edge of the stone walls, which looked almost as if they were bleeding as a result.

The hallway reached a dead end and the creature came to a prompt stop.

"Where to now?" Jo reached over its shoulder, tapping on the wall. "Don't think we can go this way, unless you want me to break it down."

She heard a soft grinding noise as the man twisted his head once more. Jo took an involuntary step backward, still not entirely accustomed to that ability. His body followed and then he stood, immobile, for a long minute, just staring at her with those blank eyes.

"Turn, please," he instructed.

Jo turned to find the hallway she had been walking in was no longer the same. Sure, it had the tracks of light, the bloody glow, and the stone walls. But now, clouded windows let in the orange glow of sunset along her left side. Along her right were a series of doors, all nearly identical.

"Third one, please," the man said from behind her.

Jo took a few wide steps. Not because she was eager to get to dinner with Pan, but because she had no interest in keeping the man at her back longer than necessary. The more distance between them, the better.

"All right, Pan, let's get this—" Jo spoke as she swung open the door, expecting some kind of dining room, but was stopped short the moment the room registered.

It was not a dining room. More like a glorified closet. A glorified, *empty* closet.

There were racks to hang clothes, shelves, and shoe cubbies on every dark-wooded wall. The carpet was a plush red velvet that muffled their footfalls as Jo and her guide entered. Directly across from the door was a mirror, and hanging in front of it was a single article of clothing—a dress.

"She requests that you dress for dinner."

"I am dressed," Jo protested.

"She requests that you wear this."

"I know what she wants." Jo walked over to the dress, grabbing the hanger and running her hands over the thin silk. "She wants to humiliate me."

In her entire existence, Jo didn't think she'd ever worn something so extravagantly impractical. And she meant her *entire* existence, because Jo was fairly certain that even as a demigod, she had worn more utilitarian garb. This, however, struck a balance between "female escort" and "got in a fight with a pair of scissors and lost." Jo didn't take issue with either in concept, but neither was *her*.

"She requests that—"

"I heard you the first time." Jo held up the dress by its spaghetti straps. "Did she say where the rest of it was?"

"This is the dress that she has requested."

Jo sighed, clearly getting nowhere with the man. She was beginning to suspect that his sentience was an illusion and he really was one of Pan's machinations. Regardless, she had no interest in tormenting a creature who was likely as much of a prisoner as she was.

"Did she say what would happen if I didn't wear this?"

There was a long pause, and Jo was expecting yet another variant of the same expressionless mantra. But he surprised her. "In my experience, if one must inquire, one doesn't want to know."

Snow's words rang clearly in Jo's ears—*there's no point in fighting, yet*. So she'd wear a revealing dress. She'd let Pan have this battle for the sake of the war. Her friends were counting on her and the sooner all this ended, the better.

"Could you turn around, please?"

The man obliged as he had before—first with his head, then shoulders.

Jo stripped down, shivering as her bare skin met the air. Surely it couldn't be that much colder than Snow's room, could it? It felt downright frigid and she felt the tingle of an icy phantom finger run down her spine. Perhaps it was just the feeling of being so vulnerable in Pan's lair getting under her skin.

The dress didn't offer much in the way of feeling less vulnerable. Jo's arms were completely bare, as was her back, and most of her front, given the drooping V of the neckline. Its hem sat high on her thigh, just barely low enough to ensure everything was covered.

Straightening her shoulders, Jo stole a second to compose herself. This whole thing was to break her down, make her feel off-kilter. It didn't matter if she walked into the room naked. Pan wasn't the one in control of Jo's feelings, and Jo was determined to show her that.

"All right, let's go."

The man's head spun, no doubt verifying that she had put on the dress as it promptly swiveled back forward. "This way, please."

He opened the door and, once more, it was not connected to the hallway Jo had used to enter. The marionette motioned for Jo to step through, but made no effort to do so himself. A strange sort of magic pulsed from the room beyond and Jo had every suspicion that it was not a place the man could go, even if he wanted to—and even if he were able to act on his own desires (which Jo was beginning to doubt).

Jo stepped into the dining room alone.

"Well, this looks more like what I was expecting," Jo muttered under her breath.

The room was a dreamscape of part-medieval hall, part-Versailles palace. The floor was the same dark wood as the closet's shelving. It, too, was polished to a mirror-shine and reflected the ornate chandeliers that hung in a row of three on the ceiling. Where Jo expected most chandeliers to be electric (magic, perhaps, in this age) or candle lit, these were neither. In an odd reverse, they dripped glowing orbs of light that occasionally fell, disappearing before they made contact with the table below.

The table could've easily sat eight—perhaps ten. But there were only two chairs with place settings, one at each end.

"I'm so glad to hear it," Pan said from where she was perched at the far end of the table. She was seated on the wide top of the wingback chair, her feet swinging happily and bouncing off the tufted navy velvet. "I want you to be happy here. Want *us* to be happy here."

Jo made no comment, heading directly for the chair at the opposite head of the table.

"I see you're wearing the dress. It looks nice on you."

Still, Jo said nothing. The sooner this was over, the better. Jo would give Pan no encouragement if she could avoid it. The last thing she wanted was to give the woman the impression that she was actually enjoying herself.

Jo inspected the silverware as she sat. It was ornate, gold, and carved in a similar pattern as the moldings throughout the walls and ceiling of the room. Jo squinted at the walls, trying to make out the paintings that hung in the heavy, gilded frames. But every time she got her focus, they seemed to shift like a mirage. In a way, never being able to make out an image was far more unnerving than seeing something disturbing.

She examined her plate. *Eat and get it over with*, Jo thought, willing the empty space to fill with food.

Movement drew her attention back to Pan.

The woman-child jumped down, both feet landing on the seat with a small bounce. The multicolored ruffles of her dress floated in the darkness, shimmering from orbs of light that continued to vanish between them. Reaching down, Pan picked up her glass and lifted it into the air. As she did so, it filled with a deep crimson liquid.

Jo noticed the same liquid filling nearly to the brim of her own crystal goblet.

"Let's begin, with a toast to us." Pan held out her glass expectantly.

Trying to feel as though the action was an indication of war rather than defeat, Jo lifted her own glass, and drank the bitter, metallic liquid.

29. EAT UP

"ISN'T THIS CHARCUTERIE just delightful?" Pan cooed, plucking a small, yellow berry up from her plate between middle finger and thumb and placing it to her lips with a long, drawn out, nearly pornographic moan. "They've really outdone themselves, haven't they?"

Jo didn't bother to ask who "they" were, too busy examining the odd array of finger foods laid out on a tray before each of them, what Pan had proclaimed to be their first course. Jo also didn't bother to ask how many courses were planned; even one was too many.

Starting from the left corner of the tray and all around in a perfectly organized spiral, were slices of something purple and gooey, the yellow berries Pan was currently devouring, cubes of what looked like uncooked chicken meat, a single leaf-like object that kept twitching, and a literal puddle of something grey and rotten-smelling.

Jo poked at one of the cubes with her golden knife, wincing when the cube deflated with a hiss like a popped balloon, dribbles of black ooze spurting out of the hole like blood from a wound. Jo swallowed back the involuntary prickle of nausea and put her knife down. She could always just spend the meal sipping the weird, metallic liquid in her goblet, but the more she looked at it, the less she wanted to.

It was going to be a *long* dinner.

"Well?" Pan's voice brought her back to the table. Jo's eyes snapped up, not to find Pan sitting all the way across from her anymore, but in the chair just to the right of her original placement. Jo hadn't heard her move seats, but she chalked it up to her mind being occupied by the unappetizing fare before her.

"Well what?" Jo asked, keeping her voice indifferent.

Pan frowned, popping one of the meat cubes into her mouth and biting down. To Jo's disgust, a line of dark black fell from her bright blue lips to make a trail from mouth to chin, one she made no effort to wipe away. "You haven't told me what you think of your food yet."

Jo looked away, not dignifying that with a response. "You haven't told me yet what I'm *doing here*," she countered instead. "Why did you do all this?"

Instead of an answer, which Jo really never should have expected, Pan responded with a piercing squeal of delight. Out of reflex, Jo turned towards the sound, tensing when Pan was now seated halfway down the table on the left-hand side—though there was literally no way she could have made it there naturally.

The cause of Pan's squeal was apparently the plate

in front of her, no longer the odd platter of finger foods, but now what appeared to be a rather large, perfectly ordinary looking steak. She was cutting into it with a vigor that reminded Jo of a starved animal ruthlessly tearing its prey to shreds. It wasn't until Pan paused to take a long swig from her own goblet that Jo realized she'd been near mesmerized by the sight.

"You should really try your filet!" she said, resting her elbow on the table and a hand against her cheek. Eyes glittering with mirth and messy lips pulled into a vicious grin.

Jo looked down at the plate before her, perfectly aware that despite no one having come to remove her tray, a new course now sat before her, identical to Pan's. Regardless of how Pan's eyes on her made the hair on the back of her neck stand up, Jo picked up her fork and knife, cutting into the meat.

There was no other way to describe the sound that filled the room other than a scream of bloody murder. It was loud and violent and terrifying, Jo's utensils falling out of her hands in her shock. At first, Jo looked frantically around the room, wondering where the noise was coming from, the acoustics and the volume making it impossible to tell. But as the scream went from a deadly yell to a pleading cry, Jo felt her stomach drop and mouth fall slack.

The steak in front of her heaved with the sound of screaming and bursts of desperate cries from between every line of the muscle. Jo pushed the plate away from her, adrenaline coursing through her veins even as she remained frozen to her seat. Slowly, the screams tapered, the cries growing hoarse, and Jo was forced to watch, horrified, as the filet of meat eventually quivered, stilled, and grew silent.

"Whoopsies," Pan hummed. "Looks like yours was still screaming a bit. My apologies. The chef doesn't always get the temperatures right."

Jo couldn't tear her eyes away from the plate, the dish looking disturbingly normal now that it had stopped its very sentient-like cries. She swallowed thickly, considered reaching out and pushing the plate away, but she couldn't move her hand, didn't want to. What if she touched the plate and it, too, started screaming or crying? She knew it was all a game—that Pan was playing tricks with her, messing with her mind—but she couldn't deny that it was working.

Right now at least, heart still thrumming in her ears, Jo was scared.

Out of the corner of her eye, Jo saw the silhouette of someone walking up to her chair. She startled, still on edge, and turned to see who might be approaching. For the second time in as many minutes, Jo felt her stomach drop.

Even after so long in the Society, even after all the changes she'd seen the world go through in its transition back into a new Age of Magic, she would never forget the sight of her friend's face. Her first friend, and—in another life—her best friend.

"Yuusuke?" Jo choked out, voice thick with fear and confusion and still-pulsing adrenaline. He stood before her, dressed in a similarly outlandish butler's uniform, this time in a bright green that reminded her of his once-ubiquitous, beat-up pair of headphones. His black hair was slicked back and his face hand been done up in makeup, but despite all that, he looked exactly the same as she remembered. Except for one thing: his stare might have fallen on her, but she saw no recognition there.

"Yuusuke, what . . .?" she started, nearly rising from her seat. *What was he doing here?* Had Pan remembered her first wish at the Society and brought him here for revenge, for bait? Was he a hostage, like Snow? He didn't seem to know who she was, but was that Pan's doing, or a consequence of their new world? She watched him move, as if on autopilot, to pick up her plate, and something in her heart broke. "Yuusuke, are you—?"

In a flash, Pan was suddenly directly to Jo's right. And a knife was pierced directly through Yuusuke's hand.

Yuusuke buckled, the first glimpse of true emotion flashing across his face before he cried out in pain. "Now, now, *Yuu—*" Pan purred Jo's childhood nickname for her friend. "She's obviously not done with that yet."

Jo was out of her chair in an instant, ripping the knife out of Yuusuke's hand and dropping to her knees at his side. She took her napkin and wrapped it tightly around Yuusuke's bleeding hand, blood soaking into the fabric almost immediately.

"What the hell are you doing?" she shouted at Pan from over Yuusuke's shoulder, but Pan had already switched seats again, now positioned unnervingly at Jo's back. Jo kept her focus on Yuusuke despite the way it made her skin crawl to let Pan out of her sight. Except, when she looked back to her friend, the cries had stopped and his face had once again grown devoid of all emotion.

A soft sound grabbed her attention, a chitter, a squeak, and when Jo looked from Yuusuke's face to his chest, she saw his uniform bulging.

Wiggling.

All at once, the buttons on Yuusuke's ridiculous butler outfit burst open, a swarm of rats crawling from the gaping hole. Jo fell backwards, raising her hand and the bloody napkin to cover her face as the rats swarmed over her in an attempt to flee. It took only a matter of seconds, but they left Jo panting and stunned in their wake. When Jo finally opened her eyes, looking past the blockade of her arms, it was to find Yuusuke's butler outfit rumpled but complete in front of her.

Jo took a breath, trying to get her heart to slow, only for the napkin in her hand to jerk wildly in her grip. When she dropped it in a fresh moment of panic, it was to the sight of a wounded rat, hole through its side, dragging itself as quickly as it could out from under the napkin and towards the door.

All at once, the terror and confusion in Jo's blood boiled over into a rage, pushing her back to her feet. She spun three-sixty until she locked eyes on Pan, pointing at her with what she was glad to see was a perfectly steady finger.

"Enough of this, Chaos!"

To her immense satisfaction, Pan actually froze in surprise at the sound of her proper name, though it was an expression quickly hidden by glee.

"Oh come now, Destruction," she sing-songed, voice playful and light as she too got up from the table. "I'm just having a little fun. You used to like my fun, a long long time ago."

"Was any of that even real?" Jo demanded as Pan stepped closer, slow, lilting footsteps practically dancing into her personal space. "Was that really—"

"Does it matter?" Pan cut her off, close enough now that she could feel the odd magical presence surrounding the woman-child. And the way Jo's own magic responded to it. . . It was an intoxicating sensation, like feeling the ground rumble beneath the wave of an explosion, or seeing a star implode and become a black hole. It was devastating and visceral and—

Jo took a step back, realizing that Pan had raised a hand as if to touch her, nails glistening neon yellow in the space between them. Understanding washed over Jo instantly.

They needed to destroy Pan before it was too late, before she lured in Jo's magic and never let go. Jo shuddered at the thought; she didn't want to be a part of this chaos any more than she had to.

"Oh dear," Pan sighed with a histrionic pout. "It seems that display really upset you." She almost looked legitimately put out by the idea, though Jo wouldn't have been surprised if it was all an act. "Unfortunately our magic is becoming more erratic, you see. More . . . intense." As if to emphasize this point, the floor shifted like shuttering blinds from a dark wood to a bright and blinding white, the table melting into a literal puddle of multi-colored paints that splashed about the empty canvas around Jo's feet. Dishes and cutlery clattered into the puddles. Jo felt the paint seeping into her shoes, dampening her socks.

"So what?" Jo asked, voice level despite the rising

air of disturbing energy soaking into the very essence of the room.

"So," Pan held out the 'o' for a long while, twirling about in the paint and making a mess of both the floor and her clothes. "I can sustain myself on Snow's magic for a good, long while. But sadly, it's not enough for three." Despite herself, Jo's breath caught in her throat.

All at once, Pan stopped her messy spinning. "This is an Age of *Magic*, Destruction. Not *Gods*—don't you remember that?" When Pan turned around then, she looked almost demure, the ruffles in her dress hanging less puffed up, the bright neon colors muted. Her hair had fallen over her shoulders in rainbow waves, but even those seemed lackluster in comparison to her usual level of outlandishness. "You must join me soon, Destruction. Or I fear you might find yourself unraveling completely."

Jo didn't quite know what to do with the seriousness in Pan's voice, or the look of seemingly genuine concern on her face. But as quickly as it had come, it was gone, replaced once again by flashy colors and a bright pink smile. As she skipped up to Jo's side, the puddles freezing in place mid-splash, Jo felt her mind and magic waver, thrown off by the complete one-eighty. Enough so that she didn't manage to move away in time before Pan was pulling her into a tight hug. She smelled like burnt sugar and gasoline.

"Why don't you . . . *sleep* on that, huh?" She giggled into Jo's hair, planting a kiss on her cheek that tingled with pins and needles, like her face had fallen asleep. Yet, all the same, Jo found herself leaning into it, her body yearning for something she didn't recognize but had once, she was sure. With a final squeeze, Pan released Jo from the hug and stepped away, snapping her fingers.

The whole room went from the mess of paint and ruined dinner to darkness, then blinked back into existence with an entirely new identity.

Though, perhaps not *entirely* new, Jo noticed as she turned around to take in her surroundings. Judging by the layout and the furniture, even the dull globs clinging to ceiling, it was obvious she was in the same place. Though perhaps if the place had aged a thousand years in a second.

Everything was covered in dust and cobwebs, cracks lining the walls and the broken remnants of the fancy tables and chairs. The large portraits which once held shifting mirage-type paintings were now either completely black or ripped from their canvases entirely.

The door at Jo's right creaked open on hinges that sounded as if they'd gone many, many years unused, and Jo caught sight of a butler's outfit beyond it. She held her breath, walking into the wash of light pouring in from the hallway, and sighed in relief when it wasn't Yuusuke but the marionette once again.

"To your room, madam," he said, ushering her towards the hall with a jerking motion that made it look as if he'd dislocated his shoulder. Jo didn't argue, didn't bother to give the room even another glance before following her orders.

Much like before, the halls shifted and changed as they passed, room after room blending into one another in a way that should have made her dizzy. But Jo kept her eyes on the golem's back, allowing him to lead her to whatever room Pan had "graciously" provided for her. Jo struggled to regain her footing, to level her mental state.

The best she could do was continue with the plan, though it was becoming painfully clear that getting a message to her team wasn't going to be easy. Especially when the golem finally led her to a room with no windows and only one door. So much for breaking one of the flag poles.

"You will be summoned," the marionette said, never setting foot inside Jo's room; she wondered if he was contained within the halls and nowhere else. "Until then, you have been instructed to rest."

"Yeah, sure." Jo shrugged, watching as he closed her door, and unsurprised to hear him lock it. With a huff, she sat heavily onto the bed, comforter plush but scratchy beneath her fingers. However, her old clothes were there. *How kind.*

As it was, she was without a means to contact the others, and only a vague idea as to where Pan was keeping the bow. She'd found Snow, and though it both filled her with rage and heartache to know what he'd been put through, to know he was so close yet still so far, seeing him again was like a boost of adrenaline, a surge of motivation that pulled her back to her feet with a determined breath.

The original plan was the best thing they had, even if it was still mostly evolving as they went along, and it was the least she could do to try and keep it playing out. She'd gotten inside, she'd found Snow; now all that was left was finding the bow and sending out a signal.

She just hoped that total destruction of Pan's

precious castle would be enough to get their attention.

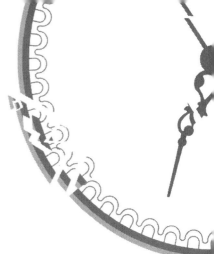

30. TIME TO DESTROY SOMETHING

SNOW'S WORDS REPLAYED in her head as Jo paced the tiny box that was her room.

Pan kept her treasures in a vault, a room, a safe place at the center of it all.

Those thoughts layered atop the memory of her visit to Pan's room in the Society—the only time Jo had achieved an in-depth look into the workings of the magical fortresses Pan surrounded herself with. But there was something more, adding a depth to her understanding that even Jo didn't want to consider too closely.

It was a quiet reassurance nearly purring in the back of her mind that she knew what Pan had done because they were one being; they were born of one mind and had never deviated too far from each other's thoughts.

Jo stopped her pacing. She closed her eyes, mentally summoning the central courtyard she'd seen earlier—the one void of decor and function. *The room was an illusion*, Jo decided, *one of many*. It was a house of mirrors, reflecting outward distorted images to keep people from finding what was truly within. But something about that room seemed significant to her. Something about that room in particular was central to everything else.

"They call me a demigod." Jo looked at her hand, balling it into a fist. "I should see if it really holds true."

She had come here for one purpose: to end it. No amount of fanfare or distraction was going to change that. Resolved, Jo turned to the door. Magic churned within her, faster and faster until it felt like she was at the eye of a storm that would be unleashed on the whole building. She would start as usual—by dismantling and cracking at the seams. But Jo was prepared to unleash a hellfire of wanton destruction, caring not for how things were decimated so long as they *were*.

Jo gripped the door, ready for a lock, ready for it to resist her.

But it did not.

It swung open soundlessly, miraculously revealing the same hallway she'd seen before. Jo stared at it, somewhat angry that Pan couldn't even let her have a dramatic start to the end.

Jo shrugged the idea away, running down the hall. The less she had to destroy—for now—the better. The longer Pan could be ignorant to Jo's movements (assuming she didn't already know them), the longer Jo would have to locate the bow. But first, she had to get to Snow.

Jo skidded to a halt at the end of the hall, a dead

end creeping up out of nowhere. Like she'd done with the marionette earlier, Jo turned in place to reveal a new stretch of hallway. She sprinted between the orbs, pushed through the door at the end, and was met with the first sitting room she'd seen upon entering.

"I choose . . . you." Jo pointed to the door opposite, pushing through it and into another hall.

She repeated the process two more times.

On her fourth try, Jo came to a stop at the end of the hall with the dead end. But this time, she didn't turn around. Jo stared at the wall in front of her, forcing herself to think of what Pan would do. She was certifiably insane, but she could calculate a long game better than a chess protégé.

Pan knew Jo would come for Snow, for the bow, and to end things once and for all. Pan knew she would ultimately escape her room—the unlocked door was practically an invitation. Which also meant Pan knew that Jo would fall prey to her maze and reach this point of frustration.

She knows I'll break something, Jo thought to herself, not daring to say the words aloud. If Jo had been herself from a year ago—headstrong and hotheaded—she would've walked right into Pan's trap and destroyed the wall before her. And why not? It was barring her path. All the doors in the room were unlocked—there was no need for her to break them.

Jo's eyes dropped. In truth, Pan might think Jo would do any number of things. But destroying the floor from underneath her feet? Jo didn't think that would be among them.

Pushing her magic downward and into the floor,

Jo felt the fractures increasing just before the large, satisfying *crack* that sent rubble and magic scattering.

Biting back a scream as she fell, Jo braced herself for impact—braced to bounce back the moment her body would be destroyed. Her magic worked in the same fashion as it had before and Jo landed hard, feeling the bones in her shins shatter and using the momentum of it to send her sprinting forward—her body as good as new in the process.

This hall felt different than the one above her. She'd landed in another one of Pan's mazes, but one a little closer to the castle's center. Here, the chaos seemed to writhe and struggle to keep its foothold. It was almost as if an invisible comb was trying to pull out the tangles and yank it into order.

Snow was here.

Using his magic like a homing beacon, Jo broke through the walls and windows and doors that would hold her back. But that wasn't all Pan would throw her way, apparently. One of the shadow creatures she'd faced before at High Luana stood at the ready, blocking her path ahead. Jo remembered what Eslar had said—these were elves who had sold themselves to the dark arts. This wasn't like the first man who'd been a civilian tainted by Pan's magic. This man stood here by choice.

She didn't even waste her breath offering to spare its life.

Jo launched in for the offensive, throwing out a wave of magic. The creature's shield unraveled, then promptly bounced back together—it seemed Pan had made some modifications. Startled, Jo was almost caught flat-footed as the thing charged.

Dodging to the side, Jo stomped her foot down as she caught her balance. It sent a shockwave of magic into the floor that crumbled the stone beneath the man's feet. He barely had time to look at her before he was falling and Jo didn't waste her time looking to see where he landed.

She started running again, only to come to a sudden stop mid-hall. Turning to a wall, she pressed her hand into the stone.

Creation, her mind, her magic, and her heart, seemed to say in unison.

The wall blasted inward with a cloud of dust.

"My demigod prince, I've come to rescue you." Jo took a shot at the dramatic, because why not?

Snow's reaction was decidedly unenthused. "What're you doing?"

"I'm breaking you out."

He looked nearly frantic. "But—"

"There's no time, Snow. We'll get the bow. I'll let the team in. We end this."

"The team is here!"

His confused panic suddenly made sense.

"What?" Jo whispered. The dust settling on the bedspread they'd made love atop mere hours ago suddenly seemed loud, as though every minute speck landed with an earth-shaking rumble. "*Here?* That's impossible. They're out—"

"Pan left not long ago. She came to make sure I was . . . aware. That she has you and the team, and that she's successfully playing you both."

The team. Pan had the team. Well, of course she did. "We were so stupid!" Jo agonized aloud. She reached up, grabbing her hair with a colossal cry of frustration at the ready, then stopped. "No . . . this can work."

"What?" Snow pulled one of her hands from her hair, taking it in his own, drawn as much by a need to comfort her as to assure himself that she was real.

"The team is here, in here already, we just have to find them. Pan meant to trap them—to show off how strong and in control she was. But all she did was bring us together. And if *you* didn't know about the—" Jo stopped herself short, not daring to say the word *arrow*. His room had been compromised by the large hole in the wall, after all. "—the special thing."

"Then she still—yes, I understand. But how will you get to them?"

Jo thought about this a moment. As they stood, speaking, she could feel ripples in the magic throughout the castle. It was as if Pan was trying to redesign things on the fly. But Jo wasn't about to give her that chance.

"I'm going to get the bow." Jo gripped his hand tightly, pulling him close and planting a firm kiss on his mouth. "You use the cracks in her chaos to find the team."

"If you can destroy her magic, perhaps I could create passages through it," Snow reasoned as she was pulling away. "When I get to them, then what?"

"Then find me! I think it'll be easy to tell where. I'll get the bow and then keep holding her off!" Jo started running down the hallway once more, stopping at a window. She put a foot on the ledge and the glass shattered outward. As the wind howled, whipping her hair, Jo took a long look at Snow. Who knew if it would be her last? She ignored the twinge in her chest, the sudden extra weight around her heart, and grinned. "Good luck, Creation."

"Good luck, Destruction."

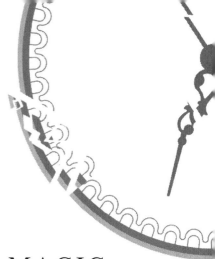

31. A CHEAP MAGIC TRICK

JO JUMPED THROUGH the window and fell onto a lower balcony. She could've sworn she'd been in the basement of the castle not a moment before, but what made sense anymore? In Pan's topsy-turvy castle, nothing did.

But that was fine. There didn't have to be any rules, because Jo wasn't going to play by them. She was making her own from now on.

Looking over the edge of the balcony, Jo saw the greenhouse-like rooftop of the strange room she'd seen before—the room she suspected held Pan's treasures, and the one she had deemed her goal. She could fall right down onto it, but that was assuming Pan didn't have any other tricks up her sleeve. Instead, Jo turned inward, turning the doors to the room beyond into splinters with a look.

She stepped into the decimated room, eerily similar to the dining room Pan had entertained her in not more than an hour ago. Jo had two missions: The first was to get to Pan's treasure room. The second was to break as many things as she could, so Snow would find the opening he needed—if he couldn't create it himself. Or perhaps her destruction would yield the fodder for him to craft a door. Jo was still learning how his magic worked, but either way she relished in the opportunity to wreak more havoc on Pan.

The doors across from her opened, more shadowed assassins rushing toward her. Jo didn't even bother with them. Instead, she rushed to the table between her and the dark elves, meeting it before they did. The moment her fingers came into contact, it exploded into shards of wood for them to impale themselves upon.

Jo knew it wouldn't work; if Takako's bullets couldn't penetrate their shields, then wooden spikes couldn't either. But her aim was to slow them down— and she did, if only by a fraction of a second. By the time they even noticed she'd moved, Jo had rushed through the doors to her left. The second they closed, Jo looked at the keystone of the arch above the door and forced it to crack to the base on either side. Fissures spread outward with a surge of magic light similar to a lightning strike, bringing the whole wall crumbling down.

For the first time since entering the castle, Jo saw daylight. It streamed through the hole in the wall like a ray of hope shining on an otherwise desperate situation. Climbing over the rubble, Jo stepped outside onto one of the narrow glass-like ledges of the castle's many spindly towers.

Knowing what was on the inside, knowing Pan,

Jo looked at it as if for the first time. It was obsidian, much like the disk she'd looked through with Samson. Jo held out her hand, thinking of the framework he'd helped her access, and raised it.

Like an architectural sketch visible only to her, the castle's magical structures laid themselves bare. She couldn't make sense of what was inside the room, but she could see its structure. And if she could see it, that meant one thing.

"This is going to break beautifully."

Jo started from one of the flagpoles and worked her way down. With a mighty heave of power, she felt the castle rumble and the tower come crumbling down. Turning her eyes to the next one, Jo exerted the same force, watching as it was reduced to glass-like shards.

After the third fell, a familiar rooftop was exposed. *There*. Pan's treasure room, finally accessible without layers of magic concealing its true nature.

Jo took a leap, not caring for the crunch of her ankles or kneecaps as she landed. She was Destruction; she could find life in death itself. In her own way, she was eternal.

Making her way across rooftops and ledges, Jo found herself on the top of the greenhouse-like roof. Crouching, she placed her hand on the semi-translucent stone. She didn't even brace herself for the impact among the dagger-like shards of crystal.

As she stood, Jo heard a slow clapping sound.

"Well done! Looks like you made it all the way here," Pan's voice echoed from the opposite side of the room. "Too bad it will mean very little in the end."

"The only end is yours, Pan," Jo threatened,

instantly feeling like some comic book hero brought to life. She had no reason to talk to Pan and she wasn't going to be lured into it again.

"Well, the bow is right here. So take it." Pan motioned to a pedestal in the center of the room. "Or, you can join—"

Jo started running.

"I didn't even finish my dramatic declaration!" Pan half-screeched, half-whined.

She barely got several steps toward the center of the room before a wall suddenly jutted out from the floor. Jo skidded to a stop, stumbling, tripping, bracing for impact only to fall through it like a mirage. Another one of Pan's illusions.

"They're not coming." Pan's voice echoed as Jo peeled herself off the floor.

She looked around the room and took it in for the first time—it was just like in the Society. There were shelves upon shelves lining the perimeter, stacked with all manner of trinkets and tokens. Jo saw rows of military medals between platemail she'd associate with a knight in medieval times. There was a whole train engine that looked to be made of jade next to a life-sized sculpture of some muscle-bound woman swathed in silks.

"Join with me. End this," Pan all but commanded. "End it all!"

Once more, Jo didn't reply. She turned her head toward the sound of Pan's voice, locating it in the cavernous room, and set the shelves behind her to exploding. Their contents scattered the floor, rolling to clutter the room.

"I really liked that one!" Pan screamed, picking up a platter from the ground. "You'll pay for that!"

She threw it like a Frisbee and midair the disc morphed, taking on a saw-like silhouette. Jo held out a hand, letting the teeth bite directly into her flesh. It gave her enough of a rush of power that she spun easily in place, sending the disk right back. But before it could hit Pan, it transformed into a raven and flew away.

Chaos and Destruction, an even match for no one to win.

Jo looked back to the bow, more resolved than ever. She couldn't end this, which meant there was only one person who could, and one plan that even had a chance of working. Putting her trust in Snow and the others, she pushed forward.

Another projectile was thrown at her and Jo didn't even bother redirecting; she merely dodged. But Pan had closed the gap faster than she expected, and the other woman caught her wrist, wrenching Jo close. Their noses were almost touching.

"Join me," she hissed. Jo could feel the heat of her breath, the spark of magic that bounced between them, turning into something dangerous. *I may want to*, a voice whispered in Jo, more tempted every minute. "End this and join me."

"I will end this," Jo vowed, finally breaking her silence. With a grunt, she yanked her hands free, feeling her bones snap and twist away from Pan's unrelenting grip.

Jo began running again, and Pan attempted to thwart her.

Back and forth it went, but Jo gained on her step

by step until her hands landed on the bow. A magic not unlike Snow's coursed through her from an origin that Jo could only suspect was the Life Tree. Like Snow, it was an antithesis to her that was as calming as it was alluring, in a far more wholesome way than Pan.

But the trance was only momentary as Pan yanked on the other end of the bow.

"Do you think you can defeat me with this?" she screeched.

Jo didn't answer. Instead, she pulled on her end and forced her magic toward Pan with the express intent of breaking the demigod's wrists. It didn't quite work— there was something about Pan that her magic refused to harm. But it was enough to startle Pan, who let go completely. Jo's force over-compensated; off-balance, she tripped, falling backward, and lost the bow in the process.

The wooden implement clattered across the pebbled floor of Pan's treasure room to the opposite side of where they now stood. It came to a stop, landing against a large piece of golden platemail and what looked to be a geode as big as Jo's head, cracked open and scattered on the ground. Jo looked to it, panting, and then back to Pan.

Pan's eyes were on her, her cat-like irises narrowed to thin vertical slits as sharp as daggers. Her shoulders heaved up and down with her ragged breathing and her hair seemed to change color with her every breath— blue, purple, pink, green—a kaleidoscope of shifting magic. Then, with a ruffle of bows and ribbons, Pan moved.

Jo was close behind, dashing in the direction of the

bow. It seemed to ooze light and life in staunch protest to the chaotic world around it.

She had to get to it before Pan did.

Lengthening her strides and pushing her legs as hard as they could go, Jo cast a hand in Pan's direction, unleashing her magic. The ground beneath Pan's feet rippled, pebbles breaking upward, free from the mortar, in shrapnel of stone. Pan responded with a jump and a snap of her finger, leaping through what were now rose petals falling harmlessly to the ground.

"Try again," she snarled.

With nothing more than a look in Jo's direction, the silver medals scattered at her feet unraveled and slithered, turned from ribbons into cobras. Jo reared back, stalling. She looked at the metal, reducing it to white-hot molten pools she quickly leapt over.

"Gladly," Jo grunted.

She threw everything she had at the roof overhead. With a look, it fractured, raining translucent black stone down on Pan. Pan stopped scowling as she leaned down. Gripping at a ribbon on her sandal, she tugged it free, the shoe falling lose. Pan wove it through the air like a whip and it slashed through the hail of stone nearly completely.

Nearly.

With her nemesis caught in the debris, Jo made her final steps, preparing to lunge. She was so close to the bow. She could feel it now, almost taste the magic in the air. And then—

"Jo!" Snow's voice called.

Jo's head whipped around at the sound of her name spoken on the tongue of her other half, her *wanted* and *beloved* other half. Snow was standing at the far corner of the room—where a stone tunnel had been crafted impossibly through the rubble. The other members of the Society were clamoring over the debris around him, Takako in the lead. Relief soared through her at the sight of them—safe and sound, if not a little bruised and beaten. She saw tears in Wayne's clothes that she had no doubt he would kill someone for (hopefully Pan), and some blood on Samson's face that *Jo* would kill someone for (also, hopefully Pan).

But *no one* was killing Pan when all their eyes were off her.

Jo never even saw it coming.

It felt like a claymore digging into her side, tearing her from the edge of her flesh nearly to the naval. It stole the wind from her lungs, stalling her, knocking her off balance. She rolled, feeling the muscles in her abdomen tense as magic pulsed in her brighter than before. Rearing upward, Jo was ready to launch the next attack. But her magic never left her body.

Pan stood over her with a heart-shaped scythe in one hand and the bow in the other, twirling it impossibly between her little fingers.

"I can't destroy it—not my magic," Pan admitted, loud enough that her voice carried across the decimated remains of her treasure room. "But I can change it."

In one movement that seemed like nothing more than a blink, Pan tossed the scythe aside and gripped the bow, thrusting it out before her. There was no flash of light, no sound to herald the end of the world. Pan simply uncurled her fingers, and the bow was transformed into nothing more than doves and confetti—an act that could've been done at any time, but Pan no doubt waited until just that moment, her intended audience gathered in rapt attention.

The hope of the world died like a cheap magic trick.

32. THE FINAL MOMENTS

J O WATCHED THE confetti fall, some of it landing in her hair, on her outstretched hand. It wasn't over. It couldn't be over. There must be something else they could do. . .

No.

But not without the bow. That had been the crux of their plan. Without it, they had nothing.

They'd think of something else. They'd come up with a new plan. But with what time? What could they possibly do now and with no weapon? There had to be a way. It was over. It couldn't be. Not like that. Not. . . Not so suddenly. Her thoughts were dangerously scattered and chaotic. Jo had no draw to pull them back together or she'd risk losing herself.

Jo lifted her head and watched the doves fly up and away, wishing she could do the same. There was no escape now; Pan had them all trapped. The hopeless truth of it filled her lungs and stole her voice. She couldn't breathe.

"This is pointless. Fun, but pointless," Pan giggled, walking right into Jo's line of sight. Jo kept her gaze steadily trained on the doves overhead, diminishing white specks in the sky. When Pan noticed the lack of attention, she glanced over her shoulder, frowning. With a click of her teeth, the doves bloated to impossible size and turned into balloons that drifted out of sight on the breeze. Jo forced her gaze to attention, though not without throwing Pan as murderous a glare as she could manage.

"This isn't over." She thought she might have heard a rustle behind her, the sounds of commotion from her friends, but she kept her focus on Pan, drawing herself shakily to her knees.

"Oh but it is," Pan said sweetly, reaching out to place a hand beneath Jo's chin. "You've played your little game of rebellion. Even I admit I had a bit of fun with it. But it's time to stop this now, my darling. It's time give up the charade and join me."

Jo's magic spiked at the idea, though whether it was in temptation or revulsion was hard to say with Pan's touch against her skin. So Jo shook that touch away, backing up. "We'll stop you." Pan frowned at Jo's words, her catlike eyes shimmering red. Despite the warning signals crackling down Jo's spine, she pressed on. "We haven't lost yet."

If Pan's magic had been a fire, everyone in the room would have burned beneath the onslaught that suddenly filled the room.

"Enough of this nonsense!" Pan suddenly stood before them in swaths of elaborate armor, her hair a flyaway mess of rainbow strands caught in a perpetual whirlwind. But it wasn't the costume change that had everyone falling into stunned silence so much as the look of pure, unbridled rage on her face. "Stop being such a *fool!*" She reached back out towards Jo, grabbing her face in a vice-like grip and squeezing her cheeks enough to bruise the flesh—if Jo had been mortal still. In an instant, Pan was back to her normal self, ruffles and colors and all. "I mean seriously," she giggled again, releasing Jo's face. "What are you going to do without your precious bow?"

And she was right, wasn't she? No bow meant no weapon. No weapon meant no shot. No shot meant no chance to vanquish Pan. It had been a plan with no failsafe because it couldn't have one; even Samson had said there was no other material from the start. Everything up until then was a last resort in a war that none of them had asked to be a part of.

Except, it was a war that *Jo* had asked them to be a part of. The members of the Society hadn't needed to fight, and might not have if she hadn't dragged them back into the fray. She'd led them all to failure, hadn't she? Just like she had with Nico.

"That's it, my sweet," Pan hummed, her tone soothing as she covered the distance between them in a single step and wrapped her arms around Jo's shoulders. "You know you've lost. So just let go, *hm?* Just do what your magic has been begging of you, destroy it all—these petty friendships, your pathetic life, this sad little world. I promise, it'll feel good."

As if in counter-argument to her words, Jo felt the lick of familiar magic against her own, not Pan's wild and fiery blend of chaos, but the swirling rush of a bonded soul easing its way beneath the cracks in her confidence. Still somewhat slack in Pan's embrace, Jo let her eyes drift towards the sensation of it, capturing Snow's eyes at once.

He stood within a circle of his own magic, eyes already searching out Jo's gaze. The moment they connected, the soothing reach of his magic began to ease her away from the chaos, willing her own magic to fall back into a semblance of order, safely out of Pan's reach.

He was trying to counter-attack Pan's sway, pulling in the opposite direction—a game of magical tug-of-war.

Jo could see the rope between them in beams of light, felt it wrap around her like a blanket, warm and comforting and desperate for her safety. It heightened her senses and called out to her in a way that Pan's did not.

"You think your pull is stronger than mine?" Jo heard Pan hiss, the words themselves slithering into her ears and attempting to block out Snow's call. Jo felt suspended between the two of them, Pan's magic seeping into her skin, dark and sticky like tar, while Snow's tried to wash away the chaotic darkness clouding her mind. It was growing impossible to tell herself apart from the whirlwind of magical sensation.

In fact, within the storm were even tendrils of her team. She could feel Wayne's magic in a distant thrum, even Eslar's and Samson's too, their magics so intertwined it was near impossible to tell them apart. She could hear their fear and taste their desperation, but among all that, with a sudden spike of recognition, she could also feel their hope.

Which was when Takako's magic tickled her senses.

While Snow's magic called to her like a song, and Pan's called to her like a demand, Takako's was a beacon on the horizon of a dark, vast ocean. And as if Takako's magic had shouted her name, it drew Jo's focus instantly.

Takako held the arrow nocked between the middle and index fingers of her right hand. Her left was curled into a relaxed fist, space between her fingers as though she was holding something invisible. The shaft of the arrow rested on her left pointer finger as she slowly raised her arms, drawing back in an invisible string.

Muscles tense and bulging, Takako stood in a perfect firing stance, her arms aligned in front of her in a way that looked ridiculous, and had Jo been unable to feel the swelling thrum of magic coming off of the woman, she would have laughed. But as Takako braced her fingers against her jaw, Jo could almost see the magic rippling in the air in the shape of exactly what they needed.

A bow.

Pan seemed to sense the shift of magic too, her whole body tensing before she yanked away from Jo, her attention suddenly consumed by Takako. Out of reflex, Jo grabbed Pan's wrist, keeping her from moving forward, and putting Pan's chest in the direct line of fire at Jo's side.

But that wouldn't be enough. Not nearly enough. It was a truth Wayne had forced her to accept at the onset of their journey—their journey to a conclusion she hadn't wanted to face.

"Where. Did. You. Get. *That*?" Pan growled in clear recognition, an inhuman sound as she tried to rip her arm out of Jo's grip, but neither of them moved an inch. Jo could already feel her magic giving in, keeping them both rooted in place, and by the way Pan flashed a surprised look in Jo's direction, she could feel it too. Jo had expected elation, maybe even a smug sort of giddiness. What she hadn't expected to see on Pan's face was relief. Maybe even . . . pride?

"Do it, Jo!" Wayne yelled, the first words to break through Jo's haze, which opened up the floodgates for a cacophony of sound, most of which came from Snow. Not from his voice, but his magic. It begged and cried against the feeling of being replaced, and Jo tried not to listen. She already knew how much it would hurt, knew that in many ways, what she was about to do could be seen as a betrayal to all he had endured for her.

Especially if it didn't work—if she didn't come back.

So Jo focused on her own magic, on how it twisted and writhed around Pan's wrist and upward, sinking into her skin in veins of color, electricity crackling along every inch of their skin. Jo could still see Takako over Pan's shoulder, poised and ready, and when she mouthed the words *"I won't miss,"* Jo could have sworn she heard them in her soul.

Pan was so consumed by the sight, the sensation of their magic sewing together into one, that she didn't notice Jo's last, desperate glance over at Snow, her love, her fated half, her Creation. He'd stopped struggling, knowing perhaps that it was too late to stop the process when she'd willingly opened herself to it. But that didn't mean Jo's heart didn't break at the look in his eyes, the devastation and the pain. But not anger. At least there was that.

"I love you," Jo whispered, sending the words to him on the last tendril of her magic that had not given itself over to Oblivion.

Once she knew he had heard, once she saw the recognition on his face and the beginnings of her name on his lips, Jo closed her eyes and made her choice. She gave in to the riptide that had been working to pull her feet out from under her from the first moment she'd entered the castle.

Takako was their champion, and she would not miss. Even as Jo slipped away, that faith did not waver. That faith freed her to spend the last moments of her awareness—the last moments of her existence as a sovereign entity, unencumbered by the mad will of Pan or Oblivion—on the only thing left that mattered.

Snow. He was her love; their bond had transcended ages, and he would be the last thing Josephina Espinosa's eyes would ever see.

33. REUNITED

"*C*ALMASE, CALMASE. ESTAS bien, mijita. You have nothing to be frightened of anymore. I am here.*"*

The words were both familiar and strange, filtering past Destruction's ears like a whisper. Part of her wanted to cling to them as they drifted by, but she had no means with which to grasp them, and no recognition of why she desired to do so. Even still, the voice soothed something in her, the words sparking a deep comfort low in her being.

"Calmase, estas bien," the voice had said. *"Calm down. You're alright."* Be calm, do not cry, do not fret, you are safe.

But the calm did not suit Destruction, just as it did not suit Chaos. There was no calm or safety in Oblivion, so what use did she have for it? And what right did the voice have to demand it of her?

"It wasn't a demand, it was a comfort. *Abuelita* had

to comfort us a lot back then."

The new voice was more familiar but still strange, like listening to a recording of herself. And where the last voice had drifted past before Destruction could properly grasp it, this one echoed loudly, wanting to be heard—waiting to be recognized.

"I don't remember the nightmares anymore, but they probably had to do with you," the new voice continued.

Nightmares felt like Chaos's doing. Too abstract for Destruction, too inefficient.

"We would dream about things we didn't understand, things we wouldn't understand until much, much later. And if our parents weren't around to ease us back into sleep, then *abuelita* would. Her voice would keep the monsters away."

There were no monsters anymore, only gods.

"You are right, my darling," another voice, the most familiar of them all, eased into Destruction like a drug. Arms wrapped around her from behind, looping around Destruction's waist in a tight embrace. "There are only gods. Would you like to be one?"

There was a power simmering to life between them at those words, a power that Destruction both did and did not understand. Something about it tugged a distant part of her mind, like a warning. But Chaos's arms tightened around her, her chin resting on Destruction's shoulder, and all warnings were forgotten. The path before them was illuminated and easy to follow—they simply had to take that first step.

"It has been an honor working alongside you, Josephina Espinosa."

A memory. One Destruction did not own, but which held something visceral and painful nonetheless. Her heart ached with it, and Chaos's arms loosened from around her waist, though they did not vanish completely

"It was my fault," that voice from before whispered. *Jo's voice*. Ink-stained fingers and a warm smile flashed behind Destruction's eyes. The taste of coffee coated her tongue.

"It has been nothing short of a blessing getting to know you."

That pain in Destruction's chest grew, overwhelming even the illuminated path before her, drowning it in a warm glow, like sunlight.

"They were the last words Nico ever said to me, filled with kindness until the very end. I will miss him every day."

But Destruction wouldn't. Why would she? These memories weren't hers. What was an end, if not a celebration of the final break?

"You are one and the same, my love."

Creation's voice. Destruction had no problem recognizing him, even if he sounded far away. She tried to turn towards it, to take a step closer, hear him better, but for some reason she remained rooted in place.

"My Destruction," he said, sounding even farther, as if fading away. "My Josephina."

Josephina. The name settled over her own like a second skin. She could hear her *abuelita* singing lullabies in Spanish, could see lines of code floating in front of her vision. But she wasn't Josephina (was she?), and when Creation spoke again, it was so far away she couldn't hear it.

"Are you ready, my darling?" Chaos hummed, voice clear in Destruction's ear. But something kept her from stepping forward. Even with the path once again illuminated before her, even as Chaos's embrace tightened until it was almost painful, something kept her rooted in place.

"You don't want to leave me behind," Jo said, voice sounding as if she were standing just inches from Destruction's face, though only the path lay before her, empty and bright.

Destruction wanted to argue with the voice, wanted to demand it let her pass, but she stayed silent. She wasn't sure she could speak at all anymore. Josephina could speak though, and despite herself, Destruction listened.

"You don't want to forget. You don't want to lose me. That's why you can't go forward."

Ridiculous. Destruction had no use for Josephina's memories. Joining with Chaos was her purpose, becoming Oblivion was her design. Why would pointless memories keep her from righting a centuries-old wrong?

"Because it would mean losing all of them too." Her team, her friends, the family Josephina had found in a world outside of time. "And you don't want to risk losing him."

She could no longer hear his voice, but she could feel the memory of him as clearly as if it were his arms wrapped around her instead of Chaos's. She could feel his lips against hers, his hands on her skin, and every nerve within her was suddenly calling out not for Oblivion but for Creation. For Snow. Jo ached for him, so Destruction did too, and all at once, it became unclear which of her was which.

"But we're doing this *for* him," Destruction said in Jo's voice. "Even if it means losing him."

Chaos's arms tightened and a giggle spilled from her lips, tickling at Destruction's neck with honey-sweet breath.

"Then we know what we have to do." For a moment, it was as if Josephina Espinosa stood before her, blocking the path from Destruction's view. It felt like looking at her own reflection and seeing a memory. A beautiful memory that she would hold on to for as long as Oblivion allowed.

Jo stepped aside, letting the path shine before them, and Chaos's laugh filled Destruction's ears. This time, stepping forward was easy. Even as she and Chaos began to merge into one, Destruction had no trouble walking the path. Even as her steps began to feel more weighted, power fracturing the ground beneath her with each step, it was easy.

Every movement was so, so easy.

It wasn't even about giving in, really. This had always been the outcome. It was just a matter of finding her way back together. The leisurely pace down the path became a skip, a twirling jog, a sprint. Her magic twirled with her, around her, licking at her heels and helping her speed down the path until she could see it: an actual light at the end of the tunnel where the world awaited her return—*their* return.

It had been too long, too *long*. And as the path came to an end, but a single step left for her to take, there was no hesitation.

Oblivion's heart soared at the feeling of existence, her body somehow both weightless and settled into the gravity of her new world. It was euphoric, intoxicating, and for a fraction of a second, she could do no more than breathe it in, her eyes falling lazily back open.

If her old and fractured memories were any indication, not even a second had passed, Takako still poised to fire in her direction. It was a laughable display. To assume any weapon held the power necessary to destroy her, Oblivion was almost insulted. Hunt had always been foolish, no better than her beasts. *Best remind them of who they were dealing with.*

"You think that little toy of yours can stop *me*?" she called out in a voice that could shatter the very foundation of the bedrock itself. "I am Oblivion! I am a *god*!"

"And I'm the Champion sent across the ages to take you down," Takako replied, not even bothering to raise her voice. Not that she had to. The arrow flew the moment the words registered, a lifetime of knowledge and experience rushing through Oblivion's head. *Champion*, Takako had called herself. For the first time in her new life, Oblivion's heart skipped a beat, just in time for the arrow to pierce it.

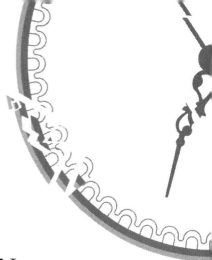

34. OBLIVION

BEADS OF SWEAT traced the outline of hair on the nape of Snow's neck, rolling down under the collar of his shirt.

Every drop of magic and focus was wrapped around Jo and Pan in a desperate attempt to combat Pan's sway. He could see the swirl of magic like a rainbow whirlpool, though he didn't know if it was visible to only him, or if the rest of the team could see it as well. Frankly, he wouldn't have even known they were standing next to him were it not for their muted words.

For him, the only thing that mattered was Jo. It had been the only thing that mattered throughout the whole of his existence. He had been made for her—for this—to shield her magic and keep her wholly separate. Then, he'd fallen in love, and after that it was hopeless to expect him to do anything less than make every sacrifice he could for her—from ending the Age of

Gods, to surrendering himself to Pan, and now this.

He was a horse that would run until its heart exploded and legs gave out, not daring to stop even a moment sooner.

Which made it an even more bitter pill to swallow when he felt the current of her magic shift. Jo would leave him, he realized. While he'd been expecting her to resort to desperate measures, he'd never expected her surrender.

It wasn't until he could feel her slipping into what promised to be a swift descent that she finally looked his way. Despite the confusion, despite the agony of loss, his heart stuttered beneath her stare. His chest ached at the thought of losing her, but the idea that she was sharing her final moments with him, in the only way she could, was a thin spackle to the cracks of his breaking heart. There wasn't long now until she would be gone, and he would fill his sight with her for every last moment.

"I love you." Her lips formed the words, silent amidst the chaos but loud within his ears, his mind. One of the few remaining wisps of her magic broke free from the rising tide, just long enough to reach out for his presence.

Then, her eyes shifted. Briefly, barely, a small change in focus that Snow almost missed. He fought to tear his sight from Jo, fearful of what it would mean when he looked back—if she'd even still be there at all.

Takako stood at his side, sure-footed atop a fallen bookcase leaning against a pile of rubble. Snow squinted at her, his mind struggling to make sense of what he was witnessing. She held her arms steady, muscles taut, and in her hands was the glittering outline of a bow, one made purely of her magic's design.

And the arrow that he had seen crafted ages ago was suspended between it. The arrow that had been made with the power to kill a god.

Snow's attention jerked back to Jo the moment he felt her magic slipping free of the protective well he'd been shaping for her. A soft "*Please*" may have escaped his lips as he searched for her eyes. But it was too late.

It was over in barely a second, swirls of rainbow colored light dancing over Pan's hair and Jo's skin, spinning about the two of them until its speed obscured them completely, the sheer luminosity of it blinding. All it took in the end was a blink against the barrage and suddenly Pan and Jo were no more. In their place was a being Snow had only ever heard tales of, in whispers between him and Destruction, in words of warning from those who'd created him.

The rubble bit into his knees as he collapsed onto it, hands swinging limply at his sides. Magic swelled in him, making him whole in a way he could barely remember being, for the first time in eons—fully untethered from Pan. For Pan was no more, Jo was no more; there was only Oblivion now, and what looked to be the end of all things he'd ever fought for.

The sheer oppressiveness of her power aside, what truly brought him down in a way that no man or god or demigod had ever been able to do before was the curve of her jaw, the lift of her cheek, and the fullness of her lips. He could see her—Jo, the woman he loved, the woman he'd been made for. But he could also see Pan in the slit of her cat-eyes, in the opalescent hair flying madly about her head.

"You think that little toy of yours can stop *me?*" Oblivion spoke with Jo's lips, the sound a rumble that seemed to come from the very heavens. Yet even in the sound, his ears objected, trying to pry apart Jo's voice. "I am Oblivion! I am a *god*!"

"And I am the Champion sent across the ages to take you down," Takako's voice pierced the cacophony like a bullet through the center of one of her targets. Or perhaps, more accurately, like an arrow through the heart of a god.

Snow wanted to close his eyes the moment he heard the magical *twang* of the bowstring. He was scrambling to his feet as the arrow shot through the air, curving true and powerful toward its target. It hit Oblivion square in the chest, piercing with an ease that should not have been possible. Her torso curled in on itself at the impact, the slits of her eyes narrowing to almost nothing as she lowered them to take in the arrow now embedded in her heart.

"*You. . .*" She gasped a noise that sounded like a chainsaw on a chalkboard. "You think that can stop me?" Oblivion lifted a trembling hand, gripping the shaft of the arrow. Snow watched as she yanked it from her chest. "Hunt was a f—"

Her final words were cut short by a scream that shook the world.

Magic filled his vision and licked like flames beneath his skin. It was as if the goddess had been tapped like a keg. Magic poured out with all the brilliance— all the chaos, all the destruction—of fireworks. She leaned backward, her spine bending at an unnatural angle, arms dangling, as though she were held up by the magic being torn from her body.

Then, she crumpled, and it was over. It was finally over.

And Snow ran.

"Snow, wait!" Takako called.

"We don't know if she's really—" Eslar began to say behind him. But Snow paid them no mind. If Oblivion wasn't dead, she would ride again to kill them all, and his distance from her would only buy him seconds.

Snow skidded to a stop, falling, scrambling, half-crawling to the corpse of the god. Her skin looked brittle, the light within no longer contained by it. It was as though she was burning alive from within and would soon be reduced to ash, scattered by the breeze.

"No," Snow whispered, tilting her face upward. The wide eyes were still Pan's, but the cheeks his hands cupped were Jo's. "It can't end this way. Not after everything we did."

For a brief second, so quick he could've missed it, her eyes gained focus. She looked at him in a way Pan never had and Oblivion never could.

Destruction.

"What must I do?" he whispered to her, to the world. "I would give my life for you now, if I could."

"You . . . can." Jo's voice, his Destruction, spoke. In an instant, there and gone. The focus in her eyes was beginning to vanish.

"I—" And it hit him. Oblivion was very much dead in his arms, and yet she was still there, the faintest of echoes trying to scream against a growing silence. Holding the limp form of the fallen god closer, Snow closed his eyes and reached deeper for that sensation, that spark of life that felt distinct and undeniable. The one that mirrored his own.

He felt no trace of Pan, no inkling of Oblivion, but just as he began to grow doubtful, worried that the feeling had been nothing but a symptom of his own grief, he sensed it. Jo was still there, burning up the last of her magic like a dying star.

"I'm sorry, Snow," Eslar's hand fell heavy on his shoulder. Snow hadn't even heard them approach. He could feel Takako's magic, still buzzing about the air after firing the arrow, and beneath that, Samson and Wayne's, familiar and dulled by their own confusion and heartbreak.

"This isn't over yet." Snow hastily laid the limp form down. Sure enough, her skin was beginning to crack and fly away in the breeze. He didn't have much time before the final casing holding in Jo's magic was gone. And then, *she* would be gone.

Unless he made a new casing for her.

"Eslar, I need you to do something for me."

"Snow?" The elf seemed startled, but already resolved.

"No one else can." He'd done it for her. When the time had come to end the Age of Gods, Snow had been the one to see Destruction split in two. He'd seen the process once before. "I need you to use the same ritual the elves would use to sever my magic and imbue it in a new form."

"What?" Eslar balked.

"Like the pillars at Springtide." For as panicked as Snow was, his voice was low, quiet, and he never took his eyes off of Oblivion's slack form. "Do it."

Eslar was at his side in a second. With a reluctance that bordered on physical pain, Snow tore himself away from Oblivion's face to stare into the eyes of his first friend, his first confidant. The first member of the Society. Eslar's brow was furrowed in concern, his expression distraught, but Snow rested a hand on his shoulder in brief reassurance and pressed on.

As pointless as it might have looked to everyone else, he knew what must be done for him to have a hope of a life worth living—a life with her.

"What are you going to do, Snow?" Samson asked, voice soft yet no longer filled with its usual tremor. There was grief there, Snow noticed, a sort of muted hope overshadowed by a sense of doubt that tainted and spread.

"I'm bringing her back," Snow offered, persistence soaking into his voice, his magic, and then blocking the rest of the world from his mind.

There was no point in holding anything back. He'd give it all to her. Snow reached deep, and held out his hands in the air in front of him as Eslar began to chant at his side.

As if Snow were sculpting from invisible clay, light shimmered under his thumbs as he drew them through the air. He traced the outline of her face, sculpting her every curve from memory. His magic eagerly filled in the blanks, creating a doll of light and life from nothing—pure creation.

Snow kept Jo in his mind all the while, the glint in her eyes and the tantalizing pull of her smile, the soft curves of the body he'd become intimately familiar with in more than one life. He thought of her voice, both as Destruction and as Jo, remembered the softness of her hair and the bite of her sarcasm. He held tight to her memory as if nothing else mattered.

And then he let it go.

"Now, Eslar!"

It wasn't a painful thing. His magic was taffy under the elf's hands. Eslar pulled and drew. Despite Snow's willingness, his magic reacted to the sensation defensively, unable to be soothed. It was like trying to convince himself to undergo a surgery without painkillers; his magic was used to being whole, and being ripped apart was met with vehement resistance.

Yet the ancient magics of the elves—handed down to them by the gods themselves for the sake of tending to the world in their absence—came through once more. Eslar pulled. He pulled and Snow willed his magic to heed his commands. As if sensing his intent at long last, his magic gave way. No longer a demigod, but a mortal. No longer one person, but two.

The sensation left him feeling hollow at first. He slouched and fell into something hard and sturdy; orange hair tickled his cheek. But as he opened his eyes, he looked to the hovering shell of Jo he had made, praying this final bid worked.

Magic filled the floating form of his love like a paint by numbers. Her long, dark hair bore streaks of vibrant color, her tanned skin glowing despite the lack of genuine life. His magic welled in the doll, filled to the brim thanks to Eslar's efforts.

"What now?" Eslar panted. "Snow, I did all I could."

"No. . . wait . . ."

A soft whisper of her magic chose the moment of his doubt to make itself known, followed by the familiar warmth of her presence pulsing from the fading outline of Oblivion and charging toward the magic he had imprinted in the doll to draw her essence like bait. It was a wave of sensation after that, her magic spilling into the new host with a weak but determined vigor. He could sense it settling beneath the doll's skin—*Jo's skin*, bringing color to her pallor, life into her dormant heart.

The world became real for her; she became real. No longer hovering, her bare foot touched down on the stony floor. Jo stood, naked as the day she was first born; on this day, she was born again.

"S-Snow?" she whispered, her eyes on his hunched form foremost. "What happened to me? Did I bounce back like bef—" Jo looked down at herself. "Why am I naked?"

The sentiment broke the deathly chill of panic with the bounding laughter of relief.

"Here you go, dollface." Wayne shrugged off his coat. "Though, for someone just come back from the dead, sorry I don't have something a little more flashy."

Even as she slid her hands into the sleeves, her eyes stayed on Snow. "What did you do? I thought my destructive magic would be impervious."

"Your magic was. The physical form . . . not so much."

"Then?"

"I split my magic to make a host for you. Your magic . . . filled it," Snow simplified.

Awareness widened her eyes and she quickly

crossed the gap between them, raising her hands to his cheeks to gently cradle his face. Watching her move was enough to make his eyes go watery. "Then, if you split, you're not a demigod anymore?"

"Neither are you," he affirmed.

"You did that for me?" She still sounded fragile, unused to her new body and voice, but she sounded alive. She was *alive.*

"I would do anything for you," Snow said, meaning every word of it. He would do anything for Jo, for Destruction, for his other half and truest love. Even living out the remainder of his life as a mortal. A life with magic, yes, but not the infinite well of forever to draw it from.

Still, as long as he shared his life with Jo, no matter how long, it would be worth it. He would split his magic a million times, and she would still be worth it.

"What does this mean?" Jo asked after a long moment of tense silence, gaze still hazy but regaining its usual brightness. Snow didn't care, not while she was living and breathing within his arms. But still, he gave her an answer.

"We live, my love. We simply . . . live."

EPILOGUE

"**W**E'LL BE BACK as soon as we can to come and see you and Jo," Samson said, pulling in for a tight hug.

Takako returned the embrace, feeling a little smile work its way onto her mouth at the mention of her and Jo, but no Snow. As if Jo would go anywhere without Snow again now that they had each other. Or, perhaps, that was just the craftsman's way of communicating his priorities.

"What about me?" Wayne huffed from Takako's side.

"You too, when you're here."

Wayne rolled his eyes at the implication that he was not worth his own trip, but hugged Samson anyway.

"We will not be leaving High Luana often," Eslar added, tempering the expectations Samson was setting. His familiar, no-nonsense demeanor was oddly comforting, something Takako had always appreciated in the man. Yet, despite his words, he took a step toward her, holding out a hand. Takako gripped it firmly. "However, we may be able to make an exception for a royal wedding, should one ever happen."

Takako gave a knowing grin.

"Wayne, do not cause too much trouble."

"I was never the troublemaker," he insisted to a wary-looking Eslar. "That was entirely Jo."

"You can only use Jo as an excuse for the last year and change of the Society, not all your antics prior. I do recall when you were meddling with an illegal—"

"Okay, okay, I get it," Wayne stopped Eslar hastily. "No need for details, old friend."

Old friend. The words stuck with Takako. Here they were, four people who should've never met. Four people who'd shared little in the way of mutual interests, thrust together in such an impossible situation that they'd had no choice but to become friends. She'd once resigned herself to seeing these faces, and no others, for the rest of her life.

Now, there was a new age upon them. They all had choices before them, paths they could take. Still, something drew them together. The ties that bound them would persist, and Takako certainly didn't find herself upset at the thought.

Takako gave a wave as Samson and Eslar were ushered into a vehicle and carried away, nothing more than the residual haze of magic left behind. She and Wayne stood in the central courtyard for a long minute, saying nothing, merely looking at where their friends had once been. It was time for them all to start anew—

as they'd tried to do when they'd first woken in this Age of Magic—but with no godly threats looming over their very existence.

"And then there were two," Wayne finally muttered.

"Not for long." Takako put her hands in the pockets of her pressed trousers, feeling where the rough starched wool met the inner silken lining. They were standard-issue for the Aristonian army, something Takako was not *exactly* a part of. But she was also not exactly *not* a part of it, either. Her new post straddled the line between garnering respect in Aristonia and not committing treason against her home country. "You're leaving soon too, aren't you?"

"'Fraid so. I should get back to Yorkton, make sure my executives haven't destroyed my company. I like being rich far too much to see them squander my success." Wayne turned, starting back for the castle. Takako followed suit.

The castle was almost done being rebuilt—construction with magic was far hastier compared to purely manual labor in Takako's time—a time that was slowly fading from her consciousness. Takako was letting it go without struggle. The world she'd been born into was gone; she'd accepted that in the Society with every granted wish. Now, it seemed like a natural evolution to settle into this reality in its entirety. She could actually put down roots here, after all; it wasn't as though timelines would be changing again.

"I'm surprised you're not taking her up on her offer. Head of the finance department sounds . . . prestigious," Takako said, throwing a brief smirk in Wayne's direction.

"She shouldn't give out every cabinet post to her friends, and you already accepted Champion." Wayne gave her a wink.

"Champion is not a political position. I am not Aristonian, so it cannot be. It's more of an award of—"

"Easy there, I'm just joshin' you. Either way, you're right, I should get to finishing up my travel arrangements," Wayne finished.

They came to a stop just inside the now perpetually open castle gates. They overlooked a recessed central courtyard—the same place Oblivion had died—that was slowly being transformed into a grassy garden. The destruction of the castle had been written off to the public as surprise renovations gone wrong. At the same time, there was a quiet mention of Pan being "out" and Jo being "in" as Snow's royal advisor.

Aristonia on the whole seemed so thrilled with the changes that no one probed too deeply. Of course, there were always conspiracy theories online for Jo to find and the rest of them to get a laugh at. Even when the truth was seemingly impossible, fiction could be made to sound stranger (and oftentimes more hilarious) than fact.

"I'm sure I'll see you again soon," Takako said with a smile, their rooms in opposite directions.

"Likely for that eventual wedding." Wayne looked across the garden. "Can't believe Snow wouldn't lock a woman like that down."

"Women aren't meant to be 'locked down'," Takako reminded him, though she'd heard the expression before and saved Wayne the unnecessary explanation by continuing. "And it isn't for lack of trying . . . after all, it's Wednesday. I'm sure he just made another attempt."

"I don't understand them." Wayne shook his head.

"Understand those two? I don't think we ever will. But wanting to live a little without Pan and the Society pressing on them . . . that at least is clear enough to me."

At that moment, the disk in her pocket pulsed with magic. Takako pulled it out, recognizing the frequency. Her eyes skimmed the message on its surface.

"I'll leave you to that," Wayne said, already starting to walk away.

"Sorry! It was from my family."

"It's all right. I'm not leaving until the end of the week, I just decided. We can have a rematch at tarith with a nightcap tonight."

Neither of them really knew how to play the elvish tile game. They seemed to have more fun arguing over made-up rules than actually trying to learn the game properly.

"It's a deal." Takako turned in the other direction and put Wayne from her mind. She had other, more pressing things to worry about now.

Takako strolled upward through the castle, amazed at how much transformation could transpire in a mere month. Originally, she had thought the castle looked like obsidian stalagmites, jutting unnaturally from the ground. Now, the color of the stone had changed to a pearly white, bright blue glowing deep under its surface. It was a reflection of Snow's magic, Takako had reasoned. Or it was merely an aesthetic illusion to cast away Pan's lingering darkness. Either way, the outer casing still pulsed with magic and the inside had been transformed into an equally bright (and far more logically constructed) space.

The one thing that had remained the same were the puppet-like creatures. Pan's assassins fled like rats, retreating to their next hideaway to lurk until a new, powerful leader no doubt organized them. But that would be a problem for another day. The puppets, however, had not been destroyed when Pan's magic dissolved.

They had lingered about the castle, listless, until Jo made the decision to accept them. Now, they played an active role in upkeep and restoration. Takako was wary of anything that changed loyalties so quickly, but they seemed harmless enough, merely happy to have a purpose. She wasn't sure how she felt about them stepping aside with a bow, though, every time she passed. It was worse when the other (more sentient, living, breathing servants) did the same. Takako wasn't used to such deference.

She came to a stop outside an unmarked door in a quiet wing of the castle. Servants, and those closest to the royal advisor, knew it was her true office—not the fancy ceremonial desk she was forced to use during meetings, to maintain appearances. This was where the woman felt most at home.

Takako gave two raps on the door.

"Come in," Jo's voice called from inside.

The room was a total wreck. Where the rest of the castle was beginning to reclaim order from chaos, this room was chaos incarnate. Perhaps Jo had the tiniest bit of Pan within her still. If Pan's only lingering mark on the world was a messy room, Takako reasoned, they'd done all right.

Clothes were strewn about the floor, and boxes stacked on boxes spilled over with pieced-together technology, wires dangling from them like gutted beasts. At the center of it all was the woman herself. Jo was lit up only by the neon glow of the monitor in front of her, her eyes glued to the magical script flowing across it.

"Still working on learning technomancy, I see." Takako closed the door behind her.

Jo turned, a can of RAGE ENERGY at her mouth. "It's being a pain. The whole 'magic meets technology' thing is nonsense."

"So you've said." Takako looked at the drink more closely. "Where did you get that? Weren't you lamenting how this age didn't have that particular flavor?"

"His newest proposal." Jo wiggled the can before taking another sip. "Thinks he can win me over with caffeine."

"I think he's already won you over."

"Don't let him know that." Jo didn't even bother hiding a grin as she spun in her desk chair.

They all knew it was only a matter of time before a royal wedding happened. Even Jo had said as much the first time Snow offered to make things official in that decidedly mortal way. But Jo had requested they spend some time *being* mortal first, just living without the Society or Pan.

Takako had thought it sensible, but she suspected it may have disappointed Snow at first. He proposed for the second time not long after. The third proposal came even faster after that. It was now a weekly thing, more like an inside joke than anything else.

"So, what can Aristonia's chief advisor help you with today?" Jo grinned over the can. "Come to give me an extra set of hands again?"

She had been, originally. Takako fumbled with the disk in her pocket, feeling somewhat guilty. Everyone was leaving all at once. . .

"There's something I'd like to ask."

"Shoot." Jo's expression told Takako the pun was intended, and Takako couldn't suppress a chuckle.

"I have received a message from my family."

"Oh? How are they?"

By way of answering Jo's question, Takako pulled her disk from her pocket, reading aloud.

"We had not heard from you in some time, and given all that has transpired in Aristonia, the family wants to make sure you're all right. Your sister's children miss you. It would be good to have a call soon. Don't be like your cousin Hiro; he left for the Kingdom of Zakon nearly three months ago and hasn't been heard from since.

"All is well here," Takako finished.

"You should go back and see them," Jo said with a smile, prompting Takako to wonder if she could now read minds. "I'm sure they'd like that."

"It wouldn't be any trouble? I had promised you I would—"

"Don't worry about it." Jo shook her head, turning back to her computer. "I have enough to keep me busy for a while. You can go over the Aristonian military with me when you get back. But take as much time as you need."

"Thank you." Takako almost felt compelled to give the other woman a hug. Instead, she let the gratitude of her words hang in the air before turning for the door. She didn't have much to pack, but like Wayne, she should still do that and square off her travel arrangements.

"Oh, one thing though."

"Hm?" Takako hummed, turning.

"If you end up going down to Zakon to find your cousin—"

"I doubt I will," Takako interjected. "Hiro has always been a bit of a wild child for his parents. This is hardly the first time he's pulled a stunt like this. I'm sure he'll be back soon, talking about how he 'found himself' in some remote mountain village."

"Still, if you do, be careful." The genuine caution in Jo's voice caught her attention. "I'm sure it's nothing . . . but I've been seeing weird reports pop up online about merfolk attacks down there."

"Merfolk attacks?" Takako repeated. "I haven't heard anything."

"It's just rumors right now. Who knows if they're true. No reporting seems to confirm. . ." Jo glanced up at her. "Still, be careful."

"I will," Takako vowed. It was easy to make such a promise. While she had jumped head-first into research about her new world when she'd first woken in this new Age of Magic, there was still much to learn, and ignorance bred caution.

In a time like this, when elves were real and dragons streaked across the sky, who knew what could happen?

ABOUT THE AUTHOR

ELISE KOVA has always had a profound love of fantastical worlds. Somehow, she managed to focus on the real world long enough to graduate with a Master's in Business Administration before crawling back under her favorite writing blanket to conceptualize her next magic system. She currently lives in St. Petersburg, Florida, and when she is not writing can be found playing video games, watching anime, or talking with readers on social media.

She invites readers to get first looks, giveaways, and more by subscribing to her newsletter at: http://elisekova.com/subscribe

Visit her on the web at:
http://elisekova.com/
https://twitter.com/EliseKova
https://www.facebook.com/AuthorEliseKova/
https://www.instagram.com/elise.kova/

ABOUT THE AUTHOR

LYNN LARSH considers herself to be a serial hobby-dabbler. She got a bachelors degree in music (which she used for all of four months), studied aerial acrobatics and classical piano for many years, worked briefly as a stunt woman in a Wild West stunt show (it's a long story), and eventually settled down into the bar tending business in St. Petersberg, FL. When she's not acting as a purveyor of fine libations, you can find her diving head first into her newest venture as a New Adult author, or simply writing Voltron fan fiction on Archive of Our Own.

Visit her on the web at: https://www.lynnlarsh.com/

Also from Elise Kova

A young adult, high-fantasy filled with romance and elemental magic.

THE
AIR AWAKENS
SERIES

A library apprentice, a sorcerer prince, and an unbreakable magic bond. . .

The Solaris Empire is one conquest away from uniting the continent, and the rare elemental magic sleeping in seventeen-year-old library apprentice Vhalla Yarl could shift the tides of war.

Vhalla has always been taught to fear the Tower of Sorcerers, a mysterious magic society, and has been happy in her quiet world of books. But after she unknowingly saves the life of one of the most powerful sorcerers of them all--the Crown Prince Aldrik--she finds herself enticed into his world. Now she must decide her future: Embrace her sorcery and leave the life she's known, or eradicate her magic and remain as she's always been. And with powerful forces lurking in the shadows, Vhalla's indecision could cost her more than she ever imagined.

Praise for Elise Kova's AIR AWAKENS

"DEAR BOOK GODS, THANK YOU. THANK YOU FOR THIS MASTERPIECE." – *Rachel E. Carter, USA Today bestselling author of the Black Mage Series*

"Avatar the Last Airbender meets The Grisha Trilogy in Air Awakens." – *RHPL Teen Book Reviews*

". . .THE book for people that love the Throne of Glass series" – *IrisjeXx*

"Phantom of the Opera meets Cinderella in a wonderfully crafted world." – *Michelle Madow, USA Today bestselling author of ELEMENTALS*

Loom with the best person to get him where he wants to go.

He offers her the one thing Ari can't refuse: A wish of her greatest desire, if she brings him to the Alchemists of Loom.

Praise for Elise Kova's THE ALCHEMISTS OF LOOM

"Kova (the Air Awakens series) crafts a fascinating divided world" – *Publishers Weekly*

"Prepare to have your mind blown. THE ALCHEMISTS OF LOOM is the perfect mashup of genres, with a killer heroine, fiery romance, and friendships that run as deep as blood." – *Lindsay Cummings, #1 New York Times bestselling author of ZENITH*

"Reading THE ALCHEMISTS OF LOOM was like curling up with a favorite fantasy classic. Yet what truly transported me was the brilliant twists and layers that make this story totally unique, totally fresh." – *Susan Dennard, New York Times bestselling author of TRUTHWITCH*

Printed in Great Britain
by Amazon